I WAS A WOMAN IN A MAN'S PROFESSION,
AND JUST BECAUSE I CARRIED A PYRE-GUN
DID NOT MEAN I WAS TAKEN SERIOUSLY.

Dallas Gutierrez, my right-hand man, strode to my side.
"What do you think, Mia? Alien?"

"Absolutely."

A little of the sparkle left his eyes. "You sure?"

I tossed him an are-you-kidding-me frown. "Can a woman lose one hundred and seventy-five pounds of unwanted fat by divorcing her husband?"

"Damn." He chuckled, the sound rich and husky in the twilight. "No wonder you're still single. You're vicious."

Damn right I was. I had to be.

AWAKEN ME DARKLY

"A fantastic read. . . . Fascinating characters. . . . Gena Showalter has created a very interesting world that readers will enjoy visiting over and over again."
—Aromancereview.com

"The final spin will shock. . . . Mia is a fabulous 'bad girl.'"
—Thebestreviews.com

"This novel sizzles with mystery and the supernatural. . . . Amazing."
—Freshfiction.com

This title is also available as an eBook

AWAKEN ME
Darkly

GENA SHOWALTER

New York London Toronto Sydney

DOWNTOWN PRESS, published by Pocket Books
1230 Avenue of the Americas
New York, NY 10020

This book is a work of fiction. Names, characters, places and incidents are products of the author's imagination or are used fictitiously. Any resemblance to actual events or locales or persons, living or dead, is entirely coincidental.

Originally published in trade paperback in 2005
by Downtown Press

ISBN-13: 978-1-4165-1717-7
ISBN-10:   1-4165-1717-0

This Downtown Press paperback edition March 2006

10 9 8 7 6 5 4 3 2 1

DOWNTOWN PRESS and colophon are trademarks of Simon & Schuster, Inc.

Cover design by Anna Dorfman, cover photo by Burke Heffner

Manufactured in the United States of America

For information regarding special discounts for bulk purchases, please contact Simon & Schuster Special Sales at 1-800-456-6798 or business@simonandschuster.com.

To the kick-ass people in my life:

Lauren McKenna—kick-ass editor
Deidre Knight—kick-ass agent
Joyce Harrison, Cynthia Watley, Esther Tolbert,
Barbara Pryor, and Paula Dowling—kick-ass aunts
Sheila Cooper, Jill Monroe, Ammanda McCabe,
Betty Sanders, and Donnell Epperson—all-around ass kickers

and

Mike and Vicki—who do not kiss my ass

AWAKEN ME
Darkly

CHAPTER
1

*M*idnight. The witching hour, some say. Since it was 12:07 A.M. and I was standing over a dead body, I had to agree.

The victim, William H. Steele, a thirty-six-year-old Caucasian male, six feet four, approximately two hundred and thirty pounds, brown hair, brown eyes, lay naked across a bed of crisp winter leaves. Moonlight spilled in every direction, and withered foliage mockingly framed his muscular physique. He bore no open wounds, no bruises. In fact, not a single blemish marred the perfection of his skin. He was only recently dead; heat still radiated from him and curled into the icy night sky.

Alien Investigation and Removal agents, also known

as A.I.R., were scouring the area, meticulously search-ing between every blade of brittle grass, every grain of dirt. The faint murmurs of their chatter echoed in my ears. I tuned them out and intensified my focus on the body. The man's legs were slightly spread and bent at the knees. One of his hands rested behind his head, and the other was bound to his penis with a—what the hell *was* that? I crouched down. Eyes narrowed, I reached out with a gloved hand and slid one finger under the material. A pale blue ribbon, tied in a perfect bow.

I scowled. Was he supposed to be a gift?

Yes. Yes, that's exactly what he was, I realized, my scowl deepening. Frost gleamed in his hair like dia-monds against dark velvet, yet he hadn't been outside long enough to acquire the frost from nature. He was a gift that had been posed to look carnal, seductive. Alluring. To the average citizen, he would have appeared eager for a long night of sexual gratification.

To me, he just looked like the corpse that he was.

His eyes were fixed straight ahead, his lips slightly blue, and he wasn't shivering from the cold. A dead giveaway, if you will. Besides that, his testicles were as smooth and shiny as marble, not shriveled like I sup-posed every other man's out here were.

With a wry shake of my head, I pushed to my feet.

Perhaps my assessment was callous and indifferent; perhaps my humor was misplaced. Dead bodies were the norm in my line of work, and I couldn't allow myself to view this man as an actual person. If I did, I'd have to acknowledge that he once had hopes and dreams, thoughts and feelings. I'd cry for the family he left behind, wonder about the life that had once pulsed through his veins.

I couldn't do that and still hope to function. With tears came distraction, and with distraction came death. My first year of fieldwork, I had spent more time crying for victims than hunting for their killers, and I had almost become a victim myself. I glanced down at my wrist. The inky blackness of my glove didn't quite meet the cuff of my jacket, leaving a small patch of skin visible. That skin boasted a tattoo of the Grim Reaper's scythe and was just one of my many reminders to remain unemotional.

I'd gotten the tattoo after recovering from a nasty beating, courtesy of a pissed-off other-worlder. While I'd been lost in my grief for a victim I couldn't even remember now, an energy-absorbing Rycan attacked me from behind—and kicked major huntress ass.

I had vowed never to cry again. And I hadn't. Tears were a weakness only civilians could afford.

I am an alien huntress. I am part of the A.I.R. team, working with or against the New Chicago PD— whichever suits me at the time. Every night I stalk and kill other-worlders, and whether I'm investigating a death or causing one myself, I have to shove sentiment aside, find humor where I can, and concentrate on the facts.

I love my job despite the blood and gore—or maybe because of it. I love solving puzzles, fitting each piece of evidence together. I love that one by one, I'm ridding Earth of our unwanted visitors.

Yes, some aliens are peaceful and are allowed to live and work among us. Those, I leave alone. But the others? The rapists, the thieves, the killers? I despise them.

Alien sympathizers often ask me if I, a hunter, a legalized killer, live with guilt. My answer: Hell, no. Why should I feel guilty for destroying a predator? I'm proud of my work. I'm privileged to do what I do. Other-worlders who survive on human carnage deserve the sting of my pyre-gun.

A glacial blast of wind whirled past my shoulders, scattering a thin sheen of snow powder in every direction. The hem of my long black leather jacket danced around my calves. Four inches of snow had been predicted, so I needed to work quickly. Twenty minutes ago, I'd received a call from my boss, Commander Jack Pagosa. He'd briefed me on the situation. He'd also informed me I had until morning to present him with a suspect, or I would spend the next year behind a desk.

William Steele, a happily married father of one, had been abducted from his home four weeks prior. His wife and newborn child slept peacefully throughout the entire ordeal, unharmed and unaware. Abductor's point of entry: undetermined.

Four other dark-haired, dark-eyed men disappeared

soon afterward. One had been taken from his work-place, and two had been snatched straight from a crowded street during their lunch hour. Oddly enough, there had been no witnesses and not a single shred of evidence left behind at any scene. Because of the enig-matic nature of each disappearance, aliens were the prime suspect.

Just half an hour earlier, a hunter on patrol had found Steele in this deserted Southern District field. Thankfully, the hunter had preserved the scene until my team arrived. The first thing I'd noticed was that Steele's body showed no indication of torture, no sign of having been restrained.

Second, I'd realized his death had nothing to do with impulse or rage—just as I knew the murder had nothing to do with stupidity or amusement. The scene was too precise, too perfectly planned. Mr. Steele had been killed for a reason.

What? I couldn't yet fathom.

I drew in a deep breath—and stilled. Slowly, I drew in three more breaths. As I exhaled the last, I smiled. Since the first kidnapping, no one had dared guess which of the forty-eight alien species were responsible, but I had just narrowed it down to three.

The victim had been killed by poison. Onadyn, to be exact. A deoxygenating drug used by the Zi Karas, Arcadians, and Mecs for survival on this planet. They couldn't breathe our air without it. To oxygen-breathers, the substance was lethal. Worse, it was virtually undetectable. Virtually, but not completely. A rare few could identify Onadyn by its scent, a subtle fragrance similar to a dewy breeze during a summer storm.

I was one of the rare few, and I smelled it now. The scent filled my nostrils, intoxicating and sweet, as lovely as it was deadly, and somehow suddenly more obvious to me than the scent of waste, rotting food, and charred leaves that made up so much of this domain. My observation wasn't as solid as a neon sign blinking over the killer's head that read I DID IT in bold red letters, but it did point us in the right direction.

Still, I wanted more.

I scanned the area to my right, paused, then scanned the area to my left. Except for the occasional twinkle from regulation halolights, the task force blended into the night.

I dragged my focus farther back, taking in the tall oaks that knifed the sky. The trees were sparsely scattered, their branches naked, their bark weighed down by dripping ice. Situated between the trees were homes and businesses. I use the term *businesses* loosely, of course. Nice people referred to this seedy, neglected district as Whore's Corner. I'd once been fined for publicly saying what *I* called the place.

Had any of the residents seen anything unusual? Would they tell us if they had?

I'd already dispatched the most charming of my agents to question every citizen within a one-mile radius. But this late at night, civilians tended to be cranky and distrustful. Besides that, the Southern District was notorious for its hatred of law enforcement— human or otherwise.

"What do you think, Mia?" Dallas Gutierrez, my right-hand man, strode to my side. He wore a black leather jacket and black combat boots that fit the hard planes of his body to perfection. At times, I thought he was too handsome to be real. His hair was dark and thick, and the inky locks hung in sexy disarray over the wide, muscled length of his shoulders. Perfect eyebrows arched over perfectly shaped eyes. Perfect cheekbones framed a perfect nose.

For some reason, he was smiling—revealing perfect white teeth, the bastard—yet even as the brown depths of his eyes glinted with mischief, he still possessed the razor-sharp edge of a hunter.

I admired him for that.

On more than one occasion, Dallas Gutierrez had flipped Death the bird and come out alive. He was a man who rushed into the middle of danger without hesitation. He considered his friends' safety before he considered his own, and he never regretted his choice, even when he lay wounded and bleeding. He'd saved my life so many times, I should have tattooed his name on my ass.

"What do you think?" he repeated. "Which group of aliens is responsible?"

"Zi Karas, Arcadians, or Mecs."

A little of the sparkle left his eyes. "You sure?"

I tossed him an are-you-kidding-me frown. "Can a woman lose one hundred and seventy-five pounds of unwanted fat by divorcing her husband?"

"Damn." He chuckled, the sound rich and husky in the twilight. "No wonder you're still single. You're vicious."

Damn right I was. I had to be. I was a woman in a man's profession, and just because I carried a pyre-gun did not mean I was taken seriously. Not even Dallas had taken me seriously at first.

His first week on the job, he fought to have me relocated. "Women aren't hunters," he'd said so many times I wanted to brand the words on his chest—while he was awake and tied to his bed.

I stand at five feet five, weigh one hundred and twenty pounds. I'm only twenty-eight years old, but I have an indomitable will. I do not take shit from anyone, especially when it comes to my job. The first time Dallas and I practiced hand-to-hand combat, I had him on the ground in three seconds flat, my palms wrapped around his windpipe while he gasped for air.

Funny enough, we were best friends after that, and he never again mentioned my relocation.

"What makes you so sure of yourself?" he asked, folding his arms over his chest and pinning me with a frown of his own. A plastic bag dangled from his fingers.

I shrugged. "Ever heard of Occam's razor?" He blinked over at me, and I took that for a no. "Occam's razor is a nineteenth-century principle that states the simplest explanation for a mysterious event is most likely the truth."

His brow furrowed, and his eyes flashed dark fire. "How in the hell did you decide the most likely suspect was from an oxygen-intolerant group?"

"I smell Onadyn," I said, biting back a grin.

"Christ," he grumbled. "I was excited that I knew something you didn't. Thanks for ruining it for me."

"My pleasure. Now what's in the bag?"

As soon as the words left my mouth, all traces of emotion drained from his expression. Silently, he studied me, as if trying to measure my inner strength. I knew what he saw. Straight black hair pulled tight in a ponytail, though several wisps had already escaped confinement. Wide blue eyes that had seen more evil than good, and an oval face that boasted delicate cheekbones better suited to a ballerina.

My appearance worked well for me at times. Suspects expected me to be feminine and delicate, and I was able to take them by surprise. At other times my appearance worked against me, bringing out all kinds of protective instincts in men. This was one of those times I wished I had a mustache and a long, hideous scar.

I kept my gaze locked on Dallas's.

A sigh slid past his lips, leaving the words *You win* unsaid, though he didn't answer my question right away.

"Notice any footprints around the body?" he asked.

I peered at the ground, studying, searching. "No."

"Neither did we. And we've analyzed every inch of dirt in this godforsaken shit hole. At first we thought someone performed a beam-me-down-Scottie."

I tossed that idea through my mind. "Maybe. But most aliens arrived here through interworld portals. Not spaceships. So they wouldn't have access to the kind of technology required for a molecular transfer. Besides, the killer is cocky. What better rush than placing the body here, in full view of witnesses, and still getting away?"

"Give us some credit, Mia. I said *at first*. We soon changed our minds." Smug now, he dangled the plastic bag in front of my face. Inside were six strands of white hair. "Found them snagged on a branch."

I frowned, studied the hair more closely. They were thick and coarse and . . . my frown deepened. There weren't six *individual* strands of hair; in actuality, there were only two. Three strands per follicle.

"Arcadian," I said, confirming my Onadyn suspicions. Only the Arcadians had three strands of hair attached to one follicle.

Dallas nodded, his features suddenly tense, determined. "You got it."

Dread prickled along my nerve endings, and my stomach twisted into a thousand tiny knots. Why couldn't the Zi Karas or Mecs be responsible? Of all the aliens to invade our planet, Arcadians were the strongest, the deadliest. The hardest to capture. Their psychic abilities proved a sufficient weapon against us, helping them evade capture. And their talent for mind control . . . Damn. I didn't even want to contemplate that right now.

No wonder there were no footprints around the body. An Arcadian could very easily use telekinesis to wipe them away.

"Good luck to us," Dallas said, his voice punctuating the sudden silence. "Finding the other men alive doesn't seem likely now."

"We'll find them," I said, pretending I didn't have my own doubts.

He pushed out a breath and motioned to the corpse with a tilt of his chin. "One thing I can't figure out. Why only men with dark hair and eyes?"

I'm pretty sure I knew the answer. "Our killer is an Arcadian female who's only attracted to men who are the exact opposite in appearance to her kinsmen."

The corners of his mouth twitched. "Occam's razor again?"

"Brilliant deduction." Another blast of wind pushed around us, causing tendrils of hair to momentarily shield my vision. I hooked them behind my ear. "I think she wanted Steele and the others as her kinky new sex toys, but couldn't obtain them through legal means."

"Let's be honest, though. No woman is strong enough to force poison down a man this size."

"You know better than that," I said, patting the gun

at my side, reminding him that I could force a steel pipe down his throat if I wanted. I knelt down and pulled at the bow tied to Steele's penis. "Look at this. Is this something a man would do?"

"No." Dallas shook his head slowly. "No, it isn't."

"Hey, Snow," one of the men called just then. I recognized Ghost's deep baritone; he was a man I enjoyed working with. He possessed a heart of honor and courage unlike anyone else I'd ever met.

"Yeah," I answered and released the ribbon. I shoved to my feet, searching the darkness for his rich, chocolate-colored skin. He stood several feet away, his grin a beacon in the night.

"Why don't you come over here and do that to me? I'll enjoy it so much more than Steele there," he teased with a wink.

Of course, Ghost also possessed a warped sense of humor. "The last breathing man who let me near his goods dropped to the floor in a fetal ball and begged for his mommy."

He gave a good-humored chuckle. "You stay the hell away from my goods." With barely a breath he added, "You want us to erect the force field and protect him from the weather?"

"No, not yet." I wanted to view him exactly as he'd been left for a little longer. I returned my attention to Dallas, who was scrubbing a hand over his jaw stubble. "What are you thinking?"

"The killer went through some pretty elaborate

measures to pose the body," he said. "The intelligent thing to do is destroy all the evidence, leave nothing behind."

"Our girl's into showmanship, but more than that, she's into punishment. She took her time here, labored over every detail. See how the victim's body is perfectly aligned? See how the frost is perfectly sprinkled in his hair?"

A pause.

"I'm guessing he did something to really piss her off."

"Damn me," Dallas said, "but I think you're onto something here. Punishment equals humiliation, and there's nothing more humiliating than going down in history as the man found in a dirty, diseased field with one hand tied to his dick." He snorted, his mouth quirking up at one corner. "Maybe we should interview a couple of my former girlfriends. Sounds like something they might do."

Over the years, I'd met many of Dallas's girlfriends. Some of them had needed icicles surgically removed from their veins—a sentiment I'd voiced aloud on more than one occasion. Not that he'd ever appreciated the genius of my insight.

I shook my head and said, "All we're likely to get from your leftovers is frostbite, so we'll forgo the pleasure of interrogating them for now."

He shot me a teasing grin. "Oh, oh, Miss Snow. Is that jealousy in your tone?"

"Blow me, Dallas."

"You wish. I'll bite, though."

He was kidding, I knew. Our relationship had never been sexual. And would never become sexual. Sex destroyed more male/female partnerships than death, and God knows it would completely negate my authority, something I would *not* allow.

I stared down at the body for a long while, a new crop of questions running through my mind. "I want you and Jaxon to interview the victim's family in the morning," I said. Jaxon was another member of my unit. Whereas Dallas was all intimidation, Jaxon was a man who could ask the most private of questions and somehow convince interviewees they were happy to answer. "I want to know every sexual secret Mr. Steele possessed, every woman he ever glanced at. I even want to know the brand of underwear he preferred."

Dallas's handsome face twisted in a wince, his full lips pursing in feigned pain. "That should be fun."

"If you'd prefer, I'll assign you to PADD." Paper and Desk Duty.

"Hey," he said, smiling like he was about to do me a huge favor, "you want me to talk to Steele's family in the morning, I'll talk to Steele's family." Before I could comment, he added, "What's next for tonight?"

I cast another glance around the scene. It was about to start snowing again, the night suddenly thicker than before. "Boys," I loudly called, "go ahead and erect the force field, then call homicide. They can finish searching the area. We've found what we need."

To Dallas, I said, "Let's go to the car." I pivoted toward our unmarked black sedan. I only set my feet in select places, using the same path I'd taken to get here. "I want to search the database."

He fell into step behind me. When we reached our destination, I placed my index finger on the passenger ID scanner. After recognition the door popped open, and I slid inside. With a tug of my wrist, I slammed the door. Moments later, Dallas occupied the driver's seat.

"Start," he commanded, and the vehicle immediately roared to life. "Heat. High." The heater kicked into action.

I glanced out the window and watched Ghost and the other men assume positions around the edges of the crime scene. Each man withdrew a small box, placed it at his feet, and pressed a button. Blue lights sparked from every box, and the air around them appeared to solidify, becoming liquid and spreading upward and out, until meeting and creating a protective dome.

"We need names," I said, turning to Dallas. "Specifics."

"That I can do." Features tightening with concentration, Dallas unfolded his computer console, located where steering wheels were once positioned. Within seconds, he was plugging away at the keyboard.

Pensive, I removed my gloves and massaged the

back of my neck. "Pull up a list of every Arcadian hunted, questioned, or wanted for interrogation in the last year."

"Males, too?"

"Yes."

"Already done." He punched a few more buttons, and twenty-six names popped onto the screen.

Ignoring the names, I scanned the crimes committed. Prostitution. Robbery. Vandalism. "Cross-reference this list with all Arcadians questioned for sex and human hate crimes. Delete those that have already been exterminated."

His fingers again flew over the keyboard. Mere seconds passed before the names dwindled to five. I nodded in satisfaction. Very few aliens linked to violent crimes ever lived long enough to gloat. Since alien supporters had yet to push through a law stating that other-worlders were entitled to a trial, hunters were often judge, jury, and executioner.

Instead of thanking us for keeping them safe, however, the supporters continued to fight us. Didn't they realize that if aliens weren't controlled, if their numbers weren't kept to a minimum, they could overrun us? That they might one day have the power to wipe us out completely? Didn't they realize that species with extraordinary powers like weather control, levitation, and the ability to absorb energy needed to know they would be punished if they harmed a human?

When the aliens first arrived more than seventy

years ago, we would have destroyed them all if we could have. From all the reports I'd read, panic had spread worldwide, and we immediately engaged them in war. Instead of causing them to flee, we came very close to destroying our own planet.

In desperation, our world leaders finally met with the commanders of each species, and it was agreed that the aliens could live here as long as they remained peaceful toward us. However, as with humans, there are those who are innately good and those who are innately evil. When several other-worlders placed humans on their dessert menu, both aliens and humans agreed something needed to be done. A.I.R. was quickly established, granting us free license to kill those who proved evil.

"We'll question each one," I said, "see what they know."

Keeping his gaze on the front windshield, Dallas adjusted the pyre-gun hooked to his shoulder holster. The lines around his mouth were taut. "To be honest," he said, his voice just as taut, as if he were embarrassed by his words, "I'm not sure I'll be much help to you on this case. I've only hunted two Arcadians since joining A.I.R., and I had no luck either time."

"Then consider tonight your lucky night. We'll split the unit into five groups of two, and each group will hunt one Arcadian." I shifted to my left, facing him more directly. "You'll be with me, and I"—I winked—"always get my alien."

"Not a bit cocky, are we?" His lips widened into a full-fledged grin, and he radioed the others and told them our plan. "Jaffe, Mandalay, you're searching for Cragin en Srr. Ghost, Kittie, you're searching for Lilla en Arr—"

"No," I said, cutting off his words. The moment he'd spoken Lilla's name, cold fingers of apprehension had crawled up my spine. "I want the woman."

His brow furrowed. "There are two females listed."

"I want *this* woman." My instincts rarely proved wrong.

His eyes gleamed with curiosity, but he nodded, corrected Ghost and Kittie's target, then continued his litany. When he finished, he returned the radio to its receiver and faced me. "So you think Lilla's our girl?"

"We'll see." I motioned to the computer with a tilt of my chin. "Pull up her voice frequency." When an alien was interrogated, no matter the crime, their voice was recorded and filed, and through voice recognition we were able to monitor their whereabouts for the rest of their stay on Earth. Alien voice was much like human fingerprints, and since high-frequency recorders decorated every street corner and were constantly monitored, we'd have the information we wanted in seconds.

"Her voice isn't listed," Dallas said, confused.

"She was questioned, so it has to be. Try again."

Silence. Then, "I'm telling you," he said, "it's not here."

No damn way. "See what else you can find on her. Every little detail."

He positioned his fingers onto the keyboard and jumped back into work. One prolonged heartbeat of time passed. Two. "Shit, take a look at this."

"What is it?" I straightened in my seat and eyed the screen.

"Firewall. All records for Lilla en Arr are deemed confidential, and no one, and I do mean no one, is allowed entrance."

"Arrests and interrogations aren't confidential." The words rushed from me, ripe with displeasure and confusion.

He shot me a narrowed glance. What little I saw of his eyes blazed with irritation. "I'm telling you, access is denied. This is one hell of a block."

Dark curiosity pounded through me because there was only one logical explanation. Someone on the inside didn't want authorities poking into Lilla's life. "Get into that file," I commanded.

"Want me to pull a rabbit out of my ass, too?" he muttered, his tone heavy with sarcasm. But he turned back to the screen, his fingers working furiously.

"If you can show me that rabbit at the same time you get into that file, I might think you've got talent."

"Shut the fuck up, Mia."

Minute after minute dragged by, the click of the keys the only sound. I was not known for my patience, and tapped my foot against the floorboard.

Finally Dallas laughed, threw his hands in the air, and shouted, "Couldn't block that, could you, you bastards."

"What'd you find?" Excitement blended with my impatience, each emotion feeding off the other.

"Still no voice recording, but she's been questioned twice. Once for soliciting sex from a human, and once for beating the shit out of a human."

"Who arrested her?"

"For solicitation—George Hudson."

I filed that information away. I didn't know the agent personally, but I would. "What about the assault charges?"

"Let's see. The arresting officer was—" He scrolled down the screen, then whistled between his teeth. "The name's been erased."

"This doesn't make sense. Alien assault is punishable by death, and only death, yet Lilla was released and her record buried."

"Why bury it?" Thoughtful, Dallas worried a hand over his shadow beard. "I mean, someone obviously wants her information to remain hidden, so why not destroy it?"

"Blackmail, maybe?" I turned my head and glanced outside. Several agents were packing their gear and loading their vehicles. Pieces of this puzzle just didn't fit, and I pinched the bridge of my nose, trying to make sense of what I was learning. I returned my attention to Dallas. "Does the database list who Lilla solicited and who she trashed?"

Another pause, then, "Shit, Mia. You're not going to believe this. The man Lilla beat within an inch of his life was William Steele. And the man she propositioned was none other than—"

He shot me a glance, and we said in unison, "William Steele."

"So there's a connection," I breathed, brushing a hand down my face.

Slowly, he nodded. "Looks like we've got our killer."

"Yes, it looks that way, doesn't it?" Yet suddenly something didn't feel right, and my mind whirled with probabilities. Here was an Arcadian female who'd desired Steele enough to try and seduce him. When that failed, she beat him. This was a female perfectly capable of murder, and the simplest answer to our investigation.

Occam's razor.

Except . . . everything inside me was screaming *Too easy!*

Oh, I was willing to bet my savings account she was involved. Had to be. But . . .

"Got anything else on her?" I asked, hoping to assuage my concerns. "Is her name linked with any of the other missing men?"

"Not that I can see. The only other bit of info here is the fact that she works at Ecstasy, and is dating the owner."

I pursed my lips and flipped through my mental files. "That name sounds familiar."

"You need to get out more, woman. Ecstasy is the most exclusive nightclub in New Chicago, and host to a slew of alien sympathizers. Mark St. John, the owner, is a hard-ass bastard with more money than God."

So the boyfriend had money and power, probably kept a few officials in his pocket. That explained Lilla's confidential file and the fact that she was still alive. "Let's go after Lilla first," I said, "and then Hudson."

"Beauty before brawn, eh?"

I rolled my eyes. "Think she's working tonight?"

"According to this, she works every night."

"Doing what, exactly?"

"Tending bar."

"It's a damn good thing I wore my dancing shoes, then," I said, leaning back in the seat, "because we're going to crash the party. And don't kill her, Dallas," I added quickly. "I want her alive."

"As if you have to worry about me. You're the one who's trigger-happy." Grinning languidly, he programmed the club's address into the console. "I do believe this night is about to get interesting."

CHAPTER
2

*E*cstasy perched atop a perfectly manicured hill in the upper East District. Moonlight cast an unholy frame around the three-story building, illuminating the deceptively virginal white walls, stained glass windows, and hanging pottery filled with bright green faux foliage. A cross rose from the roof like a direct antenna to God.

A fucking chapel, I thought. A nightclub infamous for illegal drugs and made-to-order sex was housed in a fucking chapel. I shook my head, marveling at the defiance such an act required. It was like saying, "Screw you, God."

Something about the place prodded at the corners of my memory. I stared at the silk flowers twined around the tall alabaster columns, searching my mind for . . . what? What was I forgetting?

It hit me in the next instant, and I almost groaned. I'd forgotten my brother's memorial was tonight.

My parents had me in their late thirties. My mother ran off not long after, but my dad stuck around. For many years, he'd been a wonderful father. Loving, supportive. It was only after my oldest brother's death that he became an indifferent, sometimes cruel bastard.

The only thing that seemed to give him joy was this annual midnight vigil on the eve of Kane's death. So what that my brother had died twenty-three years ago. So what that Kane had been seventeen, and I'd been five and therefore didn't remember him. My dad expected me to be there.

Anger spun a treacherous web inside me as I considered the situation. I was still alive, but my dad basically treated me as if I was dead; Kane was dead, but he still lived and breathed in my dad's heart. Maybe that was because Kane's body had never been found. I didn't know and tried not to care. I was going to take a lot of shit for missing.

Had the service been for my other brother, Dare, I would have obliterated any obstacle to be there. Dare had been my hero, my lifeline. Whenever Dad punished me, it was Dare who comforted me. Dare who made sure I had enough food and blankets.

And he'd been tortured and killed by a group of

aliens on his eighteenth birthday. The date of his death was stamped in my mind like a physical brand.

Had my dad ever once held a memorial for him? Hell, no.

"Looks like we're gonna have ourselves some trouble," Dallas said, capturing my attention.

I realized my hands were clenched, almost snapping the bones. Thinking of Dare's death always had that effect on me. "Nothing we can't handle," I said absently. My dad hadn't called yet, but it was just a matter of time before he did. This was the only night of the year he acknowledged me.

While I usually (secretly) looked forward to his call, I didn't need the distraction right now. I slipped out my cell unit and switched the tone to silent. I forced my body to relax and my mind to clear. No thoughts of my dad tonight, and certainly no thoughts of my brothers, either. I had to focus on here and now. Human lives depended on me.

At the gated entrance, Dallas eased his sedan toward the security booth. Before the wheels came to a complete stop, a uniformed guard appeared at the driver's-side window. The guard had dry, yellow skin, almost reptilian. He had no nose, and his cheekbones were so sharp they could have cut glass. Ugly as putrid water, with a smell to match, he peered into the car with wide golden eyes.

An Ell-Rollis. He was definitely an Ell-Rollis. Their race wasn't known for creativity; they rarely possessed an original thought, so they relied on the exact directives of others. And those directives were usually nefarious. Except for their physical strength, they didn't have any special powers. That I knew of. Perhaps one day there would be a manual outlining every alien species and their abilities, but until then, we operated on what little knowledge we possessed.

Dallas lowered his window, and suddenly all that shielded him from the alien was air. And that wasn't a good thing, since the alien was built like two WWE wrestlers fused together, muscle stacked upon muscle. He'd probably been ordered to kill whoever defied him.

"Do you have invitation?" the guard asked, his voice low, gravelly, and heavily accented.

Before Dallas could utter a single word, I leaned across the seat and flashed my badge. "Open the gate."

The Ell-Rollis kept his gaze locked on my partner, assuming he was the bigger threat. Unimpressed, the alien crossed his arms over his chest. His expression darkened with disdain. "No invitation. No enter."

"I understand," I replied pleasantly. Deceptively. And I did understand. He saw a badge and automatically assumed I was an average cop with no alien jurisdiction. "Maybe this will help." With a fluid, lightning-fast motion of my wrist, I unsheathed my pyre-gun and leveled it at his face. "Open the gate, or taste fire."

Pyre-guns caused maximum pain with lethal results, and that was something even a Ell-Rollis could understand, the dumb bastard. These guns were standard issue; they emitted thin talons of fire that exploded upon impact. The wielder controlled just how much fire—just how much pain. Certain alien breeds were impervious to bullets, but I had yet to meet a breed resistant to fire.

Dallas flipped on the cab light, and two glowing circles flooded the front seats, chasing away the darkness. The Ell-Rollis tugged his gaze from Dallas to my gun. He flicked my face a nervous glance. When he saw me, his eyes widened, and his mouth formed a small O. He recoiled three steps back.

"Mia Snow," he breathed on a horrified gasp.

"That's right." My gaze remained as steady as my gun.

"I let you inside, yes?" He tried for an easy, I-only-want-to-please-you chuckle that sounded more like a misfiring pyre-gun. His limbs trembled, and he edged his way toward the guardhouse.

"Stay where you are," I said, keeping my tone casual. He froze so quickly, I almost laughed. Almost. "I want my friend to open the gate. You blew your chance." No telling how many alarms the bastard would kick if I allowed him inside his booth.

He swallowed, the action followed by a jerky nod. "Whatever say you."

Dallas emerged from the sedan, always careful to stay out of my line of fire. He stepped inside the guardhouse, and moments later the thick metal bars blocking our entrance were groaning in protest as they split.

"What's your name?" I asked the Ell-Rollis.

"I called Bob," he offered hesitantly.

I rolled my eyes. Why couldn't he have picked a human name that fit his appearance? Biff? Or Hulk? "Well, Bobby," I said, "I'm feeling generous tonight." I holstered my gun, but his expression remained tight with fear. "I'm going to let you live, and in exchange, you're going to escort me to Lilla en Arr. Understand?"

"Yes, yes. I understand." The lines of tension finally eased around his mouth. "Mia Snow always keep her word, just as Bob do."

"For your sake, I hope so." My gaze remained on Bob, but I spoke my next words to Dallas. "Follow in the car and meet me inside."

"You got it," he replied with an easy smile. He always enjoyed watching me, the dainty little flower, intimidate such enormous creatures. Warped humor, if you asked me, but then we all had our quirks.

"You try anything, Bobby," I said, exiting the sedan, "and I swear to God I'll use you for target practice." The predicted snow chose that moment to pour from the sky. In seconds. Thick white flakes fell and swirled around us, descending like glitter inside a water globe.

"I no try nothing." He shook his head violently, causing his dark brown braids to swing around his temples. "No, no. No try. I your friend."

Friend, my ass. He'd kill me if I gave him the opportunity. With a tilt of my chin, I motioned him inside the gate. I kept him three strides in front of me. I didn't trust him at my back, and I didn't want him at my side.

Cars littered the grounds, all strategically placed for easy departure. One by one, we maneuvered around them, each step taking us closer to Ecstasy. Finally, we stood at the large, intricately carved double doors. Thunderous rock music boomed so loudly, the walls and floor vibrated.

I wiped the snow from my face and wondered at the lack of entrance security. Yes, they had Bob posted at the front gate, but as I'd just proved, he wasn't insurmountable. I doubted they relied on cameras. Unlicensed surveillance had been restricted years ago because even the average citizen knew how to splice "tamper-resistant" film, and after numerous false claims, the courts had decided to restrict all video usage. This nightclub had never been issued a license. Sure, they could have hidden cameras, but why gamble on the loss of a business over something so trivial?

I wondered again at the reason for only posting one guard. Stupidity on the owner's part? Or simple cockiness? Or maybe he was just too cheap to spring for more. I voted for all three.

Just get this over with, Mia. I silently palmed my gun and adjusted the control to stun. I'd said I wouldn't kill him, and I wouldn't. But I never promised not to immobilize him for a few hours. Hand steady, I aimed at Bob's back.

As if sensing my intent, he turned and cast me a glance over his shoulder. His expression was comical, really, since he had no nose. His sharp, yellowed teeth were chewing on his bottom lip. I stupidly paused for a second too long, allowing his expression to distract me.

Panicked, he slapped my arm. The gun went flying and skidded across the porch. He dove for it, but only managed to push it farther away. Cursing myself, I jumped onto his back and pressed my fingers against his temples, preventing his fishlike gills from raising and lowering. The action cut off his air supply. He soon forgot all about my gun as oxygen was denied him. He fought me, legs flailing, hands tearing at my fingers. When that didn't work, he jabbed his elbow into my stomach, and though breath exploded from my lungs and pain rocked me, I held tight.

Finally he went still. His body collapsed, and he thumped to the ground. I jumped to my feet, but remained doubled over as I sucked in a deep, much-needed breath. "You'll thank me later, you bastard."

Dallas barreled up the stairs, his gun cocked and aimed at Bob as I picked up my own gun and fired a round of stun lasers at the sleeping giant. My hand fell to my side, and I sucked in another round of air.

Dallas pinned me with a concerned gaze. "You okay?"

"I'm fine," I said, but damn it, my stomach felt like an overused punching bag at boxing practice.

"Want me to kill him? He assaulted an officer, after all."

I thought it over, then shook my head. "Nah. Too much paperwork. He's not who we came for, anyway."

Dallas's lips twitched at the corners. "You going soft on me? First you allow an Ell-Rollis to disarm you, and then you—"

"Go fuck yourself."

Chuckling, he slipped his gun back into place. With his hands free, he locked his arms under Bob's armpits and began tugging the giant out of the way. "I'll hide him beyond the edge. No need to help."

"Don't worry. I wasn't."

He shot me a frown. That frown quickly changed to a grimace as he strained under Bob's weight. "Did I tell you I've got a date tomorrow?" he asked conversationally, changing the subject just to annoy me.

"With who?"

"Jane Marlow."

"Christ. The porn star?"

"She prefers the term *professional sex advocate*," he replied, huffing from exertion.

I arched a brow. "At least with this one you'll know there's more than ice in her panties."

"I resent that. Especially from you, a woman who hasn't gone on a date since the Great Heat Wave."

My back straightened, and my shoulders squared. "I had dinner with Kedric Coners last week."

"He doesn't count. His legs are so skinny, I could use them as chopsticks."

"He's not that skinny."

"You can't deny he's got no heart, though. Hell, I bet he tosses widows and children out of that fancy apartment building he owns and into the cold, wet streets."

Dallas rounded the corner, out of sight, and I heard a thud as he dropped Bob to the ground. Within seconds, my partner was striding toward me. When he reached me, he leaned down until our noses were only inches apart.

"Why do you only date men like that? Men you can walk all over? There's no way in hell you can respect someone like that."

My eyes narrowed. Anger rushed through me, growing hotter and hotter, darker and darker. I liked being in control. So what? I liked things done my way, when I wanted, where I wanted. I rarely dated, but when I did, I picked men who took what I gave them and didn't ask for more. If I were a man, Dallas would be slapping me on the back and offering me a beer instead of chastising me. "What I like is solving a case," I said with false calm. "I think we've wasted enough time outside, don't you?"

A muscle ticked in his jaw, but he held up his hands and shrugged. "Whatever you say. You're the boss, right?"

The entry doors swung open.

In unison, Dallas and I spun, weapons drawn. From the open doorway, smoke billowed like a thick morning fog. Amid the haze, two Delensean females emerged. Both appeared to be in their mid-twenties, with flowing azure hair, azure skin, and four handless arms. Both wore only drunken smiles and wraparound chains. The thin silver links wound around their curves, hiding mere inches of skin.

The women giggled when they saw us, not the least concerned by our presence. We allowed them to pass without a word, then each turned and fired, stunning them. They froze in place.

All Delenseans acted like rebellious teenagers, anyway. Throw drugs into the mix, and no telling what kind of havoc they would create.

"You gonna help me this time?" Dallas asked me.

We each dragged one around the corner and dropped her beside Bob. If we didn't get inside soon, no telling how big the pile would become.

I strode to the front door and pushed inside, Dallas right beside me. Music blasted my ears, a fast rhythm that lured in the unwary. The mingled scent of sweat, sex, and alcohol filled my nostrils, almost obscene in its headiness. Illegal cigarette smoke, too. Shadows and light constantly battled for control, blending together at times, illuminating, then hiding each other, but all the while creating a dreamlike atmosphere.

The foyer possessed no furnishings, yet still overflowed with half-dressed, undulating bodies, both human and alien. One man was bound to the wall by thick ropes, and he moaned in rapture as the woman standing behind him spanked him with a spiked, wooden paddle.

Another group was in the middle of a dog-and-pony show. Three naked human women were on all fours, a spiked collar wrapped around each of their necks. A glowing male Mec paced them up and down the walkway.

"I'm feeling a little overdressed," Dallas said.

I'd never seen so many people getting off in so many different ways. "Come on. Let's find Lilla before we lose our concentration."

"Too late for me, but go ahead and lead the way."

As I strode in front of Dallas, a man latched his fingers around my wrist, trying to draw me into his waiting embrace. I attempted to jerk myself free, but found my efforts were paltry compared to his determination.

I was just about to introduce the man's groin to my knee when Dallas slammed his fist into the guy's face.

I was suddenly freed. "Thanks," I said with a half grin.

"No prob."

We continued toward the main room. My boots stuck to the floor in several places, and I shuddered at the thought of just what was making them stick.

Once in the center of the action, I cataloged the entire scene. Crosses decorated the walls, and moonlight dappled through red velvet curtains. Pillowed

chaises in brilliant golds and purples snaked around the
far corners. Sashaying in every direction were waitresses
dressed as slutty nuns, each holding a tray piled high
with drugs, alcohol, and sex toys. Amid the moans of
titillation that rivaled the music's volume, bodies
bumped and writhed.

"Think I can get a membership?" Dallas asked, the
warmth of his breath fanning my ear.

"You're perverted enough."

"Yes, I am," he answered proudly.

I rolled my eyes. "Do you see her?"

"Honestly?" He slowly smiled. "I haven't been looking. There are too many other, more interesting sights."

I couldn't chastise him, since I'd been distracted as
well. I slid my gaze to the bar. Lilla's file claimed she
was a bartender, but I didn't see her peddling drinks.
Determined to find her, I studied every individual,
every corner, every hollow. I counted two Arcadians,
both female, neither Lilla.

Then suddenly . . . joltingly . . .

My gaze connected with the seductively uptilted
violet eyes of an Arcadian male. Breath froze in my
lungs, and everything around me receded. Time
slowed. The music faded from my ears. My vision tunneled to this one man as a foreign energy sizzled under
my skin. I rubbed at my arms, trying to rid myself of
the odd sensation.

The Arcadian was taller than anyone else in the
room, his shoulders broad and muscled like a savage

Pict warrior from long ago. His cheekbones were high, his nose straight, his lips full, lush, and sensual. He wore danger like a cloak, erotic danger, lethal danger, and there was a hard, granite edge to his expression. It was the same expression cops and hunters wore, one that proclaimed he'd seen the darkest life had to offer and had survived. I couldn't see his clothing, couldn't tell if he wore traditional earth clothing or something more daring. I only knew he looked like living power.

At last you arrive whispered so clearly across my mind, I almost turned to see who had spoken. I watched a knowing—and perhaps a little mocking—smile half-curl the corners of his lips, and then he was gone, his warrior body somehow hidden in the crowd. I searched, but couldn't find him. Besides the energy flowing through me, there wasn't a single indication of his presence.

Where was he? Who was he? And how the hell had he disappeared so quickly?

I frowned.

"Hey, Mia," Dallas said, slicing into my preoccupation. "You okay? You were in a trance or something. I had to call your name several times to get your attention."

"I'm fine," I offered weakly. Disgusted with myself, I scanned the masses again. *Lilla. I'm looking for Lilla.* The man didn't matter.

I resumed my search and was quickly rewarded. There, at the back altar, was a black overstuffed lounge that curled at the end like a lover's palm. Atop the cushions, I saw a cascade of white hair and a perfectly sloped back. Anticipation zinged across my nerve endings. Sometimes I just knew, *knew* things without any explanation why, and I knew this was Lilla, though I couldn't see her face.

She was poised above a human male. His legs were bent and spread to offer her a libidinous cradle. I couldn't make out his features. On Lilla's left and right sides were two catlike Taren females; both wore flimsy white robes and were licking and kissing Lilla's shoulders.

As if she sensed my gaze, Lilla tossed her hair over one shoulder, turned, and met my stare. I felt a slight hum of energy whiz through me, the same type of odd hum I'd felt with the Arcadian warrior. It was . . . bizarre, something I'd never encountered before today. I had no idea what it meant, and I didn't have time to analyze. Lilla gave me a slow smile before returning her attention to her lovers.

My eyes narrowed. "This way," I said to Dallas, giving his shirtsleeve a tug. Side by side we strode across the dance floor, ignoring wandering hands and gyrating bodies.

When we reached our destination, I received my first full look at the man beneath Lilla. He had thick red hair and freckled skin, big ears that probably flapped in the wind. His eyes were spaced too far apart, but the color was nice, a mixture of green and brown.

"Mark St. John," Dallas supplied. "Ecstasy's owner."

I had a few questions for Lover Boy, but knew those would have to wait. A man with a hard-on had trouble concentrating on facts. Besides, interrogations worked best with one suspect at a time.

I shifted my gaze to Lilla. She wore a flesh-colored halter top and skirt that almost made her appear naked. I reached out and tapped her on the shoulder. "Lilla en Arr?"

"Yes?" she said, not sparing me a glance.

"We need to speak with you."

Languidly, deliberately, she turned to face me, and our gazes collided again. As if on cue, the music tapered to silence.

"Mia Snow," she said, her tone as soft as a caress, each syllable well modulated and punctuated precisely with an almost hypnotic rhythm. "I am so glad you have, at last, joined us. We have been expecting you."

CHAPTER
3

*W*e have been expecting you.

The words reverberated in my mind amid the unexpected silence.

We. Not I. Kind of like the words that had whispered through my mind only minutes before. *At last you arrive.*

I stared down at Lilla. Her features were as delicate as butterfly wings, incandescent and angelic. Pale. Wholly innocent. And somehow the absolute essence of sexuality. On the surface, she was beauty personified. Yet there was an underlying hardness to her gaze, a tightness to her lips that gave her an emotionally untouchable veneer.

I didn't have to glance at Dallas to know he was

foaming at the mouth for a taste of this woman. He was a sucker for ice queens.

I fought the urge to grab her by the shoulders, slap a pair of laserbands on her wrists, and haul her ass down to A.I.R. headquarters. I had questions, and most likely, she had the answers. However, taking her to the station might have the same results as her former arrests—swept under a nice, tidy little rug—and I wouldn't risk that. I didn't want Lilla released, her file once again buried. Maybe even destroyed this time.

I'd interrogate her here, in front of God and every pervert present if needed.

"We need to speak with you, Lilla," I said, my tone as hard as her expression.

"Then speak," she replied. Still watching me, she traced a fingertip down the center of her flesh-colored top. She was the very picture of carnal seduction, and I was amazed by just how *human* she appeared. "I have nothing to hide. No secrets lurking about, waiting to nibble on me."

"Let's go somewhere private."

"Whatever you wish to discuss, we will discuss here, with my friends. Or . . ." Her gaze swept over me. "Perhaps you would like to join us first?"

"I'm not interested in dying like William Steele," I said.

Lilla's smile lost some of its arrogance, and something dark flickered in the depths of her eyes, turning the violet to deep purple. I almost regretted that I'd punctured some of her casual disregard. After all, I admired strength in a woman. I admired the courage it took to look a hunter in the eyes and casually dismiss him. Or her. Still, I found it interesting that she'd betrayed such a reaction to my words. There were definite emotions here.

Uncaring of the happenings around him, St. John snaked his arms around Lilla and caressed her bare stomach. Lilla regained her easygoing facade.

With one wave of her hand, she dismissed the two Taren women. Or cats. Or whatever they were. They hopped down on all fours without protest and slinked to the bar. Lilla whispered something in St. John's ear. He shook his head, intent on getting his piece of ass. She whispered something else. I couldn't make out the words, only the fierceness of her tone. This time, he gave an abrupt nod. His expression dark, he pushed to his feet, the action causing Lilla to bounce on the couch. St. John stalked away.

"Smart move," I said, the mechanics of their relationship suddenly clear. Lilla was the puppet master, and little Markie was her puppet. Whether she controlled him through simple feminine wiles or Arcadian mind control, I didn't know. Didn't care. "We wouldn't want St. John to hear about your dealings with another man, would we?"

Keeping her gaze locked on mine, Lilla rose, her movements slow and elaborate, somehow making the simple act of rising a seductive dance. Her eyelids lowered in an enticing, come-hither blink. "Please," she said on a breathy murmur. "Follow me. We will chat somewhere private, just as you wished."

The music kicked up, filling the club with a syncopated beat and claiming the attention of the patrons. Lilla turned, flicking her luxuriant white hair over one shoulder, and strolled toward guarded double doors. Dallas followed right behind her, as if it were perfectly natural to follow a murder suspect wherever she might lead.

Were they pumping drugs through the ventilation system? I thought sarcastically. Dallas wasn't usually this foolish. Lilla was beautiful, yes, but the only thing worthy of such blind adoration was a giant vat of fresh, steaming synthetic coffee.

Ever watchful and guarded, I remained five steps behind. When I found myself searching for the Arcadian male who'd caught my eye earlier—for reasons that had nothing to do with safety—my lips curled back involuntarily in a scowl. I was as bad as Dallas. I forced my gaze to focus straight ahead.

We were led into an empty hallway and up a flight of creaking stairs. The long, narrow corridor we entered next had dancing nymphs painted on the walls and soft, wine-colored carpet. Finally, we entered a small office. There were no windows adorning the plain white walls. A desk crowned the center, and four chairs formed a half-moon at the front. The air was clean, devoid of smoke. In fact, the air smelled faintly of dried rose petals and lavender sachet, a scent any grandmother would have applauded.

Lilla settled on the edge of the honey oak desk. No papers were on top, I noticed.

"Would you like the door open or closed?" she asked. The seductress was gone, and in her place was a polite but formal hostess.

"Closed," I answered.

"Excellent choice." She pushed a small button on a remote control, and the door snapped shut, cutting off all traces of music. "We are more intimate this way."

I refused to have my back to the door, so I claimed the high-backed swivel chair behind the desk. Dallas stayed beside the entrance, just in case someone tried to enter—or Lilla tried to leave.

"Well," Lilla said with a little laugh. She hopped off the desk and eased into one of the seats facing me. She folded one leg over the other, the action slow and sensual. "You certainly have my full attention now."

I placed a voice recorder on the desk's surface and pushed record. Then I waited, allowing silence to stretch around us like long fingers of ice. I wanted Lilla to wonder, even stress, about what I had to say. An old trick I'd learned my first year of duty.

"I am patient," she said with a knowing smile. "I can wait as long as you can."

Fine. "Did you murder William Steele?" I asked, my voice steady and clear.

Her eyes widened, and I knew she hadn't expected me to be so direct. "Wh—what?"

"William Steele was found in an abandoned field, stripped and dead. We're here to give you a chance to clear your name," I lied. I truly doubted she could clear her name; she was involved somehow, some way, I just didn't know the specifics. But I would. "So I'm going to ask one more time. Did you murder William Steele?"

"No. No, no," she said with a shake of her head. "I did not kill William."

"You're going to have to prove that by giving me a detailed list of your whereabouts today."

"I would never hurt him," she continued as if I hadn't spoken. "Ever."

I arched a brow. "Ever?"

"That is right."

I glanced to Dallas. "Now correct me if I'm wrong, but wasn't it Lilla en Arr who beat the shit out of William Steele six weeks ago?"

"That'd be correct," he answered.

Lilla's already pale skin grew more pallid. "I do not have to respond to that. Nor do I have to answer any more of your questions." She held out the remote, intending to open the door. I grabbed it and slammed it onto the desk.

"Let me break it down for you," I said. "Other-worlders are allowed to live and work among humans as long as all of our laws are obeyed. The moment a law is broken, aliens lose all rights. My job is to enforce and punish. The fact that I even suspect your involvement in a human murder grants me the authority to kill you. You're alive now only because I allow you to live."

Silence.

Silence so thick it cast an oppressive fog throughout the room.

"I didn't hurt him," Lilla finally whispered, each syllable ragged and broken, giving her tone an underlying pain, a deep hurt that was totally at odds with everything I'd concluded about her. She gazed down at her hands, and locks of white hair fell forward, shielding her face. "I loved him."

Yeah, she'd loved him so much she hadn't looked for him or helped the police find him before he died. But I had to give two thumbs up for her performance. She deserved an Academy Award for best actress during a hunter interrogation.

"I still need that list," I said.

"I did *not* murder him."

"Where were you this afternoon?" I insisted.

"At the club." She sighed. "I was here at the club."

"You were here all evening? You never left? Always had someone around you?"

"Yes."

"I'll need names of the people you were with and the times that you were with them. And Lilla?" I added, blinking over at her. "I *will* verify this."

"Then you will find I have spoken the truth."

Without glancing my way, she clicked off the names and times I wanted.

"I did love him," she said, almost absently. "He simply would not listen to my warnings. I tried to force him to my will that night, but he refused to heed me. I used physical force, yes, but I did not mean to hurt him."

"What were you trying to force him to do?" Give people enough rope and they'll hang themselves.

She eased up, her hands wringing together. "I tried to make him leave. He thought he could handle them. He thought, as all humans do," she added bitterly, "that nothing bad could happen to him."

"Them?" I demanded. "Who is *them*?"

Her mouth fell open, as if she couldn't believe she'd given so much away. She didn't answer.

"Who is *them*?" I insisted.

"That is none of your concern." She arched her brows. "And you, I think, will not ask me such a question again. I won't hurt you; that would anger my brother. But there are other things I can do—"

"Your brother? Why would he care?"

"No more questions."

Phantom hands shoved their way into my mind, grasping, reaching. I went on instant alert, using all of my strength to erect a mental block. "Mind control is a crime," I ground out. A sharp ache pounded in my temples, growing deeper and more intense with every second that passed, and I wasn't sure if the pain stemmed from her attempt at mind control or my attempt to block her powers.

When I thought I might cry out from the strain, she whipped around, and the dynamism of her gaze was broken. All of a sudden my pain ceased, and dizziness overtook me. Unable to focus, I dropped my head into my waiting hands.

The air began to spark with electricity, and the intensity only increased.

"Dallas," I said, forcing myself to glance at him.

He ignored me. He was focused completely on Lilla . . . and he was opening the goddamn door for her.

"Dallas!"

Still no response.

I had the sense of mind to grab my voice recorder before lunging to my feet. My knees buckled. By the time I regained my balance, Lilla was gone. I raced around the desk, saw that Dallas was slumped against the wall, eyes closed. I flew into the hallway, but only emptiness greeted me. Damn, damn, damn.

I stomped my foot, and the weight of my boot caused a heavy thud. Inside the office, I slapped Dallas across the face, hard, putting all my strength behind the blow. "Damn it, why did you let her go?"

"I—I don't know." His expression bemused, he shook his head, blinked his eyes.

"Why?" I demanded.

"I felt like I *had* to open the door for her, or I'd

die." A moment later, his eyes darkened with anger. He rubbed three fingers over his reddened cheek. "Why the hell did you hit me?"

"I think the better question is, why didn't I slap you twice?"

He left that alone, because he knew I was angry enough to follow through. "Do you know where she went?"

"She's smart, and she knows we'll find her here. My guess is she's run to another location—or to someone," I added as an afterthought. Then I swore under my breath. "I can't believe we let her get away."

"Look at it this way," he offered. "Now the true fun begins. We're going hunting."

CHAPTER
4

*S*ide by side, Dallas and I pounded down the steps, taking them three at a time. Still dizzy from Lilla's mind control, Dallas wasn't as agile as he normally was. He stumbled once and had to grip the banister to keep from tumbling face first.

A group of men, obviously hired muscle, waited for us at the bottom. They were human, which meant we couldn't kill them without a shitload of consequences. Too bad, too. A little killing might have worked off some of my tension.

We ground to a halt in the middle of the staircase. We either had to arrest them or fight them, and I didn't have time to take them to A.I.R. headquarters. What's more, anyone who attempted to hinder an alien investigation deserved an ass kicking.

I counted five idiots, all grinning because I probably looked like I'd never been dirty, never perspired, and never said a naughty word in my life, and Dallas was only one man. What harm could these two do? they were thinking.

A slow grin played at my lips. I'd spent my childhood in one fight or another, trying to prove to my dad that I was strong, capable, and fearless, just like my brothers had been. Living in the Southern District, the poor side of town, I hadn't been able to fight like a cop or a sweet little lady. No, I'd learned to fight dirty. And mean.

Maybe if my mom hadn't run off when I was a kid, she could have instilled some feminine qualities in me. But she had, and I wasn't a "lady." A tide of anticipation was already rushing through me at the thought of putting these men in their places—at my feet.

"You ready for this?" I asked Dallas. I knew how to inflict damage, yes, but I couldn't do this alone.

"Absolutely." He sounded completely sure of his ability.

"This is going to be fun," one of the idiots said.

The speaker was a handsome man, probably only twenty years old, and he had a hard-on the size of a police baton. Impressive, but it wasn't going to save him from a beating. He wore a come-and-lick-me smile, and I noticed he had a mouth of straight white teeth. Too bad he was about to lose some of them.

To the beat of the music rocking in the next room, Dallas and I darted into action. The moment I neared them, I kicked out one leg and struck one of the men in the balls with the heel of my foot, all without missing a step. He screamed in pain. The starting bell, you could say, because the fight had just begun.

Another man came at me, and I let my fist fly forward. Bone crunched against cartilage. Blood squirted from his nose. Never pausing for breath, I elbowed two throats, broke one man's kneecap, kneed a couple groins, and jabbed a pair of eyes before slamming a guy's head into the wall. One of the men recovered sufficiently to grab me by my jacket lapels. I brought my arms up hard and fast inside his grip and quickly ground my palm into his trachea. Eyes wide with horror, he struggled to scream, the sound broken. He released me as if I were radioactive waste and clutched at his throat, unable to breathe.

He'd probably die, and I'd be written up. Oh, well. "You shouldn't have come back for seconds, dumbass."

Beside me, Dallas fought like a champion boxer. He punched, ducked, then punched again, intermittently landing solid blows. Finally all five men lay unconscious at our feet. Blood pooled from some of the bodies, a crimson river of pain. A tooth lay next to the far wall—it probably belonged to the guy who'd thought this would be fun. Ha!

I had endured several fists to my stomach and now had a cut lip, and a bruised thigh. One of the men had actually pulled my hair and scratched my cheek, like a sissy girl who hadn't gotten her way. What a pussy.

I ignored the fact that I was doubled over and panting like a sissy myself. "You okay?" I asked Dallas.

"My side and face hurt like hell, but other than that, I'm fine." He gently fingered his swollen, blackening eye. "You?"

"About the same." I took a moment to catch my breath, dragging each intake into my lungs as if I was on life support. Smoke had seeped inside this little alcove, so the air wasn't fresh and left an ashy taste in my throat.

"If we go through there," Dallas said, pointing to the double doors that led into the club, "another fight will break out, and I'm not sure my body can go another round right now."

"Big baby," I said. I wasn't going to admit that I felt the same way. My bones throbbed, and my muscles burned. "There's a window on the north wall. If it opens, we might be able to get outside without drawing any attention to ourselves."

"That's worth a try," he said.

We limped to the window in question and paused. Our curses mingled together in a long, heated sputter as we surveyed the potential exit. The thick stained glass was welded to a copper frame, which was welded to the wall. I wouldn't have been surprised if the wall was welded to a steel support beam.

Dallas shifted his attention left, then right. Not a

single piece of furniture, not a single decoration, occupied the hallway. Muttering more curses under his breath, he removed his left shoe. "If this doesn't work," he told me, "we have to go through the club. Start praying."

"I gave up prayer a long time ago."

"Do it anyway." He placed the boot over his fist and hit the glass, dead center, using all his strength. Nothing. He punched and punched and punched. Finally, thankfully, the glass gave way and shattered. The sound blended with the booming music like wind chimes on a blustery day. I'm sure we tripped some sort of alarm.

I removed my jacket and threw it over the jagged threshold. Dallas gave me a hand up. He came through behind me, tossed me my jacket, and we were on our way. I welcomed the cold, fresh breeze as darkness and snowflakes swirled all around us.

"I hear footsteps," Dallas said, grabbing my hand. "Move faster."

Together, we dashed to his car.

Two hours later, we were no closer to finding Lilla than we had been when we first left the club. We now had her voice on tape, but wherever she was, she wasn't talking, so we couldn't pinpoint her location. We'd tracked down and spoken with several people she'd listed as contacts, but had no luck with any of them.

"This sucks ass," Dallas said.

I agreed.

I sat in the passenger seat of his sedan. We were maneuvering down the East District's winding streets, made slick from the snow. Though the car guided itself, Dallas kept his eyes on the road, ever conscious of our surroundings. Music rocked softly from the speakers, and heat trickled from the vents, both as oppressive as my thoughts.

Someone close to me was going to die before the night ended.

The premonition took me by surprise. I blinked, and just like that I saw a scene unfold in my mind, though I could not make out all the specifics. I saw the blast of a pyre-gun, the fall of a man. I couldn't see his face, nor could I see who had fired the shot; I only knew the shooter was a woman, the victim was my friend, and every fiber of my being was screaming of the approaching death.

Dallas sometimes teased me about being psychic. I always denied it, said my instincts were simply better than most. But I lied. I *was* able to predict certain events.

I was fourteen years old the day of my first vision. In my mind I had seen my youngest brother lying in a crimson river, three aliens standing over him, laughing and pointing. I'd pretended then that what I'd seen hadn't been real, had only been a figment of my imagination. But the next day I found Dare unconscious, his body drained of blood.

My next vision came a year later. I saw my dad get drunk and step in front of an oncoming car. Vehicle sensors hadn't been as sensitive as they were today, and the front end slammed into him. Of course, I immediately told him what I'd seen. He'd laughed, waved me away with an indifferent sweep of his hand. Two days later a sedan barreled into him. He broke his hip and leg and had to endure bone replacement surgery. He'd never spoken of it, but I know my ability scared him.

That's when I began to realize just how different I was. I realized, too, that I had to push myself harder than everyone else, had to be better, stronger, and smarter if I wanted to be seen as one of the boys.

I rubbed a hand over my face. With this new vision, I was going to take measures to prevent it from coming true. I had to. Yet with each second that ticked by, dread churned inside me, growing colder than the glacial snow whipping outside the windows.

Just what could I do? Delay our hunt until tomorrow, perhaps? Radio all of my men and send them home?

As soon as those thoughts entered my mind, I discarded them. Civilian lives depended on me. On us. I wouldn't abandon my job, even for one night. And my men wouldn't either, even if I begged them. Our jobs came before our emotions. Always.

So what could I do? My teeth ground together as helplessness claimed me. Over the years, I'd lost my brother Dare and many, many friends to rogue aliens, and I wouldn't lose another friend without a fight. I didn't have many left, and those I had meant something to me.

"Stop the car," I managed on a shaky catch of breath.

Dallas cast me a quick glance. "Why? We're almost—"

"Stop the fucking car!"

"Stop," he commanded the vehicle. The sound of squealing tires filled my ears, and I was suddenly thrust forward with the momentum of our skid and ultimate stop. Another car honked and swerved around us.

Dallas leveled me a frown. "What the hell's the matter with you?"

I didn't know what to tell him, so I simply said, "I need a moment to think."

"Of what? How to find Lilla?" He lost some of his anger. "I've already loaded her voice frequency, but she's not goddamn talking, so there's nothing we can do."

"Just get on the computer and see what else you can dig up about her." I didn't spare Dallas another glance. "Open," I commanded the door, and the hatch slid open. I stepped into the bitterly cold night.

I strode a few paces away, my boots crunching snow with every step. I realized I stood at the edge of State Street, alone, silent, the cloak of twilight and stars all around me. Several snowflakes floated onto my lashes, and I blinked the crystals away, hoping to blink my fears away, as well.

Both remained.

Maybe I had missed something in the vision, some obscure detail that would help me prevent the death from occurring. There was only one way to find out. . . .

I closed my eyes, manipulated my consciousness until I stood at the periphery of my thoughts, and allowed the gruesome scene to replay in my mind, along with a deep, pounding ache.

Through a thick, gloomy fog, I see two women; one is a human, the other is alien. They are facing each other. I can't make out their coloring, can't make out anything except the shape of their bodies. A man bursts into the room, behind the alien. I know this man, his scent, his energy, but his identity escapes me. He shoves the alien aside. The human woman fires a pyre-gun. The man falls in a puddle of his own blood.

The vision left me in the next instant.

I cracked open my eyes. My hands clenched at my sides as my helplessness intensified, more real than the aches and pains of my battered body. I didn't know why the man had pushed the alien aside, or why he'd taken a blast of fire for her. Nor did I know why a human would want to hurt him. And I still didn't know the identities of the victim or the killer.

I drew in a deep breath, then slowly released the air through my lips. No friend of mine was going to die tonight. I simply wouldn't allow it. I would suspect every human female I encountered, and I *would* save this man.

If we could just find Lilla, we could lock her up, and Dallas and the others could go home, away from danger.

My movements were clipped, jerky, as I spun around and strode back to the car. The passenger door was still open, so I slid inside and slammed it shut beside me.

Dallas was plugging away at the computer console. He shot me a glance. "Better now?"

"Yes." I didn't explain further.

The edges of his mouth twitched. "You always have PMS this bad?"

"This is actually a light case," I replied dryly.

He chuckled, the husky timbre of amusement mingling with his next words. "God help us all when it's bad, eh?"

I opened up to tell him to go to hell. Before one word emerged, however, his expression sobered, and he cursed under his breath. He pounded a fist into the keyboard. "I'm having a hell of a time getting back into Lilla's file. Damn it! If I could match her voice frequency, we'd be set."

"Forget voice. We're missing something," I said on a frustrated breath. In my mind, I pored over everything I knew about her, everything I'd learned from our meeting. "The woman isn't very discriminating. Is she linked to any more men?"

"Not that I'm aware of. She's been seen with William Steele, of course, and Mark St. John, but no one else. Well," he added, "unless you count George Hudson, her arresting officer."

The moment Dallas spoke those words, several pieces of the puzzle connected in my mind. "You're a freaking genius, Dallas." I flopped back against the headrest and laughed with excitement. "Hudson. We haven't yet talked to Hudson. He's involved somehow."

"But why did Lilla allow him to arrest her? Her capacity for mind control is staggering, as we both found out."

"Wait. Remember what she said? That she couldn't force Steele to do what she wanted? Maybe she can't control everyone. Maybe she can't control the men she screws."

"Oh, that's good. That's very good. Since she couldn't convince Hudson to forget her arrest, she must have clocked in a few hours between the sheets with him."

I was intrigued—and disgusted—by Hudson's supposed behavior, which didn't fit with A.I.R. standards. Agents did not sleep with other-worlders. Ever. For any reason. "If they were sleeping together, though, why didn't he simply let her go? Why go to all the trouble of taking her down to the station, booking her, and then burying her record?"

"Maybe he was jealous of her association with Steele and wanted to teach her a lesson: obey me or pay the consequences."

"There are other ways to teach an alien a lesson. Ways that don't include incriminating himself."

"Witnesses," Dallas said, slapping his thigh. "There would have been witnesses to her crimes, and Hudson had to make her arrest appear real."

My eyes widened. "God, this all seems so clear now," I said, and with that, relief hammered through me. Knowing exactly who had hidden Lilla's file wiped away my worries about the station house. I could take Lilla into custody now; I could interrogate her on *my* turf.

This didn't mean my friends were completely safe, of course. It just meant I had one less worry on this shit-filled night.

"What do we know about Hudson?" I asked.

Dallas punched some keys. A picture of George Hudson filled the screen, his information posted beside his smiling face.

"Forty-one. Brown hair, brown eyes." Dallas paused. "I'd forgotten his coloring. A perfect match for our missing men." He rolled his neck, and the bones popped. "Do you really think she'd go to him? That she'd go to the man who arrested her?"

"Oh, yeah. She'd feel safe with the A.I.R. agent who's protected her twice already."

"Should I call for backup?"

I nodded. "Have Ghost and Kittie meet us at the old warehouse on Water."

Dallas radioed the two agents, then programmed the address into the car. Our tires squealed as the vehicle veered onto the street, high-tech sensors guiding it and keeping it from crashing into objects. "I told you the night was going to be interesting."

"Interesting?" I shook my head. "No. It's about to get ugly."

A flash of movement captured my attention. My eyes narrowed, and I intensified my focus, my head turning as the car sped farther and farther away. When I saw a second flash, a peculiar, familiar energy washed over me. Just like at the club. And I knew. It was the male Arcadian.

"Stop the car."

"Again?" Dallas asked.

"Pull over," I shouted.

At his command, the car once more jerked to a stop, and I propelled forward in my seat, then back. At this rate, I would have whiplash by morning.

"Stay on your guard," I told Dallas, then said, "Open," to the car. As the hatch lifted, I added, "I spotted someone I want to question." I jumped out, my weapon already drawn, my feet already moving, causing me to leap into a run the moment my shoes touched the ground. This was not the setting of my vision, so I had no compulsion to guard Dallas.

"Why the hell—" I heard Dallas shout behind me, his voice traveling with me. I didn't slow down to explain. Couldn't. He'd follow. He always followed when I took off. His protective instincts wouldn't allow him to wait passively behind.

My eyes continually searched the area around me.

Damn, where had the Arcadian gone? I kept running, following his Onadyn scent.

With each pump of my feet and arms, with each jagged rock that beat into my boots, it became more and more clear that this man meant only to taunt me. When Dallas had ground the car to a halt, I had seen the Arcadian smile—smile, damn him—before sprinting away at full speed.

My footsteps continued to pound into the pavement. My heated breath mingled with the icy wind. Buildings towered on both my left and right sides, causing even greater darkness to swell around me. My senses were alert, my nocturnal vision excellent, and I finally caught another glimpse of him. I watched a trench coat whip around a corner and followed.

"Stop!" I shouted. "A.I.R."

His laughter floated to me, rich and smooth, like warm brandy during a summer storm, unbelievably, suggestively sensual.

I'd catch him, the bastard, if for no other reason than to cut out his voice box so he'd never laugh again. As I ran, I adjusted my pyre-gun to stun, aimed, and fired off several rounds. With each shot, blue lights blazed a trail in front of me, illuminating the shocked faces of the alley's inhabitants. The lights quickly faded.

I'd missed him. Every time. He dodged each round as if he knew exactly where they would land. *Faster, Mia,* I commanded myself. *Don't lose him.* Ragged breath burned in my throat and lungs and clanged in my ears, but I forced myself to keep moving.

Abruptly my run came to a stop, for reasons that had nothing to do with stamina. A wall blocked the end of the alley. Turning, panting, I eyed every inch of this bricked enclosure. The Arcadian was nowhere to be seen. How the hell had he gotten past that wall?

In the next instant, something soft brushed my ear. I whipped around, fired. Hit only the wall. The same softness brushed my other ear, renewing my awareness, propelling that odd thrill of energy through me. I spun, fired, and cursed. Still, nothing.

"You are being followed," a husky male voice said. *His* voice. The warrior. He sounded serious and grave now, and I couldn't tell which direction his voice came from. He was moving too fast.

"I know I'm being followed," I said through clenched teeth. "By you." Steady. "Are you a coward? Reveal yourself."

"Another has already been taken, Mia Snow, and another will soon become a victim as well." He continued to move around me so swiftly I couldn't get a lock on him. "Will you protect these victims," he said, "or will you help the killer?"

What kind of question was that? One so stupid, I wasn't going to answer it. "Who has been taken, and who *will* be taken? Give me the names," I demanded.

"Will you protect these victims?" the Arcadian demanded in the same hard tone I'd used.

Where the hell was he? "Of course I will protect them. That's my job. Now give me their names."

A long pause surrounded us. Finally, he said, "What do you know of Rianne Harte?"

"Ryan Heart," I echoed, committing the name to memory. "Nothing. What do you know of him?"

He chuckled, the sound dark rather than amused. "Surely you have gotten further in the case than this. Surely you——"

"Mia," Dallas called behind me.

"And so our time together ends," the alien said.

"Stay," I demanded of him. "I'm not finished with you."

The Arcadian didn't respond. In fact, I no longer felt his presence. The gentle charged hum of his electrical output was gone. Damn it. Obviously his powers were exceptional. Maybe that was why I'd felt his energy twice now. To escape as quickly and easily as he had, he either levitated or walked through that brick wall.

God help us if aliens could now mist through solid objects.

My free hand fisted. Had he told me the truth? Had someone else already been abducted? Was another man soon to die? If so, the Arcadian might even be the one responsible. He could have been bragging. I found myself nodding. That made sense and fit part of the killer's profile.

"Where's the Arcadian?" Dallas asked, panting. "I got a look at him and then he disappeared."

I pivoted and faced my partner. "I lost him. Fucking lost him."

"Who the hell was he, anyway?" He bent over and sucked in a breath. "And why the hell were we chasing him?"

"I saw him at the club."

Dallas's eyes went wide. "You think he knows something?"

"Yeah." With my hands on my hips, I searched the alley one last time. Nothing. "Let's go back to the car, and I'll explain."

We strode briskly to the vehicle, ever alert to the happenings around us, and managed to settle inside the car's warmth without incident.

"He mentioned a name," I said. "Ryan Heart, male. Check for a missing person's report."

Dallas typed the name into the console, then glanced at me. "Nada."

"Try Ryan Hart," I said, changing the spelling. "And if that doesn't work, try Harte."

A moment passed before Dallas uttered a dark chuckle. "I hate to break this to you, Mia, but there are two Ryan Harts. One is sixty-eight, not the appearance of our victims. The other is his ten-year-old grandson. They both have blond hair."

"Are you sure?"

"Positive."

The Arcadian had lied to me. My muscles tightened with simmering fury.

"Get both Harts on the phone," I said. "I want to personally hear that they're safe in their beds."

It took Dallas fifteen minutes, but he finally confirmed that both Grandpa and the boy were safe.

"I want a guard on both of them," I said. "I want to know who they talk to, where they go. And keep it low-key. I don't want anyone to know, not even the commander."

"There are a couple of humans who owe me a favor." Dallas made the necessary calls.

I didn't like this. I didn't like this at all.

CHAPTER
5

When we arrived at the warehouse, Ghost and Kittie were already there.

They stood beside their cruiser, each loaded down with multi-sized guns, knifes, and ammo. They were wearing typical hunter attire—black leather pants, black shirts, and black jackets. Where Ghost was tall, with chocolate-colored skin and a well-muscled body, Kittie was short and as pale as vanilla ice cream. His spindly arms and legs hid a dangerous strength and an ability to take down the most menacing of suspects.

Kittie's real name was James Vaughn, and on his first day at A.I.R. he roamed the halls, introducing himself as Mad Dog. He deserved a tough nickname, he'd said. I decided then to call him Kittie.

The name had stuck.

Dallas commanded the car to park next to them, and the vehicle smoothly obeyed. We exited.

"Evening, boys," I said.

"Evening," Kittie said with a grin. His lips were almost imperceptible, only two thin slashes of pink, and he had a chin that pointed like a leprechaun's shoe, but damn if he didn't have a beautiful pair of eyes— two brilliant emeralds framed by spiky black lashes. He dragged one last puff on his cigarette, then tossed it to the ground.

"That's a nasty habit," I said, my gaze following the glowing orange butt as it rolled across the pavement. "And completely illegal."

"Only way to control my advanced schizophrenia and narcissistic rage." Those green orbs glowed with amusement as he lovingly patted the cigarette pack in his coat pocket.

"Mia, you're lookin' as fine as always," Ghost said, "but Dallas . . . man, that's one hell of a shiner. Did you piss Mia off again?"

"Nah." Dallas shrugged. "This time she hit me for no reason."

"There's always a reason," I muttered.

He only chuckled.

"Did you have any trouble finding your first target?" I asked the others.

"None whatsoever," Kittie said, his deep voice a vivid contrast to his physique. "We put the little bastard in lockup. But I gotta tell you, he couldn't find his ass with a miner's hat, the stupid son of a bitch, and it was pretty obvious he knew nothing about Steele."

"Well, the Arcadian we're about to apprehend *does* know about Steele, so listen up." I clapped my hands to make sure I had everyone's attention. "Hudson's house is only a block away. We do this quietly and as quickly as possible. And I want all of you, *all of you,*" I stressed, my earlier vision suddenly filling my mind, "to be careful around any and all women we encounter. Got it?"

They all just stared at me with narrowed eyes, like I'd just called them stupid-ass morons. Maybe I had. They knew to take care with everyone they encountered. I held each stare for a few seconds, then crossed my arms over my chest and waited. I wasn't going to apologize.

Finally, Ghost broke the silence. "You want this girl Lilla dead or alive?" he asked.

"Alive. I have questions, she has answers. Now enough talk. Let's move."

We stealthily maneuvered on foot to Hudson's backyard. Our black clothing was like a neon sign set in the paleness of the snow, so we stayed crouched low to the ground, trying to stay in the shadows. At some points we crawled. Others we ran. The lights were out throughout the entire house; all of the curtains were drawn. Our heated breath misted the frigid air, and the only sound was the gentle patter of falling sleet.

I doubted Hudson was stupid enough to leave a

hideaway card for the guest scanner outside, but I searched anyway. Unfortunately, I found nothing more than a few shiny rocks and a fistful of dirt.

Kittie spent a few minutes at the power receiver, cutting the alarm and backup battery. A risky move, really, because the stilling of a ceiling fan or the flicker of a clock could alert the residents of our presence. Risky, but necessary.

Ghost crouched down in front of the doorknob and extracted a black velvet pouch from his side pocket. He removed a tiny saw blade and fit the shiny silver metal into the scanner. Wireless systems were still uncommon among the middle class, thank God, but even the most basic of houses used print IDs or guest cards for entry. In this Hudson was no different. I couldn't pick an ID unit to save my life. I didn't have the patience.

Smiling, I said softly, "I love it when you do this." His ability to break past any barrier gently and efficiently, without anyone the wiser, was how he'd earned his name. "I swear to God it turns me on."

"Any time, baby," he said. "This is just one of my many talents with my hands."

I already had my weapon drawn, so I lined up behind him and covered his back while he worked. Moments later, the ID was disarmed and the door popped open.

Quick as a snap, I spun and placed my back against the wall, preparing for entry.

Which one of these men would die tonight?

Unbidden, the question flashed in my mind. For a moment, I couldn't move, could barely breath. No. *No!* I would *not* let them die inside this house. I would protect them, with my own life if necessary. With that thought, I calmed. I would keep them safe with my own life. Shaking my head, I cleared my thoughts.

"Ready?" I asked, not voicing the words, just moving my lips.

Dallas got into position on the other side of the door. He nodded.

Ghost and Kittie stepped back, guns drawn. They, too, gave a short but sweet nod.

Every nerve in my body on alert, I silently stepped inside. My gaze darted, and my gun moved with it. Clear. I stepped deeper inside, careful to place my boots exactly to prevent any type of squeak. I paused, absorbing the silence. Dallas entered behind me, followed quickly by Ghost. Kittie stayed at the door, guarding our rear.

Legally, we didn't have to announce our presence like PD had to do. We were hunting a predatory alien, and that gave us the right to enter any home we wanted without advance notice. So we didn't give any. Lilla was a slippery creature, and I wasn't going to give her any warning.

I scanned the immediate area. A kitchen. Broken dishes littered the floor. Chairs were upturned. My heart sped into overdrive. There had been a fight in this room, and my gut told me Lilla was the instigator. Just like in the club, just like with the Arcadian warrior, I felt her energy, caught a lingering trace of her scent, sensual and exotic. My guess: I felt her because she was as powerful as the other Arcadian. I'd have to be careful with her.

I might not know what had suddenly allowed me to sense Arcadian energy today, but I was damn glad for the ability at the moment.

I motioned for the men to remain behind me, and I didn't have to see their expressions to know I'd just pissed them off royally. Usually they moved ahead and cleared the way before I took the next room. Not this time. I wasn't taking any chances. Screw their egos.

Noiselessly, I entered the moon-washed living room. A big bay window decorated the far wall, and the curtains gaped slightly down the middle. Couch cushions were strewn across the floor, the television was smashed to bits, but no life.

My heart slammed inside my rib cage, and I had to fight to keep my adrenaline rush under control. This was just like my vision. Total chaos, angry energy. Then death. I shivered and forced myself to breathe. I had to keep my mind cool. Calm. I paused a moment and simply listened. Silence.

No. No, there was a muffled sound, low and hurried, erratic, but there all the same. I waited, breath bated. There were three open doorways in the hall, no light emanating from any. Which room was the sound coming from? Damn it, I didn't like this. The best course of action would be to check one myself and allow Dallas and Ghost to check the others, all at the same time.

I rejected that idea as soon as it formed and skirted around the wall ledge, the men close to my heels. I moved into the first room. Almost immediately, I noticed a woman sleeping on the bed. Pink silk sheets draped her from toe to shoulder. I was able to make out blond hair, but nothing more.

Four steps later, I stood at the side of the bed. Keeping my weapon locked on her chest, I freed a pair of laserbands from my waist and locked her wrists around the headboard. The bands pulsed with a slight, golden light as they bonded to her skin. She muttered something as she stirred. Her eyelids slowly opened.

The moment she spotted me, her jaw dropped, and she prepared to scream. I covered her mouth with my free hand, cutting off any sound. A second later, Ghost was beside me.

Someone moaned, and it wasn't the bound woman. The sound had been too deep, too far away. Ghost put his hand over the woman's mouth to replace mine. I spun, ready, and watched the doorway. The sound had come from one of the other rooms.

"We're A.I.R. agents, ma'am," Ghost whispered to the woman. "Be quiet, and you'll be fine. Understand?"

She was glancing from one to the other, trembling so violently I feared she was having a seizure. Tears were filling her eyes, but she nodded. Shit, I inwardly cursed, as

I looked at her more fully. She was just a kid. Probably eighteen, give or take a year.

Behind me, I heard a woman groan and shout, "Oh, God."

I spun again and saw no one. And that's when it hit me. We had been so careful, so discreet, and in all likelihood, we wouldn't have been heard if we'd blown a trumpet to announce our presence. Hudson and Lilla were too busy screwing.

"Stay behind," I told Dallas.

He gave a quick, jerky nod in the affirmative. Fury burned in his eyes.

Since the bedroom door was open, Ghost and I took opposite sides of the frame. Kittie made the end of the hallway his focal point. I concentrated on the couple. They were crouched on the floor, and Hudson gripped Lilla from behind. Her pale hair swayed each time his naked ass pounded forward. His hands roamed all over her, through her hair, over her breasts.

I had to admire his technique.

"On my count," I mouthed silently.

I raised my index finger. One.

Middle finger. Two.

Another finger. Three.

We burst inside.

"Hands up," Ghost shouted. "A.I.R."

"Do it now," Dallas yelled. Of course, he hadn't stayed behind like I'd commanded.

Lilla screamed and jolted to her stomach. Hudson

didn't even turn. He was too busy reaching for his gun on the bedside table.

"Touch your weapon, and you die," I told him calmly. "You're fucked, Agent Hudson. And I don't meant that literally."

With his back still to me, he held his palms up and out as he eased back on his ankles.

"Keep your hands where I can see them," I said. "Understand?"

He gave one almost imperceptible nod.

"Good boy. Now turn toward me. That's right." I arched a brow as he sat himself next to Lilla. I couldn't help myself. My gaze was between his legs and I almost smiled. "At ease. I'm not that impressed with your equipment."

Hudson scowled.

Lilla was crying, her sobs echoing off the walls, and I switched my attention from Hudson to . . . "Fuck!" I shouted. "That's not her. That goddamn isn't her." Hudson hadn't been screwing Lilla, after all. This woman wasn't even an Arcadian. She had long blond hair, yes, but her eyes were dark blue, and her skin was perfectly sun-kissed.

I almost blew Hudson's face apart just to appease my growing rage.

But I paused and took stock. Okay. So this woman wasn't Lilla. Didn't matter. Lilla *was* here. I still felt her presence.

"Where is she, Hudson?" I demanded. When he

didn't respond immediately, I leveled my gun at his dick, so proudly displayed.

"I don't know what you're talking about. I swear to God I don't." He licked his lips and tried to scoot himself behind the woman's back.

"Using a civilian to shield yourself," I muttered. "You're practically the Antichrist, you know that?"

He stilled.

"In A.I.R. training, did you watch instructional halograms of my work?" I asked.

"Yeah," he hesitantly answered.

"Then you know I have no conscience, and I'll do whatever it takes to get what I want." I gave the trigger of my gun a little pressure, not enough to grind off a shot, but enough to make my target squirm a little. "I'm not going to ask you about Lilla again. I'm just going to hurt you."

"You'll go to jail if you hurt me." Sweat beaded on his forehead, and he worried a shaky hand back and forth across his brow. "Assaulting an agent of the law is a federal offense, and there are too many witnesses here."

One by one, my men turned around and faced the wall. Hudson's face grew paler and paler. A cruel laugh pushed past my lips. "Wrong answer," I said, and switched my gun's setting to its highest level. I aimed.

"She was here," he rushed on, hands up to ward me off, "and she tore my place apart. I kicked her out. I swear."

He was lying.

Lilla didn't control him, but he cared enough for her to risk his career and his freedom by burying her file. I truly doubted he would have kicked her out for trashing his place.

"Who's your friend?" I asked, motioning to the crying female. My men turned back and faced us. We'd made our point.

Hudson glanced at each man. "She's my wife."

He was lying. Again. His record said he was single. Most likely, he didn't want us to be able to question the woman about him. "Georgie, Georgie, Georgie," I said, holstering my gun, "you've really pushed me too far this time." With that, I closed the distance between us and slammed my palm into his nose. The cartilage snapped on contact. Amid his shrieks of agony, I turned and said, "Three noses in one night. Not my record, but not bad either."

Behind me, I heard Dallas give a short bark of laughter. I pivoted, but wasn't quick enough to catch his smile. He frowned at me, still angry with me for not letting him lead. I could handle his anger, though, because that meant he was still alive.

I turned back and knelt in front of the woman. Her body was violently trembling, and her eyes were slits of fear. "I'm not going to hurt you," I assured her. "You're safe."

Watching me, still unsure, she nodded.

"What's your name?" I asked.

"Sherry. Sherry Galligher."

"Did an Arcadian female come here tonight, Sherry?"

She nodded again.

"Is she here now?"

"Yes," was the hesitant reply.

"Shut up, bitch," Hudson spat, slamming his fist into her stomach with such force she banged against the nightstand.

My eyes narrowed on the bastard, and I held out my hand toward Kittie. "Hand me your lighter. I think I'll light a cigar." I glanced pointedly at Hudson's dick. "Well, a cigarette, anyway."

"Bitch," Hudson growled, his anger and desperation making him forget his fear. "You'd do it too. Well, if you want to light up my cock, why don't you try sucking it first? Because that's the only place you belong. On your knees."

"Oh, shit," Dallas said, suddenly behind me. "He's dead now."

Kittie slapped the lighter into my outstretched hand. "Thanks." I kept my attention on Hudson. I held the flame close to his nose and slowly moved downward. He tried to scramble backward, but the bed frame stopped any form of retreat. "You want to rephrase your last words?"

His lips compressed in a tight line as his ball hairs singed. "I'm sorry. I didn't mean it. I'm so sorry."

"Good boy." I stopped the flame but kept the

lighter within his view. "Sherry," I prodded, returning my attention to the woman, "where's Lilla?"

She answered only after Ghost had grabbed Hudson by the leg and dragged him beyond reach.

"George locked her in the basement," she said. "Lilla threatened to tell the police about him if he didn't help her."

I squeezed her hand in reassurance. "You did good. Real good." I'd find out more about the Antichrist's "activities" later. Right now, I had to take care of Lilla.

"Can I—I, I mean, may I get dressed now?" Sherry asked hesitantly, tearfully.

Pity welled inside me. I hated to see a human woman so beaten down. "Go ahead." But I watched her all the while, making sure she didn't make a move toward my men. I didn't think she would, but still . . .

As fast as her hands would allow, she gathered up her clothing from the floor and dressed. I didn't want to, but I banded her afterward—just in case.

My vision was making me damn careful.

That done, I pocketed Hudson's gun. Then, just for the hell of it, I strolled over to where Ghost was holding him and kicked the bastard in the stomach. His breath whooshed out of his mouth on a pained cry. "You like how that feels?" I girt out.

His only answer was a muttered, "Bitch."

"Band him," I said to Ghost, "before I kill him."

"With pleasure," Ghost answered.

"I need clothes first."

Ghost hefted him up and pinned him against the wall, his arms stretched behind his back. Blood dripped from Hudson's nose in a red river. "I can't go outside like this," he cried. "You can't fucking take me downtown until I'm dressed. I want my attorney. Get me my attorney, goddamn it."

"We don't have to get you a damn thing," Dallas retorted. "We're A.I.R., not the local PD."

I grinned. The situation was completely under control, and I was able to relax my vigil—well, I *slightly* relaxed my vigil. I wouldn't be totally relaxed until it was morning and I knew all of my men were alive and well. Now, at least, I felt free enough to leave them here with Hudson and Sherry while I took care of some much-needed business downstairs.

"Dallas, get him some clothes and lock him in the car," I said. "Ghost, you and Kittie see to the women. I'll handle Lilla."

"Do you need backup?" Dallas asked.

"No. After I've dealt with her, I'll meet you at the car." With that, I strode from the room and prepared myself to descend into hell.

CHAPTER
6

I brandished my own personal ID pick—my pyre-gun—as I inched down the creaking steps to the basement. Once there, I proceeded to blast the scanner to hell and beyond. *Boom.* The scent of burning wires filled my nostrils. My methods were swifter than Ghost's. Messier and louder, too. But then, I didn't have to be subtle anymore.

Lock taken care of, I kicked the seam in the center of the door with one solid strike of my foot. Wood chips rained to the floor as the door split open. One lone halo-light hung from the ceiling, swaying, casting thin beams around the small room.

Lilla occupied the far left corner of this small space. She was huddled on the bare ground, her knees drawn to her chest, her fingers locked over her shins. The air here was as cold and damp as it was outside, yet she was dressed only in the half-shirt and skirt she'd worn at the club. At least she was wearing boots.

She calmly turned her chin until she faced me, and I saw a thick streak of dirt across her right cheek. "You do realize you are wasting your time?" were the first words she spoke, her tone matter-of-fact.

"Whatever. Stand up." I kept my gazed focused on her face, watching for any sign—a twitching eye, teeth nibbling on her lower lip—that she planned to bolt. "Hands against the wall."

She slowly stood. "My brother will punish you for this."

"Perhaps you didn't hear me. Hands against the wall."

With a long, drawn-out sigh—hell, she was acting like a martyr here—she did as I'd commanded.

"Do you care so little for your life, Miss Snow? My brother *will* find me, and when he does, you will suffer greatly for all you have put me through."

"Story of my life. He'll have to take a number." My motions expeditious and efficient, I frisked her with one hand while holding my gun at her temple with the other. I found a sharp little blade strapped to her inner thigh.

"Are you enjoying yourself?" she asked as I confiscated the weapon.

"More than you know." I holstered my weapon and banded her wrists behind her back.

She protested weakly but allowed me to lead her back upstairs and outside without fighting. I kept one hand on her arm as we trekked up a hill. The snow was deeper than I remembered, and with every step, powder shifted onto my boot tops, freezing my toes.

The closer we came to the warehouse, the more she talked about her brother. On and on she went. "He will kill you," she threatened. "Kyrin has killed more humans than any of our kind," she boasted. By the time we reached Dallas, I longed to cut off my ears and give them to anyone who would take them, just so I wouldn't have to hear another word about her brother.

I gazed around expectantly, and discovered Ghost and Kittie were missing. Only Dallas remained, with Hudson situated in the back seat of our car. Dallas leaned against the door with his arms crossed. His eyes shot daggers at me while Hudson, who was inside with his hands still banded behind him, valiantly tried to remove the blue tape covering his mouth by rubbing his face against the headrest in front of him.

I raised a brow in curiosity.

Dallas shrugged. "He was too chatty."

"Kyrin will—"

"Oh, for God's sake," I said, cutting Lilla off. "Shut the hell up and get into the car."

Dallas commanded the door to open, and I stuffed Lilla inside. A bulletproof shield separated the front and back compartments, so I had no fear she'd try to jump into the driver's seat and speed off without us.

When the door slammed shut, locking her in next to Hudson, I glanced up at Dallas. "Where are the others?"

"They took the women in for questioning."

"They shouldn't have left without my permission."

"Your permission?" Dallas laughed, the sound cruel and laced with rage. "Who gives a shit about your permission right now? What the hell were you thinking in there? That you knew better than we did? You took each goddamn room by yourself." His tirade echoed through the darkness, as black and lethal as the night. "Not only is it dangerous, it's stupid. You could have gotten us all killed."

I had to swallow my first reply, the truth. He wouldn't acknowledge the fact that he was as susceptible to death as every human, that he was only a mortal, not a superhero, without serious damage to his ego. So I simply leaned against the car and said, "I have my reasons."

"That's it?" he barked, incredulous. "That's all you have to say?"

"Look, you did your job, and I did mine. It worked out. So drop it."

"No, Mia." He slammed his fist on the hood of the car, then leaned down until his breath mingled with mine. "I did *not* do my job. You wouldn't let me."

Scowling, I shouldered him out of my way and took my seat inside the vehicle.

Dallas remained outside for what seemed an eternity. Finally, he plopped into the driver's seat and said, "I've already phoned Pagosa. He's waiting for us at the station." His tone was distant, the way he'd speak to a hated ex-wife.

He was pissed, yes, and felt betrayed. While I hated the distance between us, I'd rather deal with those emotions than with his death.

I gripped the tops of my thighs. Heavy silence filled the car as we wound down the roads. Blissful silence. And in that silence, a thought occurred to me. I almost grinned. Dawn was only an hour away; Dallas and the others were alive. He was going to be okay. They were going to be okay. We'd soon be at A.I.R. headquarters. Nothing bad could happen there.

Suddenly Dallas began reprogramming the car, giving it a new destination. It jerked to the side of the road. We fishtailed before a snowy embankment abruptly stopped our spin.

"What are you doing?" I demanded, glaring at Dallas.

His brow was smooth, his lips relaxed. He blinked once, twice, but didn't speak.

What the hell was going on? "Dallas?"

"I have to free her," he said.

"What! Why?"

"I have to free her," he said again. His tone was as expressionless as his features.

Mind control.

Shit, shit, shit. I threw Lilla a furious glance. She

was staring intently at Dallas, watching as he stepped into the night, skirted around the vehicle, and paused beside her door.

I shoved my way out of the car and positioned myself just in front of Dallas, blocking his way to Lilla. "Look at me," I commanded.

He didn't.

"Look at me, Dallas." I waved my hand in his face and even snapped my fingers.

Again, it was as if I weren't even there.

"If you'll just look at me, I can help you through this."

"Get back in the car, Mia."

I knew by the coldness in his eyes that he would kill me to free Lilla. I was left with no other choice. "I'm sorry, Dallas," I said, but I didn't wait another second. I wrapped my hands around his neck and squeezed, pressing against his carotid artery, cutting off the supply of oxygen to his brain. In his altered state of mind, he didn't realize what I was doing until it was too late. His eyes widened, and he wrapped those large hands of his around *my* windpipe. Before he could do any damage, his knees collapsed, and he sank to the ground, unconscious.

Getting his muscled frame buckled into the passenger seat required more strength than I thought I possessed, but I was somehow able to do it. "Go on a freaking diet," I bit out. My body was already sore, and this just intensified every ache.

Damn, but I'd be glad when this hellish night was over.

I plopped in the driver's seat while Dallas slept peacefully, his features as relaxed as a child's, his snore as loud as a freaking foghorn. Lilla and Hudson—who needed to share a little of my pain—remained still and silent. They probably realized I was about to snap. All it would have taken was one gesture—one damn gesture!—from either of them, and I would have beat some ass.

I programmed the station house back into the console, and the car leaped into motion. Soon the A.I.R. building came into view. The outside was plain, brown, and nondescript. No windows, no landscaping. A towering eyesore, really, that boasted flame-resistant walls and bulletproof glass.

As we eased into the parking garage, I noticed Commander Jack Pagosa waited impatiently at the head of my parking space. Once the car had stopped, I emerged. I stood beside the open door, relieved that I was finally here. "Hey, Jack. You ready for this?"

"What the hell took so long?" he demanded in that gruff voice of his. "And why the hell is Gutierrez sleeping on the job?"

From the corner of my eye, I watched Lilla shift her body and attention toward Jack and I knew what she was planning. My fists clenched. Damn it. That woman was a menace.

"I'll explain in a minute," I told the commander.

Right now, I had to neutralize Lilla before she brainwashed the entire force.

I freed my pyre-gun, shifted the lever to stun, and flopped back into the driver's seat. This time, I was facing the back. Lilla's eyes widened as I lowered the separation shield and levered the barrel of my weapon at her forehead.

"My brother—"

"Fuck your brother." I squeezed the trigger.

A single blue beam blasted and paralyzed her, slicing her words to a halt. God, that felt good. I nodded with satisfaction. I should have done that when I found her in the basement, but I hadn't wanted to carry her. The downside now was that I wouldn't be able to question her until tomorrow night, when the stun wore off. Oh, well. That's the price I paid for peace. And I was now very willing to pay it.

Beside Lilla's motionless form, Hudson blubbered like a baby. He'd somehow removed the tape over his mouth. The moment he realized I was watching him, he uttered a high-pitched, girlish scream that resounded through the sedan.

"I'm sorry, Mia. So sorry," he babbled. "I swear I am. I'll do whatever you want, tell you anything you want to know—just put the gun away."

I longed to squeeze a round at him, but the stun only worked on aliens. Something about their chemical makeup. The fire beam, however, killed everything in its path, and I knew that's what he feared. "We'll chat a little later, Georgie boy," I said, tapping his cheek with the side of my gun, "don't you worry. And I'll expect this same eagerness from you."

"Whatever you want." His already pale cheeks became even more pallid. I wasn't sure, but I think he wet his pants. I didn't want to look too closely to find out.

"Now, Commander," I said, once again exiting the car. "What was it you asked me?"

His mustache twitched—I knew the sign. He wasn't amused; he was furious. He didn't like being brushed off, didn't like being treated like one of my lackeys. His dark brown eyes were ablaze with emotion, and the lines around his mouth were taut. Just then, with his thick head of silver hair, his round belly, and his red flannel shirt, he looked like a psychotic Santa Claus.

"I'm this close, Snow. This close." He pinched his index finger and thumb together, leaving only half an inch of air between them. "Do you know what I'm this close to doing?"

"Kicking my ass into next week, sir?" I said, because he'd made the threat a thousand times before.

"That's right." He straightened his shoulders and adjusted his collar, most of his bluster deflated by my lack of concern. "You have to follow the rules, Snow, and that means answering your phone like everyone else."

"I turned it off. Didn't need any distractions."

"Every member of my unit is issued a phone so I can distract each one of you any damn time I want. Remember that." He pushed out a breath. "Ghost and Kittie are inside, but they haven't told me anything. I'm the head fucking commander of this team, and they want to wait for you."

"No need to do any ass-kicking yet, Jack. I brought you a present." With a sweep of my hand, I motioned to Lilla and Hudson. "A suspect and one of the A.I.R. team's finest. George here has been a naughty boy and I think he can help us with the Steele case."

Dallas moaned.

He was finally coming around. Both of his hands massaged his neck as his eyes slowly opened. He blinked, focused. I knew the exact moment he remembered the evening's events—our little jaunt into Hudson's, my refusal to explain . . . the fact that I'd almost choked him to death. Fire kindled to life in his eyes, making those perfect brown orbs blaze.

"Mia!" he shouted.

I backed away from the car, my hands up in a gesture of defenselessness. "I had to do it, Dallas. You know I did."

"I'm still waiting for my explanation," Jack interjected darkly.

"Help me get the prisoners in isolation, and I'll explain everything. To both of you," I added.

One at a time, they nodded.

*   *   *

Thirty minutes later, Jack had his explanation—minus a few of the seedier details. I breathed easier because daylight was quickly approaching. Hell, I even felt like gloating. I'd thwarted my vision. I'd won this time. Dallas was still furious with me, but he was alive. Even Ghost and Kittie were healthy and whole.

Nothing else mattered.

Life was good.

Lilla and Hudson had been separated and placed in isolation chambers. While Hudson complained during the trek to his cell, Lilla had thankfully remained silent, locked in the stun as she was. Sherry and the other woman from Hudson's—I now knew her name was Isabel Hudson, George's seventeen-year-old daughter— were being questioned by Ghost and Kittie.

The only thing left to do was talk with Dallas, but at the moment, that was impossible. Jack wasn't finished with us yet.

The commander leaned forward in his high-backed gray leather chair. He was seated behind his large oak desk, the picture of authority as he shuffled papers to the edge of the cluttered desktop. The walls around dripped with pictures of Jack's twenty-three-year-old daughter. His wife had left him years ago, so the only picture of her was the one decorating his trash can.

"You've done good work tonight," he said. "*Good* work. Both of you. You found the break in the case we needed, and you brought in suspects for questioning. Albeit damaged, but at least they're alive. Unlike last time." His eyes lit on me when he emphasized his last words.

"What?" I muttered with a shrug.

Dallas and I were seated side by side. We hadn't looked at each other since we'd entered Jack's office. Tension radiated between us.

"Problem is," Jack added, "we've had another disappearance. Victim's been missing since last night. The roommate only filed a missing person's a hour ago."

"Why weren't we notified immediately?" I asked.

"At first, the officers in charge weren't sure this one had any connection. However, I had Jaffe review the notes, and he's one hundred percent sure this case is connected to the others. Too many similarities, and too little evidence—which adds a bitch of a ripple to our case. This latest victim is female."

Dread rolled through me, dark and dangerously sharp. I glanced at Dallas for the first time since stepping inside this office. Dallas glanced at me. This wasn't good news we were getting. In unison, we both turned back to Jack.

"A female?" I asked.

Jack blinked over at me. "That's what I said."

"What's her name?" I shifted in my seat, hating and loving every moment that passed and he didn't answer.

"Rianne Harte," he said, glancing down at his papers.

"Spell it," I said, ice crystallizing in my blood.

He did.

My stomach churned, and I closed my eyes. The

Arcadian hadn't lied. He had said Rianne Harte, but he hadn't spelled the name, and he hadn't specified that the victim was female. I'd misheard and assumed. A dangerous combination.

He'd also mentioned that someone else would soon be dead.

At least I could take the guard off Grandpa Ryan and the boy. A real fucking silver lining.

"Jack," Dallas said, "Mia and I chased down—"

I gave Dallas a barely imperceptible head shake that said, *Do not mention the Arcadian male.*

"Chased down a bottle of tequila earlier," he finished lamely. "Sorry."

"Thank you," I mouthed. I wasn't sure why I wanted to keep Jack in the dark, but I did. I wasn't sure who this Arcadian was, or which side he was truly playing for. I just knew I was going to be stingy with the information I shared until I figured out exactly what motives lay behind those amethyst eyes.

"You know better than to drink on the job," Jack said, eyes narrowed. "First I catch you napping, and now you confess to drinking. What the hell is the matter with you?"

"Got a description of Miss Harte?" Dallas asked, quickly getting us back on track.

"Red hair. Green eyes. About five foot six." Jack shrugged. "She's a lab tech with Kilmer, Peterman, and Nate Pharmaceuticals. They specialize in fertility drugs."

"What similarities did they find between her abduction and the others?" I asked.

"Arcadian hair laid on the woman's kitchen counter like a rose. As with the others, there are no witnesses to her abduction. No sign of foul play. She simply disappeared from her home."

"That it?"

"Hardly," Jack said with a dark chuckle. "She had contact with two of the men before their disappearances. Sullivan Bay and Raymond Palmer. She was seen with each on two separate occasions."

"This is getting complicated, Jack," Dallas said.

"I know. And I need these missing people found ASAP. Alive," Jack added. "If you fail, well, you might as well prepare your assess for PADD." There was no humor in his tone. "I'm getting pressure from the top. They're afraid the story will break soon, and they want answers."

Fabulous. We were working as fast as we possibly could. Being ordered to work faster was fucking-tastic.

"Right now, I want you to go home, get some rest," Jack continued. "We'll debrief at noon tomorrow with Ghost, Kittie, Mandalay, Johnson, and Jaffe."

"One thing, Commander," I said. I'd worked under Jack for nine years. He was old and mean, but honorable. "Keep everyone—and that includes yourself—out of Lilla's chamber. Her powers for mind control are staggering."

"I doubt she can penetrate *my* mind."

"The government has yet to produce a workable mind shield, and until they do, you're in danger from her."

He tapped a pen on his desk. "If I stay away from her and command everyone else to do the same, you'll owe me. Big."

He should be grateful for my warning, should be telling me how sensible I was. But no, the sneaky bastard wanted a favor, so he was pretending this was some big hardship. Last time I'd owed him a favor, he'd made me teach his daughter—who reminded me of Barbie on drugs—how to shoot an old-fashioned Road Kill .48. For my troubles, I'd spent a few nights in the hospital, having a bullet removed from my ass.

"What do you want?" I asked wearily.

"I need you to work next weekend. We'll be short several agents."

"Done," I said, and felt a keen sense of relief. Working extra hours was no problem. It wasn't like I actually had a life. I had no hobbies. No friends outside of work. Never attended family gatherings. That was . . . sad, I realized with a frown.

"No one enters," he promised, stroking his beard. "Not without your permission. I'll even have her meals delivered by mechanical tray."

"Thank you."

"Now get out of here," he said, waving a hand through the air. "The sight of Dallas's beat-up face is turning my stomach." To Dallas he said, "A word of advice, sport. The next time you're in a fight—duck."

"Yeah, I'll try to remember that," Dallas said, his gaze darkening on me.

We pushed to our feet and filed out. The door closed behind us with a click. Then, silence. Benches and desks were empty, and only a few agents milled about. Most of the A.I.R. teams were patrolling the streets.

"Dallas," I said, then paused. I noticed Ghost standing down the hall, motioning me over with the crook of his finger. His bald head gleamed in the overhead lighting.

"Don't leave this building," Dallas said. "We've got a lot to discuss."

"You're right." He'd reached his bullshit tolerance, and I didn't even try to stall. "Why don't you come with me to talk with Ghost, then we'll go to Trollie's for coffee."

He stared down at me, his expression hard, determined. "All right," he finally said. "You've got ten minutes. No more."

I arched a brow at his I-am-commander-of-the-universe tone and vowed to take eleven minutes, even if I had to sit in the corner and pick my nose for most of those. We strode down the hall, the sound of our footsteps pounding in my ears. The air was sterile here, as if someone had doused the walls with cleaning solution. Ghost led us into a small private room.

"That girl is a certifiable whack job," he said the moment the door snapped closed.

"Which one?" I asked, stepping toward the large two-way mirror that dominated the side wall and offered a secret glimpse into a smaller room. I had my answer before he replied.

"Isabel Hudson, the Antichrist's daughter," I said, at the exact moment he said, "Sleeping Beauty, the Antichrist's daughter."

I studied her. She sat at a scarred wooden table, her hands hidden in the folds of her clothes. Her hair was long and blond and as straight as mine. Her skin was sun-kissed, porcelain smooth, though it was her eyes that truly drew attention. They were faultless ovals, a rich, deep violet framed by long, sooty lashes.

"She looks like an Arcadian," I remarked.

"Can't be," Ghost said. "That's not a wig, and dye doesn't take to their hair, and if you hadn't noticed, she's got a head full of blond locks, not white, not silver."

I shot him a thanks-for-stating-the-obvious frown.

"Anyway," he continued with a shrug, "there isn't room in her body for alien blood. She's twenty percent human and eighty percent insane." He threw up his arms in a the-things-I-do-for-my-job gesture. "Insane, I tell you!"

"What?" Dallas chuckled. "Did you make a pass at her, and she said no?"

Ghost shuddered, and his face wrinkled in horror.

"She's seventeen," I reminded Dallas. "If he had made a pass at her, I'd have him arrested."

"What'd she do that was so bad?" Dallas asked.

"The moment I stepped into the room, she began mumbling under her breath about mind control. One of her hands made continuous stabbing motions. And when I questioned her, she threatened to cut off my balls."

"So she mumbles and likes to cut things," Dallas said, trying hard to hide his grin. "Big deal."

"Hey, I don't see you rushing in there." Scowling, Ghost gestured to the door. "By all means. Go ask the little darling a couple of questions."

"No," I said. "I want to talk to her. Girl to girl."

Ghost's shoulders slumped in relief. "If anyone can deal with that psycho, it's you. You've got panties of steel, Mia Snow. Me? I'd have pissed in my pants if I hadn't had my gun." He patted his jacket under his left pec. He paused. Patted again. His smile fell inch by inch, and he gave a disbelieving gasp.

I was already at the door, had already turned the knob, stepped out of the observation room, and inside interrogation, when I heard Ghost say, "My gun! She has my fucking gun!"

I barely had time to react, didn't register that this was my vision coming to life. Isabel held a pyre-gun, and the barrel was aimed at my heart. She had a blank look on her face, the same look Dallas had worn when he'd been mind-controlled.

No. *No!*

Behind me, someone shouted, "Mia!" as I reached

for my own weapon. Suddenly I was shoved out of the way and felt myself falling in slow motion. Isabel fired. A blast of sound and light enveloped the room. A scream of frustration, fury, and fear lodged in my throat, and I ground off a round of my own before landing on the floor with a thud. Air abandoned my lungs in one mighty heave, and my vision became a spiderweb of black and white.

Dragging in a breath, I shook my head to clear my thoughts, realizing Isabel's shot had missed me. I was unharmed.

Then a male body fell on top of me, bleeding and lifeless.

CHAPTER
7

The *drip, drip* of an IV harmonized with the *beep, beep* of a heart monitor, creating a symphony of sound—an opera of death. My head rested in my upraised palms, and my elbows perched on the hospital bed in front of me. I was tired, so very tired. The chair I occupied was made of hard, uncomfortable wood, but I couldn't force myself to move.

When I was younger, after my dad stopped loving me, he'd punished my every indiscretion by forcing me to sit in a chair very similar to this one. Of course, he locked the chair and me inside a small, dark room. I'd sit there, terrified and lonely, silently sobbing, sometimes screaming until my voice went hoarse. The memories always left me ripe with loathing, but because of them, I could now remain motionless for hours and not utter a single complaint. That little talent came in handy right about now.

Dallas lay on the bed, his eyes closed, a machine breathing for him, slowly inflating what was left of his right lung, expelling the air, then repeating the action again and again.

Only an hour ago, he'd been declared dead. Yet one of the surgeons assigned to his care had refused to give up and had stood over him, beating on his chest, pumping him full of drugs. Incredibly, Dallas had been resuscitated. I'd never had faith in anything I couldn't aim or fire, but when the heart monitor sprang to life, I began to believe in miracles again.

A.I.R. agents had come and gone throughout the morning, just as doctors and nurses had. Not a single person that entered this room had left a ray of hope behind; they'd left only dismal condolences. Dallas's injuries were fatal. Most of his internal organs had been scorched, and there was a six-inch hole in his chest, the surrounding flesh burned beyond repair.

No, they'd offered no hope.

But Dallas was a fighter. He was hanging on to his life with every ounce of strength he possessed.

Right now, I was alone with him, trying to force my life force inside him. I wished to God he had family here, someone to cry over him, pray for him. Unfortunately, his parents had died years ago, and he had no brothers or sisters, no aunts or uncles, that any of us knew of.

Helplessness overwhelmed me, helplessness so intense my body trembled with the force of it. Morning had come and gone, and now an afternoon storm beat outside. I hadn't slept, hadn't eaten. I couldn't. My stomach was a painful knot of fear, dread, and grief. Dallas was my best friend. My rock. He was an extension of Dare, I guess, the brother I'd worshipped and lost. We balanced each other in a strange sort of way, and my life without him . . .

A shudder racked my spine, compounding the burn in my throat. I gulped. Squeezed my eyes tightly shut.

"Damn you, Dallas," I whispered brokenly. I wanted to slap him, to scream at him. I was furious, so furious, that he had pushed me aside and taken the hit himself. *I* should have been the one to fall, the one to suffer. The one to ultimately die.

I'd failed him.

My shoulders slumped from fatigue as the surge of anger abandoned me. My eyelids slowly opened, and I reached out with trembling fingers. The pads of my fingertips stroked his cheek, along his jaw. He was cold, and his once bronzed skin was now pallid, an almost translucent white. If I'd had tears to give, I would have cried until my ducts burst from the strain. As it was, I could only sit here, helpless, and watch him die.

My hands fisted so tightly my nails bit half-moon

crescents into my palms. Isabel Hudson was dead. In my mind, I saw the continuous flash of my gun, the girl's horror-filled expression as multiple rounds of fire exploded in her chest. Saw her slowly slump to the floor. I'd killed her, killed a young girl who'd had yet to experience adulthood. On some level, I hated myself for what I'd done, yet that didn't dull my desire to kill her all over again, this time slowly, lingering over every painful detail.

Damn it, how had this happened? Who had controlled Isabel's mind? Not Lilla, she'd been deep in stun. That left . . . no one.

I must have missed subtle details in my vision. God knows I'd gotten some of them wrong. I'd had the human and the alien in the wrong places, thinking a human killed Dallas. How could I have known it would be a humanoid alien? I didn't know what species Isabel had been, I just knew she couldn't be Hudson's daughter, as reports claimed.

"How could this have happened?" I whispered brokenly.

"Go home, Mia," a masculine voice said from behind me. Jack.

I didn't turn to face him. "I can't leave. I *won't* leave. You know me better than that."

He sighed. "You're no good to me like this. No good to *him*."

"Then fire me."

"Like hell."

"I just . . . I can't leave him. He needs me. He has no one else."

Jack paused a moment, and I knew what was rolling around inside his mind. Always business first with Jack. "Want me to reassign your cases?" he asked. "Give you a week or two off?"

"What about Steele?" I asked, though I was unable to summon true curiosity.

"I'll put Ghost and Kittie in charge. They'll get the job done."

With those few words, Jack sparked the first stirring of ire within me. He'd made it sound as if *I* couldn't get the job done. "That case is mine," I said with a trace of bitterness. Still, I didn't spare him a glance. "I'll finish it."

"No need. It's almost wrapped. Lilla's in custody, and once she's released from stun, I'm sending Kittie inside her cell. Hopefully, we'll know where the missing men are by evening."

I gazed past the bed, past the far window, my eyes listless as swaying trees and glistening pavement came into view. "You promised me no one would talk to her without my permission."

"That was before."

"You're making a big mistake. If you allow Kittie near her, you can kiss Lilla good-bye. She'll be gone before you can pull your head out of your ass. Besides, I doubt she knows where the missing men are."

"You're saying she's innocent?" he choked.

"Not innocent." I pushed out a breath. "Just not the mastermind behind the murder or the abductions."

His brows winged up. "And you think this because?"

"She lives by her emotions, doesn't think things through. Steele's murder was emotionless, thought out to the last detail."

"Mia—" he said, then stopped himself. He uttered another sigh. "If you want to close this case," he said, "I'll let you. If you want to interrogate Lilla, I'll let you do that, too. But you gotta get some rest."

"Losing faith in me, Jack?" I asked with a humorless chuckle. My head arched back, and I blinked up at the sterile, white ceiling. I didn't blame him. I'd lost faith in myself.

"No. Never," he said, shoving his hand into his coat pocket. "There's no one I trust more than you. Hell, you've never let me down."

"That's not true. I let you down last night. I let everyone down. Dallas wouldn't be here if I'd acted more quickly."

"Would you listen to yourself?" Jack scoffed. "That's the most ridiculous thing I've ever heard. You didn't know this was going to happen. Dallas made his own choice, and God Himself couldn't have stopped him from protecting you."

"You're wrong. I could have stopped him." I pounded a fist onto the bed. "I could have kept him unconscious until morning, unable to work. I could have postponed the hunt. I could have made him wait for me at Trollie's while I spoke to Ghost."

So many things I could have and should have done differently. I'd known, damn it. I'd known he was in danger, and still I hadn't protected him.

"Mia," Jack said softly. "You're not thinking clearly right now. You haven't slept in two nights. You gotta get some rest," he repeated.

I turned my head, and our gazes locked. His cheeks were pale, the perpetual red glow gone. His flannel shirt hung loosely over his shoulders like he'd lost a few pounds. "I'm not a child, Jack."

"Your eyes are red," he continued, "your skin is colorless. Honestly, you look like shit."

"Thanks for the compliment, but I'm fine," I said, though I knew he was right. My mind was foggy, filled with thick morning dew I just couldn't seem to penetrate. My eyelids felt heavy, my body weak and shaky.

"You're about to collapse. I'm ordering you to go home."

"Fuck your orders." I couldn't summon the strength to yell, so my words emerged as a small, hollow whisper. Surprisingly, though, my ire grew a bit more. I pivoted back to bed. "Dallas needs me."

I didn't hear Jack approach, but suddenly he stood beside me, his hand on my shoulder. "Staying isn't going to make him live."

"At least—" I gulped. "At least he won't die alone." God, that hurt so much to say. I almost screamed then, screamed at God, at Jack, at the doctors who couldn't help this once vivacious man. I had to bite my cheek to keep the sound inside me; I bit until the metallic tang of blood filled my mouth.

Jack gave my shoulder a squeeze. "He was a good man. One of the best. I already miss him."

Shut up, shut up, shut up! my mind shouted. I covered my ears to block Jack's voice. He was talking about Dallas as if he were already dead.

Perhaps he was.

I focused on Dallas's face, so pale, so withdrawn. There truly was no hope for survival.

I couldn't say those words, however, so I said, "He isn't dead yet."

"No, but he'll need a miracle to survive." He gave my shoulder another squeeze. "It's amazing how quickly a man's life can change, isn't it? A blink of an eye. A snap of fingers." He paused. "A heartbeat."

One of his tears splashed onto my palm. I watched as the clear liquid slipped through my fingers. I'd never seen this strong man cry before. And knowing his own emotions mirrored my own . . . A tremor racked my spine. He had found some sort of release, yet I had none. My emotions were trapped inside me.

I scrubbed a hand down my face, resisting the urge to bang my head against the bed rail. Maybe physical pain would eclipse my emotional pain.

"Is he suffering?" Jack asked softly, ripping into my thoughts.

I shook my head. "No pain. They've got him so high, he's probably flying with the angels."

"I'm glad. I don't want our boy in pain." Jack released my shoulder and strode to the room's only window. "Jaxon is taking care of the funeral arrangements. I thought it would be too much for you."

"I'll do it," I said, my irritation rising another notch. "As his partner, it's my right. I want my cases, too. Don't give them to anyone else."

"Very well." Then, donning his usual gruff demeanor, Jack said, "Be at headquarters tomorrow, one o'clock sharp." He turned on his heel and strode to the door, only to stop before stepping over the threshold. Gazing over his shoulder, he pinned me with his stare. "I know you're grieving. We all are."

"I—"

He cut me off. "You asked to keep the Steele case. *You* asked. I didn't command you. Therefore you have a job to do, and I expect you to do it."

"I know," I said, massaging my temples. I was grateful for his abruptness. I would have crumpled under pity or gentleness, and he knew it.

"I need you to question Lilla and report the results at our debriefing. Can you do that?"

"Yes," I said, determination creeping into my tone.

"Good girl." With that, he shuffled from the room.

I was once again alone with Dallas. Clasping his cold, lifeless hand, I laid my cheek on the edge of the bed. Those two little actions caused every emotion I'd experienced in the last hours to drain out of me, leaving only emptiness. Lethargy washed through my every hollow and crevice, claiming my limbs and, lastly, my eyes.

The last thought to drift beneath my consciousness before a swirling fog engulfed me was, Please God, send me another miracle.

I came awake slowly and realized three things all at once, only one of them significant.

First, I realized that I hadn't suffered through any dreams. Very unusual for me; I always dreamed. Second, I wasn't sure how much time had passed since I'd fallen asleep. Third, the hairs on the back of my neck were standing on end.

As my senses became more attuned, I felt an invisible pair of eyes upon me, intense, observant eyes hovering over my shoulder, watching . . . waiting. I knew I was inside Dallas's hospital room, and I knew it wasn't Dallas watching me.

Keeping my motions slow and deliberate, I reached for the gun at my waist. Then I froze. My gun was gone. Fucking gone. I didn't panic, though. I had a backup strapped to my ankle, though this one wasn't as competent, since it only offered "hot" and "extra hot" settings. No stun. I curled my fingers around the trigger.

Fighting the urge to jolt to my feet, I allowed my eyelids to crack open a little at a time, gradually taking in my surroundings. Darkness had fallen, and muted beams of luminescence seeped through the beige hospital blinds. I kept my head and body completely immobile as I shifted my gaze around the room.

There, in the corner, a man lounged casually in a chair. I stifled a gasp when his features came into view. No, not a man. An Arcadian.

The Arcadian.

The warrior I'd chased through the alley.

His energy wrapped all around me, strong, pure. Deadly. A shiver tingled along my nerve endings. His hair was thick and white and fell to his shoulders. I pictured his eyes, knew they were the palest violet, almost crystalline, with a thin veneer of calm, like nitroglycerin just before detonation. I knew his lips were full and lush, a perfect contrast against his ultra-masculine features, making him seem all the more dangerous.

He must have sensed my perusal because he blinked, a sensual sweep of his lashes, and said huskily, "Your friend rests at death's door, Tai la Mar."

Angel of Death, he'd called me. I jerked upright. My chair skidded behind me and collided with the wall. I had my firearm drawn and pointed at his heart before he could take another breath. I knew Dallas still lived because the gentle hum of his monitors filled my ears, and I could see the rise and fall of his chest from the corner of my eye, courtesy of the machine breathing for him.

"Where's my pyre-gun?" I asked, keeping my voice

calm, even though my heart was tripping inside my chest.

"Your weapon is safe."

Safe, my ass. "Where's Rianne Harte?"

"I tried to warn you about her, did I not?" He shifted slightly, creasing his black slacks. The sleeves of his white tailored shirt were rolled to his elbows. "But did you heed my warning?"

I didn't answer him. Instead, I asked a question of my own. "Did you take her?"

"No," he answered without hesitation. "I did not."

"Then prove it. If you can."

"I warned you about her, didn't I?"

I switched the safety off, making sure he saw, then narrowed my gaze, focusing on which part of his body I wanted to hit first. Between the eyes, I decided, leveling my aim. One move from him, and I would fire first, ask questions later. "I'm left wondering if your warning was meant to help me or taunt me."

He only laughed, a rich, throaty rumble full of genuine amusement. The sound moved over me as softly as a caress. "You humans are so silly. Put your gun away," he said. "Had I wanted to hurt you or your friend, I would have done so already."

Unwavering, I held my weapon steady. "I'm still interested in hearing why you gave me Rianne's name."

He shrugged, his stare becoming hard and gauging. "Perhaps I was testing you." He paused. "Perhaps you failed."

"And you're here to give me another chance? Or to gloat over my failure?"

"Actually, I am here to offer you a trade. If you are as honorable as I have heard, we can help each other."

I snorted. "The only thing I'm going to help you do is find your way into a cell."

His eyes slitted. "I am Kyrin en Arr, and I have come for my sister."

Lilla's brother. I should have guessed. Automatically I applied pressure to the trigger, but stopped myself before actually firing. This man knew about the victims, and now he was connected to the case through other means. He would better serve me alive. "So you're the Arcadian who's murdered more humans than any of your kinsmen, are you?"

"Some would say so, yes," he said without shame or regret.

"Well, guess what, Kyrin? Lilla belongs to A.I.R. now, and with her history of violence and being a prime suspect in a murder investigation, we're keeping her. I'm sure you're aware that her crimes are punishable by death."

His face paled. He was definitely aware.

"I plan to see her executed," I finished.

"She is not a criminal." Something cold and hard washed over his features, returning his color. His eyes gleamed with dangerous intent, like the sharpest of daggers, exquisite to view, lethal to touch. "Let her go."

"Yeah. Right."

"I would not be so quick to deny my request, were I you."

"And why is that?"

"Because I," he said, studying me with an unnerving intensity, "can save your friend."

I can save your friend.

Those words beat inside my mind, causing white-hot fury to pound through every fiber of my being. Bastard! How dare he utter such a lie? How dare he attempt to offer false hope, simply to save his sister? Eyes compressed to tiny slits, nostrils flared, I began adjusting the level of power on my gun to its highest setting. I was going to have myself an Arcadian barbecue.

A nurse entered the room. I saw her in my peripheral vision, but didn't switch my position or my focal point from Kyrin. She dropped her chart when she caught sight of my gun. She froze in place, her eyes a tableau of horror, her mouth open.

"I—I heard a noise," she stammered, her features ashen with shock.

"Exit the room, ma'am," I told her. I meant for the words to elicit calm and reassurance, but they exploded from my mouth with all the rage I felt. "I've got the situation under control."

"I—I—should I call the police?" she stuttered to Kyrin, as if he was the one in charge here.

"I am the police," I shouted. "Now get the fuck out!"

Nurse Idiot didn't move.

Then Kyrin gave a slight tilt of his head, and she raced from the room as quickly as her feet could carry her. My lips curled in contempt.

"Do you prefer original or extra crispy?" I asked. "Because I'm willing to fry you up either way."

He ignored me, and instead replied with, "I gave Dallas—that is his name, yes?—some of my blood. Only a drop, mind you, but he will live a few days more because of it. Were I to give him more, he would live out the rest of his life, healthy and whole."

"If you won't choose, I'll choose for you. I say"—I pretended to mull it over—"extra crispy."

"Is his heartbeat not steadier? His color not brighter?"

I flicked my partner a quick glance, and my eyes widened. Yes, on both counts, I realized, shock pounding through me. My hands stilled. "That doesn't mean *you* helped him."

"You disappoint me. I thought a woman of your talents would be more insightful."

I bared my teeth in a scowl. "Perhaps you require a demonstration of exactly what my talents are."

"Perhaps you require a demonstration of *mine.*" Kyrin slowly rose. He was so tall, I was forced to look up, almost at the ceiling. I scanned his body, but I saw no evidence of weapons. Still, my heart slammed inside my chest, and my palms sweated. I didn't understand my reaction. I'd squared off with aliens just as intimidating and won. I was the one in control here. I had the authority. I held the weapon.

"You'd say anything to save your sister," I said.

"I would say anything to free her, yes, but in this, I do not lie." He stretched out one hand and reached inside his slacks pocket with the other. Gaze locked on mine, he withdrew a small but deadly blade.

Okay, now he had a weapon.

"Stop right there," I commanded. "I'll kill you without a qualm."

"Then you would never know the truth, would you?" Calmly he clasped the blade and placed the tip at his palm. I was too fascinated by his words and actions to follow through with my threat. His features remained expressionless as he sliced a deep incision from one end to the other. Blood sprang from the torn tissues, and the scar on my arm throbbed in reaction.

As I watched, his wound slowly closed itself, the tissues weaving themselves together and leaving the blood pooled in his hand. He wiped away every crimson drop on his shirtsleeve, a red smear against pristine white, then revealed the perfect smoothness of his hand.

"Do you see?" he said. "I cannot die, and those who consume my blood will live, as well."

My God, this alien was some sort of immortal being.

I didn't know what to think of that fact. A lot of aliens had special powers, but I'd never heard of one with accelerated healing. I told him so.

"That doesn't mean it isn't so. There is only one other like me," Kyrin said with a shrug, "but you will never find her. So right now, I am your friend's only hope. My blood *can* save him."

That's when it hit me, truly hit me. Dallas could be saved. The knowledge rocked me to the core. I was almost afraid to speak my next words. "In exchange for his life, you want me to set your sister free?"

"Yes," he said. "That is all I require."

Yes, I'll set her free, I thought in the next instant. I'll slip inside A.I.R. headquarters, unlock her cell, and escort her from the building. Yes, that's exactly what I'll do. Excitement bubbled inside me. Then . . . the enormity of the situation slammed into me with the force of an antique 9mm Glock. I closed my eyes, lowered my gun. I couldn't let Lilla go. Six other lives were at stake here—the lives of the five abducted citizens . . . and my own.

By setting Lilla free, I would severely damage the Steele case. I might doom the very people I'd sworn to protect. Breaking the very rules I worked so hard to enforce meant losing my job, my honor, the respect of my coworkers. And quite possibly gaining a lifetime of imprisonment.

I'd always feared small, dark places—a reminder of my childhood and a fear I had yet to overcome. The cold, the complete and utter blackness. The silence. But I wanted Dallas healed. God, I did. Desperately, I wanted my friend to live a long, healthy life. I hadn't saved Dare, but now I had a chance to save Dallas.

Opening my eyes, I gazed down at Dallas, at the helpless man who now had a single hope of survival. I tore my gaze away and faced Kyrin imploringly. "What you're asking is impossible," I said, guilt already crashing through me because I hadn't shouted "Yes!" immediately. "My boss would never okay such a trade."

"I do not recall suggesting that you ask your boss." No, he hadn't.

I chewed on my bottom lip. Damn it, what was I going to do? I couldn't allow Dallas to die now that I knew there was a chance to save him, but I couldn't release Lilla, either. "The law states I must eliminate Lilla once she is no longer useful to my case. What if I vowed to keep her alive? To let her live inside a cell for the remainder of her life?"

"Were I to say yes to that, I would be supporting the very laws I despise," he growled. "Laws that were made because your people fear what they do not understand."

"Our laws were made to protect us from uninvited visitors," I replied just as darkly. Then, as quickly as my anger appeared, it vanished. "Please. Please help me. Help Dallas. I'll beg you, if necessary, to save him. I'll fall to my knees right here, right now. I'll do anything you ask. Anything . . . except free Lilla."

His eyes glinted like opalescent steel. "Mia Snow on her knees before me? Tempting, I must say."

"Is that what you want?" Currents of sexual energy sparked between us as we both pictured me doing more than begging. "Me on my knees?"

"Actually, right now I would rather have your gun."

Everything inside me shouted to deny him—a good agent never relinquished her weapon—but I closed the distance between us and pressed the barrel into his cheek. I lingered there for two heartbeats.

"I could kill you right now," I said, staring up at him.

"But you will not."

No, I wouldn't. Scowling, I removed the gun from his face, saw the impression I'd left there, and felt a small surge of satisfaction. I turned the weapon hilt first and placed it into his waiting hand. I didn't mention that I had other weapons. Blades were strapped all over my body.

I watched as he removed the detonation crystal from its chamber, rendering it completely useless, then tossed the gun in the far right corner of the room. At least he didn't plan to shoot me.

"I did as you wanted," I said, my eyes narrowed. "Now you owe me something in return. Give Dallas more of your blood."

"I never promised you anything. I merely asked you to give me your gun."

"Damn you," I whispered hoarsely. I longed to jam my fist into his nose, but I couldn't spill his precious blood unnecessarily. I bared my teeth in a scowl. The bastard wasn't going to give an inch. Wasn't going to negotiate. He'd stated his terms, and I either met them, or he walked. "I need time."

"And so I will give you some. But do not take too much." His expression stubborn and determined, he strode past me, saying over his shoulder, "Without my help, Dallas will die in four days. Remember that as you consider my offer."

As if I could forget.

He exited the room.

I didn't think about my next actions, or the consequences they could bring. I knew what I wanted, and I was going to fight for it. I followed quietly behind him. The moment Kyrin stepped from the building and into the cold air, I sprang forward, and my leg shot out; I focused all of my anger, all of my frustration and helplessness, into the blow. Contact. My foot hit the middle of his back. Kyrin stumbled. "Say hello to size seven A.I.R. special-issue all-terrain boots with my own personal cleat attachment," I growled. "In black, white, red, and camouflage, you sorry son of a bitch."

I was going to force him to help Dallas.

When he caught his footing, he whipped around to face me. A muscle ticked in his jaw, and his lips pressed in a tight line. "You would strike a man from behind?"

"I would strike *you* from behind." My fists were clenched and ready for the fight I knew was to come. "I want your blood, and I'll have it, by God. Every precious drop."

"I am disappointed." He *tsked* under his tongue. "Such a cowardly action from one so brave."

"Not cowardly. Smart. You'll help Dallas whether

you want to or not, and you'll help him *now*." I kicked out my leg, but he sidestepped the action.

He once again uttered that husky chuckle of his, renewing my irritation. "Would you like to bet on that?"

"Absolutely," I said, and like a deadly catapult of fists and fury, I launched myself at him.

CHAPTER
8

irst rule of fighting: Stay calm.

Second rule: Never let your emotions overtake you.

I'd broken both rules the moment I began following him.

Kyrin swept out of my way, and I flew past him. The storm had died, but the sun hid behind angry gray clouds, offering hazy visibility. Because of the sheen of ice at my feet, I had trouble stopping and turning.

Definitely not optimal conditions; however, I wouldn't back down.

"You do not want to fight me, Mia."

I whipped around. "Wanna bet on that too?" I sprang forward again, intending to kick out my leg and knock him flat this time, but he reached me first. He grappled me to the ground, pinned my shoulders to the ice, and imprisoned me with his body. Cold at my back, pure heat on top. Neither was acceptable to me.

"Still want to fight?" he asked.

"Fuck yes." I quickly landed a blow to his groin. Yeah, I intended to fight dirty. He doubled over, and I shot to my feet, slipped, then steadied.

Slow down, I commanded myself, drawing in a deep breath. I couldn't fly at him again, couldn't give him another chance to evade or capture me. A full frontal attack wouldn't work with this man; his strength was simply too incredible. I had to strike from the side, from behind, and I had to strike hard.

I relished the challenge.

Using his prone position to my advantage, I was able to land a blow to his left side and knock the deoxygenated air from his lung. He grunted in pain and sudden breathlessness. Arcadians were equipped very much like humans. Vulnerable in the groin, stomach, and head.

While he was busy gasping, I punted his left side again. Satisfied with my progress, I darted to his right and gave a booted strike. This time, he grabbed my ankle and toppled me to the ground. I lost my satisfaction, felt a moment of desperation. We struggled there, rolling on top of each other, fighting for dominance. I could smell the sweetness of his breath, the Onadyn that kept him alive.

Physically, he had me at a disadvantage, and we both knew it. He could have attempted to smother me, but he didn't.

"It doesn't have to be this way," he panted.

Think, Mia, think.

I still had full use of my legs, and I made total use of them. I gave a scissor-lock squeeze around his midsection, forcing him to release my arms and focus on my legs. That's all I needed. With a four-finger jab to his trachea, his air supply was momentarily cut off in a whoosh, giving me the perfect opportunity to spring free.

My old combat instructor would have been proud.

I took stock of my options. I had to render him unconscious if I hoped to win. He'd defeat me, otherwise. I would have to be merciless, but stop short of killing him. I needed his help, after all. His blood. I didn't want to spill a single drop on this cold, hard ice.

"Concede, damn you," I growled, circling him like a tigress locked on her prey.

"You first," he said, still on his knees.

I kicked out, aiming for his head. He swept sideways, dodging me, sending me spinning. Before I could regain my bearings, he was on his feet and coming straight at me. Just as he reached me, I linked my fingers together and swung, connecting with his temple. His head whipped to the side. He remained in place, hands balled into fists, knees slightly bent. Determination gleamed in his eyes.

"I am almost done playing with you," he said.

"Play with this." I launched a flying spin punt into his side. I anticipated the crack of a few ribs, not a block. But block me, he did. I tried again. Somehow he was able to counter my every move. He was fast. Unnaturally fast. I followed the second punt through, letting my own momentum spin me again. Then I crouched on the balls of my feet and went low. My leg struck out in a hard sweep as I tried to knock his feet out from under him. He leapt above my leg like I'd meant to play jump rope. Damn him. His speed—no one was that fast. No one human, that is.

Quicker than I could blink, he advanced on me. He used his weight to push into me, stumbling me backward. When my body came into contact with his, the strength hidden beneath his clothing jolted me. He was made of solid muscle, easily outweighing me by a hundred pounds, but he didn't once use the power hidden in his fists to strike me down. Why? I wondered, even as I punched him hard in the nose. His head jerked to the side; he made no move to counter. Why didn't he return attack? Why did he go out of his way *not* to hurt me?

There wasn't time to ponder the answer. Too much was at stake. The answer didn't matter, anyway. Right now I needed this man for one reason only, and his benevolence wasn't it. With some fancy footwork, I managed three successive lateral blows. The last sent him flying into the windshield of a parked cherry red Mustang. His body bounced onto the hood, denting the shiny metal on impact. He shook his head, trying to clear his vision, I'm sure, since a jagged cut slashed down his forehead.

A shame about the car, but I wanted like hell to save the blood dripping off the tip of his nose. I quickly jumped him, wanting to pin him, but he rolled out of my reach.

Before my eyes, the flesh on his forehead sealed, turning from red to pink to normal. That was twice now I had watched him heal so quickly, and I was still amazed.

He shot to his feet. Studying me all the while, he wiped the blood away from his face as if it were a pesky fly. Bastard. He was taunting me.

His main blood vessel, the one that supplied deoxygenated blood to his brain, ran just below his breastbone. If I could just apply enough pressure, he would crash like a test dummy.

I circled him, intending to do just that, but he surprised me by grabbing my jacket and tugging. The ice at my feet aided him. Suddenly off balance, I tumbled into him, keeping a viselike grip. His warm breath washed over my face as he leaned close.

"Now you will concede this victory to me," he ground out low in his throat.

"When you haven't hit me once?" I said, a cocky edge to my tone. I'd fought enough opponents to know Kyrin had had plenty of opportunities, but I wasn't going to admit *that* aloud.

His eyes darkened, revealing a hint of wickedness, and he leaned down until our lips brushed once, twice. Soft kisses, languid kisses. Innocent kisses.

And all the more searing because they lacked heat.

"Why would I hit a woman I'd rather fuck?" he asked raggedly. I felt the thickness of his erection between my legs.

I found myself dragging in air—not from exertion, but from arousal. This wasn't like me. Couldn't be *my* feelings. My eyes narrowed. "Get out of my head," I shouted.

"I am not inside your head." He nuzzled his cheek against my jaw. "Your mind simply recognizes what your body craves."

"No! You're an alien. An other-worlder."

He paused and our gazes locked. "What are you, Mia Snow?"

"A pissed-off woman," I ground out, trying to push him off me. I only managed to rub him against me. I gasped, savoring and despising the sensation all at once. I positioned my hands over his pecs, meaning to give a hard shove, but I only caused his nipples to press into my palms like little needles.

I wanted him off me. Now! *End it!* my mind shouted. *End the fight.*

I had to find his weakness; that was my only chance for victory at this point.

Where was he vulnerable?

The answer sprang to life the next instant. I could

use his unwillingness to hurt me to my advantage. With luck, he'd leave himself vulnerable simply to protect me.

With that in mind, I pretended to go limp. As I'd hoped, he released his grip on my jacket and caught me, holding me upright, leaving the rest of his body unguarded. Quick as a cat, I spun behind him, jumped on his back, and wrapped my arms around his neck. I jerked him against me, hard, holding my fists square in the middle of his windpipe.

One, two, three, I counted. He remained conscious.

"I am different from my kind," he said casually, as if I were giving him a hug instead of trying to immobilize him. "Just as you are different from your kind."

How did he know how different I was? I squeezed harder, but all I received for my effort was sweat running down my temples. *I* was struggling to breathe. *My* energy was quickly draining.

I had to try something. Not knowing what else to do, I slammed the back of his knee with the heel of my foot. His legs crumpled, and as he fell to the ground, I doubled my fists and cracked him in the head. His face snapped sideways and struck the slick concrete. A pool of rich blood seeped from his mouth, and a murky stream formed where the warmth melted the ice.

My knuckles throbbed from the impact.

Once again he healed quickly. Almost immediately,

he pushed to his feet and whipped around to face me. Our gazes locked.

"It seems neither of us will concede," he said, his tone raspy.

I was happy to note he finally appeared winded.

Shattered glass and car parts were scattered about our feet. The cold flurry zipped and gnawed at our battered flesh, but neither of us seemed to notice or care. His hair danced in his face, but he never removed his gaze from me.

My skin felt too tight for my body; my blood sparked with newly awakened awareness. It had since the moment I'd first seen him, but only in this moment of stillness did I become unable to mask the sensation. I couldn't force my heartbeat to slow. I cursed under my breath. I killed aliens. I did *not* desire them.

"What is Dallas to you?" Kyrin asked.

What I shared with Dallas was none of his business. I knew that, but found myself answering, "He is my friend."

Kyrin's stare became piercing. "Not your lover?"

"No."

"That is good. I do not like to share."

I forced myself to sound as cold and callous as any hunter. "Is that what it will take to save Dallas? Sex?"

"You will sleep with me because you desire me, and for no other reason."

The surety in his voice I could have ignored, but I couldn't ignore the dark premonition that swept through me. Somehow, I maintained a neutral expression. "You're that sure of yourself?"

"Oh, yes." He gave me a knowing perusal that mentally stripped away my clothing. "I am that sure."

I fought a shiver. "If Dallas dies, I *will* kill you. You do know that, don't you?"

"I know that I have not changed my mind," he said. "Until my sister is free, I will not help you. You have four days to decide. Then I will return."

Damn him. I closed my hands into fists and stepped toward him, ready to strike.

He only grinned. "Until we meet again, Tai la Mar." He spun around and began to stride away, his footsteps echoing in my ears.

"Kyrin," I called.

The sound stopped him.

I don't know why I'd called his name, didn't know what I'd wanted to say. I only knew it tasted good on my lips. I said nothing else. When he began walking away for the second time, I stupidly called out again. "Kyrin."

Once more, he paused.

"I will hunt you down," I said this time, "and when I find you, you *will* help Dallas."

He glanced at me over his shoulder, and said, "I look forward to your attempts. *Your* attempts," he said after a pause. "And no other. If I learn that other agents are searching for me, I will disappear completely, and your friend will have no chance of survival." He left me then, his body swallowed up by the fog, his words echoing behind.

I stood alone in the hospital parking lot. Sure, I could have run after him. But I didn't. What would I do with him if I caught him? I didn't have my pyre-gun, so I couldn't stun him. And he'd already proven we were an even match in a fight. Well, maybe not even.

Our time of reckoning would come, I had no doubt; sultry anticipation was already working through me. Now, however, was not that time.

Exhausted, I stumbled back inside the hospital. I'd never been in a situation like this before, and I was unsure how to proceed. I needed—God, I wasn't sure what I needed.

"This miracle sucks," I muttered.

Nurse Idiot stood sentry outside Dallas's room, sur-rounded by security guards, as she tearfully stammered her experience with me. She dabbed her eyes with a tis-sue, short strands of brown hair dangling at her tem-ples. Her face was flushed pink from her tears, the perfect offset to her bright purple scrubs. The guards drank in her every word, every expression, offering soothing murmurs of comfort each time she paused.

"You've got to be kidding me," I said on a wave of irritation.

"That's her," she cried. She pointed a finger in my direction. "That's her," she said again, cowering behind one of the guards.

All three men eyed me with distaste and edged toward me. I didn't bother with an explanation; I simply flashed my badge, and they backed off. "Get me the doctor in charge of Agent Gutierrez's case. Now."

Eyes wide, Nurse Idiot propelled herself to the nurse's station and shakily snatched up the phone. Five minutes later, I was about to pull out my hair—and the nurse's hair—because Dr. Hannah hadn't arrived.

"Page him again," I said.

"But I—"

"Who paged me?" a man asked behind me.

I turned. Dr. Hannah was short, only five feet five. He had a thick head of silver hair and equally thick glasses. "I need you to check Dallas Gutierrez and tell me if his condition has changed in any way."

Dr. Hannah frowned. "I thought this was an emergency."

"It is."

"Nurse Walden—"

"Is busy," I finished for him. "I want you to do it."

Obviously exasperated, he rubbed a hand down his face. "Surely this can wait. You called me out of prep. I've got an artificial limb attachment in"—he checked his wristwatch—"fourteen minutes."

"Then you'd better hurry." With a tilt of my chin, I motioned to room 417. "Unless, of course, you want me to call my boss and have him run a crime search on your name and every member of your staff. I can return later and discuss the results with everyone."

"Uh—I'm sure that won't be necessary." He readjusted his collar. "Dallas Gutierrez, did you say?"

"That's right."

"Very well, then." A long sigh seeped from his lips, and his eyes became heavy-lidded with resignation. "Let's have a look at him."

After taking Dallas's pulse and blood pressure, Dr. Hannah flashed a thin beam of light over Dallas's eyes. He uttered, "Hmm," then repeated the action. Brow furrowed, he cut away the bandage over Dallas's chest and inspected the wound.

"I don't understand," he said, glancing at me, then back to Dallas.

"What?" I was at his side in an instant.

"He's actually improved." Excitement dripped from his voice. "His pulse is stronger; his BP—blood pressure—is higher. His eyes dilate and contract perfectly. And look at this." With a gloved finger, he pointed to a portion of the burned tissue. "See how the flesh here appears pink?"

"Yeah."

"Well, pink indicates life. This morning, that tissue was black, dead, and completely unable to rejuvenate. Now it's alive and trying to grow."

When he began muttering about writing an article for a national medical journal, I gripped his shoulder and forced him to face me. "So Dallas will live?"

"I—I—" Grinning, Dr. Hannah scratched his head. "Yes, I believe so. For a while longer, anyway."

That was all I needed to hear. "Call me if there's any change."

"Yes, yes," he answered, distracted. "I'm going to order a complete blood count and an intralateral biopsy. Maybe a CAT scan to check brain activity. In all my years of medicine, I've never seen this happen before."

I wanted to smile and frown at the same time. How could something so wonderful for Dallas be so disastrous for others?

Damn it, I only had four days to save my friend's life.

CHAPTER
9

I went home and hit the bed fully clothed. I didn't check my messages, didn't eat or shower. My weary body ached and demanded rest, and the softness of the mattress beckoned like a knowing siren.

Sleep claimed me instantly.

As always, dreams soon followed, though these were different than any I'd ever experienced before. I dreamed of Kyrin. I dreamed he stripped me down, peeling away each layer of my clothing. His tongue moved against mine the entire time, his taste as warm and rich as brandy on a cold night.

Unbidden, my hands tangled in the silkiness of his hair.

He tore his lips from mine, and I moaned at the loss.

"Touch me," he whispered.

Even in my dream I tried to resist him. "No."

A slow smile teased his mouth before he crushed our lips together once again. I released his hair, ran my palms down the sleek brawn and sinew of his chest, then cupped the hard mounds of his ass. His skin felt like velvet, the hardness of his muscles a perfect contrast.

His body was as shaped and honed as any human. Better even. Bigger. His limbs were laced with sinew, so hot, so powerful. A girl could become addicted to such raw intensity.

"I need you, Mia," he intoned.

I clasped my hands over his jaw and brought him down for yet another kiss. I tasted a swirling storm of hunger as his tongue swept into my mouth and attempted to conquer me. Utterly conquer me.

He groaned my name.

I awoke shouting his.

Panting, sweat-soaked, I lay there, my hands fisted in the covers of my bed. Frustration clawed at me, his heady taste still in my mouth. Cool air stroked my naked, heated skin. I sucked in a broken breath, hating that I felt seared. Branded.

Kyrin was nowhere to be seen.

Only a dream, I reminded myself. Only a dream. Except, when had I stripped?

God, I need a hobby, I thought, rolling to my side. However, nothing appealed to me. I didn't have the patience to create things. Didn't like to paint, knit, or shop. My only activity in my free time was to work out or train in street combat. Sometimes I read, but that was only research for work. Maybe it was time to stop living, eating, and breathing my job, though. Maybe then my dreams would quiet.

At least I wasn't dreaming, as usual, of the aliens I had killed or the victims I failed to save in time.

I lumbered out of bed. My legs were shaky. After downing an entire pot of vitamin-enhanced synthetic coffee, I showered. I'd read that our ancestors had used water to bathe. I couldn't imagine such a thing. Dry enzyme and glyceride spray was the norm now, blowing over us from head to toe in mere seconds. Water would have cost a fortune and taken too long.

Once dressed, I headed for the station house. There I picked up a new pyre-gun, replacing the one Kyrin had stolen.

I rode the elevator to level five, then underwent a retinal scan and fingerprint ID. I felt revived, centered, as I entered Lilla's small, cramped cell. The *click, click, click* of the triple lock resounded behind me.

I'd left my gun and blades at check-in. Physically, Lilla was no match for me, and we both knew it. I could take her down without the aid of a firearm. Mentally, though . . . I just prayed I was prepared.

I was going to have to pump this stubborn, emotional Arcadian for every bit of information she possessed. I'd probably have to lie, cheat, and threaten. Whatever I had to do, I'd do it. I couldn't set Lilla free—God, I couldn't believe I was even considering the possibility—without finding the missing first.

Not even for Dallas.

I'd admitted that much to myself already, and it still hurt like hell.

But . . .

If I found the missing men, as well as Steele's killer, I could set Lilla free with a clear conscience. Sure, I'd be breaking the law—all predatory aliens were to be executed. I'd fought to put that law into place, and Lilla was definitely predatory. I didn't care, though. I'd set her free and never regret it.

Urgency, and a small trace of fear, embraced me as I took stock of my surroundings. Urgency for Dallas, fear for the enclosed space. The walls were stark white, padded, and there wasn't a single window. A cot was pushed against the north wall, and a toilet occupied the south. There was nothing else in the way of furniture.

Lilla lay on the cot, her hands folded neatly over her stomach, her legs crossed at the ankles. She no longer wore her seductive clothing. Now she had on a plain blue shirt with matching pants, both made of stiff poly. Her eyes were closed, but I knew she wasn't sleeping. Serenity might radiate from her every pore, yet I knew better; I sensed her inner turmoil.

"I know you're awake," I said. I crossed my arms

over my chest and waited. When minute after minute ticked by and still she said nothing, I added, my voice taunting, "How are your accommodations? Satisfactory, I hope. If the warden forgot to put a chocolate on your pillow—"

That had the desired effect.

"Damn you," she spat, jolting up. Her nostrils were flared, her eyes ablaze with hatred. "Who are you to ruin the lives of others?"

"I save human lives. If I must ruin yours to do so," I shrugged, "so be it."

"You are so smug, so sure. You will come to regret all that you have done, Mia Snow. Of this you can be sure."

A prophecy? Or merely words of hope? Either way, I suppressed a shudder.

"My brother—" she began in her familiar chorus.

"Yes, yes. I know. He'll eat me up and spit out my bones. The fact is, Lilla," I said, casually placing my hands in my pockets, "I've already had the pleasure of meeting your brother, the procurer of human death." I emptied my expression of all emotion. I couldn't allow her to read me, to see the truth, once I spoke my next words. "Kyrin is in custody right now."

Gasping, she stared at me, hard, searching for any hint that I lied. When she found only a blank slate, shock and fear flitted over her features.

I had to contain my sigh of relief. Until that moment, I hadn't known the depths of her feelings for her sibling. I'd only known how I would have felt if Dare had been alive and taken captive. Desperate. Knowing Lilla felt the same way about her brother gave me the leverage I needed. As long as she thought I held Kyrin's life in my hands, I could use her love against her.

"You are lying," she ground out.

Yes, I was. I held her angry stare.

"Kyrin would never allow himself to be taken." She gripped the edge of her cot, her knuckles quickly losing all color.

"Allow? Oh, no." I chuckled. "He allowed nothing. My pyre-gun gave me all the authority I needed. You do remember the effects of stun, don't you?"

Another pause.

"Is he hurt?" she half growled, half sobbed. She leaned forward, anticipating my answer. "If you hurt him, I swear by your God I will destroy you and all you hold dear."

"He is unharmed." Maintaining my casual facade, I leaned against the wall. I stared her straight in the eye when I added, "For now. If he is to remain that way, however, I need an act of good faith from you. A token of your appreciation, if you will."

"You are a bitch."

"Yes. Yes, I am." I slowly grinned. "But compliments are not what I want from you."

Her fists clenched and unclenched, and her pale cheeks brightened with color. "What do you want, then?"

"Information."

"About William?"

"Yes."

She chewed on her bottom lip. "Is that all?"

"For now."

A long moment passed while she considered my offer. "How can I be sure you will release Kyrin?"

For one brief second, I hesitated in my deception. I'd always prided myself on my honesty, and each time I uttered a lie, a little piece of my integrity melted away. Then, like the click of a camera, an illumination of black and white, a picture of the four missing men, and now the missing Rianne Harte, flashed beneath my thoughts, followed quickly by an image of Dallas, hovering close to death.

"You have my word," I said in the next instant.

Her neck arched back as she studied the white, patternless ceiling. "Very well, then," she finally said, and crumpled back onto the cot. "Where shall I begin?"

"Start with the first day you met William and end with you in this cell." I wanted to know everything. Knowledge was power, and in this situation, power was everything.

"I met him about six months ago. He came to the club. I knew he was married. I knew his wife was pregnant, but I didn't care," she added defensively, daring me to challenge her.

"I'm not judging you," I said. Whether the man had loved Lilla or not, he hadn't been as happily married as his wife claimed in her report. Jaxon would have to talk to the wife about that. "When did your affair begin?"

"A few days later. He came back to the club."

"Mark St. John didn't mind that you and Steele were sleeping together?"

"Oh, please." She waved a hand through the air. "His opinion matters nothing to me."

"Then why are you seeing him?"

She gave a dainty shrug. "Because it amuses me. George likes it rough, violence excites him, but Mark likes to be dominated. Sometimes I like one way, sometimes another."

"Did George Hudson care about the affair?" I stepped forward. Her relationships were about more than sexual preferences, I'd bet.

"Oh, yes. He hates William."

I closed a little more distance between us. "Did he hate William enough to kill him?"

"He is guilty of many things, but not murder."

There was conviction in her tone. "What are your feelings for George?"

"He was a means to an end. A bastard, yes, but I must admit it was nice to have an A.I.R. agent at my disposal." Her expression frosted, and I could tell I was entering territory she didn't wish to discuss. "Surely I have answered all of your questions. Will you release Kyrin now?"

I ignored her. "At the club, you mentioned that

you'd tried to tell Steele he would be hurt if he didn't leave with you. You said you tried to warn him about *them*. Who is *them*?"

A moment passed, then another.

"Who were you talking about, Lilla?"

She wrung her hands in agitation, twisting and untwisting the sheet between her fingers. Finally, she replied, "A group of exiled Arcadians."

"Exiled from what?"

"Arcadia. What do you think? Idiot," she muttered.

I'd been called worse. "Why would these people want to hurt Steele?"

More hesitation. "He had something they wanted."

I almost growled in frustration. The woman refused to elaborate without direct prodding. "I'm tired of prompting you, Lilla. Tell me all of it. What did he have that they wanted?" Edgy tension worked its way into my voice. I was getting close, very close, to the answers I needed. "What did he have that they wanted?"

"Life," she cried. She jolted to her feet and paced the length of the far wall. "Life."

"Life. I don't understand."

"Then you are stupid."

My jaw clenched. "Do you know any of the other missing people?" One by one, I ticked off their names.

With the questions now veering away from the exiled Arcadians, her features softened, though she didn't slow her frenzied pace. "I am only familiar with the last one. Sullivan Bay."

"How do you know him?"

"I do not *know* him. I have heard of him."

"From the exiled Arcadians?" I couldn't help but bring us back to them.

Her lips pursed. "Yes. From the leader."

"And just who is the leader?"

Her lips pressed together in mutinous silence, and her steps became wilder.

Okay, I would come back to that question. "Was your brother involved in any way with Rianne Harte?"

Grinding to a halt, she blinked over at me, and I could tell she was considering each of her coming words. "He spent some time with her, but what they did when they were alone, I know not. So if you want to know if he slept with her, I cannot verify that."

An image of Kyrin in bed with another woman had me fighting a crest of irritation. With Kyrin and with myself. "Who is the leader of the exiled Arcadians? I'll need to speak with him."

"The leader is—" She squeezed her eyes tightly shut and drew in a deep breath. Her back was pressed against the wall. "The leader is Atlanna en Arr. A female. And the others are inconsequential."

Atlanna . . . the name sent a strange wave of that humming energy through me. I don't know why. My chin tilted to the side, and I watched Lilla for any sign of emotion. "Is this Atlanna your sister?"

"No." Lilla chuckled, an amused sound that danced throughout the room. "Unlike your people, we are not named after our parents. We are named according to class."

Interesting fact, and one I hadn't known. "And just what class is en Arr?"

"Royalty."

She could be lying to impress me. I wasn't sure, and I didn't have the time to delve further on that subject just yet. Kyrin en Arr, however, had the bearing of a king, so that fit. "Let's talk more about Atlanna. How did she know Sullivan Bay?"

"They were lovers."

"Were? Is he dead?"

I received no response.

I tried not to let my temper overcome my intentions. Most witnesses forced me to mentally beat every bit of information out of them, so in this Lilla was no different. Usually I handled the situation with patience—at least, I liked to think I handled each situation with patience. Today, I was hanging at the razor's edge of tolerance.

"Is he dead?" I demanded again.

"I honestly do not know," she sighed.

"Where is Atlanna now?"

"I do not know that, either."

We were getting nowhere this way, so I tried another line of questioning. "Who killed William Steele? Do you know that?"

"No." She glanced away from me.

"I think you're lying. I think you and your brother

are involved. I think your brother needs to be interrogated. Violently."

A raging fire flared to life in her eyes. Had I been closer, she would have attempted to claw my face apart. "No matter what you discover," she growled, "my brother was not involved."

My back straightened, and my pulse leaped. "No matter what I discover, huh? That means there's evidence against him."

A gasp slipped from her, as if she'd just realized she'd said too much. "He is not responsible." Nostrils flaring, she pointed a vengeful finger in my direction. "I'm finished speaking with you. I've told you everything I know. Will you now free my brother?"

"No. You answered some of my questions, but not all. I want to know about Kyrin. I want to know what the exiled Arcadians desired from Steele. I want to know—"

"Get out. Get out before I kill you. I do not know any more. I do not remember."

My fists curled at my sides, and I remained in place. "You *do* remember."

She remained silent, but small phantom fingers began to pry at my mind, suggesting I leave peacefully. The woman dared to try and control me again. I ground my teeth together. "You want to be stunned again?"

"Get out!" she screamed, and the pressure in my mind eased.

I'd get nothing more from her now, that much was clear. Just how long would I be forced to wait for her to calm down?

Time was quickly becoming my greatest enemy.

"I'll leave," I said, "but don't think for a single moment that our conversation is over. You *and* your brother's lives depend on your memory improving."

CHAPTER
10

I spent an hour in the gym, sweating out my frustrations, pounding my fists and feet into the punching bag. I even utilized the virtual combat program, beating the shit out of computer-generated other-worlders. Unfortunately, my dark mood loomed even blacker when I strolled into the conference room fifteen minutes late.

I was determined to sit through this meeting and gather all the information I could. Even if it killed me—or I killed someone else. I'd already stuffed my car with the case files and secured documents from each abduction case. Secretly, of course. I'd paid Mandalay to hack into the mainframe and add my name to the list of those allowed inside the "Confidential" storage area. As soon as I exited, she removed my name. She hadn't asked me why, just thanked me for the money. When I got home, I planned to go through them line by line and see if anything had been left out of the copies given to me.

See, agents were always given *copies* of the main file, never originals, and the main file was locked away and strictly for top brass. Supposedly, the practice was meant to preserve the original document from tampering. Pure crap. The government wanted their sticky little fingers in everything, that's all; they wanted to control what we knew. And what we didn't.

Conversation ceased as I eased into the only unoccupied chair at the table. To my left was Jaxon, and to my right sat Jack. Ghost, Kittie, Jaffe, and Mandalay, the only other female, were facing me. Behind them hung a virtual screen that contained five vertically lined pictures of the abducted. Beside each photo was the date, time, and location of each abduction. Below the photos was a map, each location pinpointed.

Jaxon gave me an encouraging smile to show his support.

I nodded in acknowledgment. Jaxon was a good man, one of the best on the force. A scar slashed from the top right side of his face to the bottom of his jaw—compliments of a rogue alien—yet he always managed to appear saintly. Maybe that was because he never spoke out of turn, never uttered a single sexual innuendo.

"How's Dallas?" Ghost asked, his deep, rich baritone filling the space with sadness.

"The same." I wanted so badly to tell them the truth, that Dallas might survive. But I didn't. If they knew about Kyrin's blood—and what I needed to do to get it—I'd be banned from Lilla's cell forever.

Silence hung in the air, heavy and heart-wrenching, as each of us became lost in our own private thoughts of Dallas.

Finally, Jack cleared his throat and said, "Mia, Mandalay's been telling us about the Harte abduction. She's taken over since Johnson is sick. Mandalay?"

"Yes?" she said briskly, shuffling the papers in front of her.

"Continue."

"Yes, sir. Harte was taken from her home a little after two P.M. Her roommate, also her sister, claims they were watching movies. Harte went to the kitchen to make a sandwich and never returned. There's no sign of a struggle. No indication of foul play or unlawful entry. We haven't been able to track down the boyfriend. Kyrin something or other. The sister didn't know his last name. Only that he's Arcadian."

"Interesting, isn't it?" Jack interjected with a raised brow. "That another Arcadian is in the picture."

I didn't comment. My stomach was too busy churning with dread. Kyrin had known Harte, had dated her. Even Lilla had admitted to that. Having an entire A.I.R. squad know it, though, didn't bode well for Kyrin.

"Mia," Jack said. "Tell us what you learned from Lilla."

I drew in a calming breath, then pushed the air from my lips. "She mostly glossed over things we already know. However, I did learn that there's another Arcadian female involved. Her name's Atlanna en Arr, and she was seeing one of the abducted men, Sullivan Bay. She's also the leader of a band of Arcadian exiles."

"Mandalay?" Jack said with a quick glance to our computer expert.

"Already on it, sir." Mandalay's fingertips flew over the keyboard in front of her. Curly locks of red hair fell around her temples and brushed her wrists. By appearance, she was a commanding woman, tall, big boned. By nature, she was not a fighter. She worked better with probabilities and possibilities. She paused, faced Jack. "There's no Atlanna en Arr mentioned in our database."

"What about this Kyrin guy?" I asked, trying to be subtle.

"He's not listed either," Jaxon said. "We already checked."

"Did Lilla give any clue as to where this Atlanna is?" Jack asked me.

"No," I answered honestly.

"Think you can find her?"

What I thought didn't matter. I *would* find her. "Give me two days."

"Done. Okay, let's recap the rest of what Snow

missed." Jack shot me an irritated glance, and I hoped that would be my only chastisement for my tardiness. "Ghost and Kittie questioned Isabel and Sherry yesterday evening. Nothing was learned from Isabel, now deceased."

I heard several men mutter, "Bitch."

"From Sherry we learned a bit more," Jack continued. "According to her, she's known Hudson for three months. Apparently, Lilla paid her to have sex with him regularly, and the man never knew. Sherry said Lilla promised to pay her a huge bonus if she got pregnant. No luck, though."

Very interesting. "Why did Lilla want Sherry to have Hudson's baby?"

"Sherry didn't know," Kittie said. "Lilla introduced the two at Club Ecstasy." He tapped his blue lighter against the table surface. "Hudson had no problem screwing the two women, but the moment Lilla started seeing Steele, the man flipped."

"Possible motive for Steele's death," I said. "Hudson was jealous."

"Possible, yes," Ghost said. "But it doesn't explain the other abductions."

I said, "Anyone talked to Hudson? Maybe he can help us wade through the crap and find the diamonds."

"He won't help willingly, that's for sure. But no, no one's talked to him yet." A frown marred Jack's face as he twisted a pencil between his fingers. "He had his nose repaired this morning, and only returned to his cell a little while ago. Jaxon plans to question him after this meeting."

I eyed my boss, gauging his reaction. "So Hudson doesn't know about Isabel?"

"Oh, he knows," Jack said. "The good doc let it slip before surgery. Hudson didn't give a flying rat's ass, though. Said his life would be calmer now that the girl was gone."

My eyelids twitched at such blatant heartlessness. "I want to be there when Jaxon questions him." Maybe I'd destroy a little of Hudson's attitude while I was there.

Because he knew me so well, Jack shook his head. "I don't want you in the room. You're not his favorite person right now, and the sight of you may make him violent. Worse, he might refuse to talk. I'm not budging on this," he added when I opened my mouth to argue. "I'd say the same thing to a man."

I needed to be there for that interview. I needed to know what Hudson knew—and I didn't want to wait for Jaxon's formal report. "I'll observe from a two-way," I suggested.

Jack studied me for a long while. I fluttered my lashes, trying to appear innocent. A sigh slipped from him. "All right. You can go, but if I find out you stepped one foot"—he held up one finger—"one damn foot out of observation, I'll kick your ass into next week. Understand?"

"Absolutely."

Jack turned his attention to Jaxon. "What did you learn from Steele's family?"

"When I reinterviewed her, the wife admitted that he was seeing another woman, but she doesn't know who it was."

I crossed my arms over my chest. "She claimed they were happily married in her first interview. If she knew about his infidelity, why did she stay?"

"I asked the same question. Says she was pregnant when she found out and couldn't stand the thought of raising her baby alone. Says she loved him."

"Could have been lying," Mandalay said.

"True," Jaxon acknowledged.

"Does she have an alibi?" Jack asked.

"Yeah. Since Steele's disappearance, she's been staying with her mother. Already verified. I learned something else, though. Steele had dinner with an Arcadian male the night before he was kidnapped. Kyrin," he said, checking his notes. "The same Kyrin who dated Rianne Harte, is my bet."

My stomach rolled. This was what Lilla had warned me about. This was what she feared would implicate him. And by God, it did.

"We need to find this man," Jack said. "I want him questioned ASAP."

I couldn't allow other agents to search for him, not with Kyrin's warning ringing in my head. If anyone other than me searched for him, he'd slip into hiding so fast he'd have windburn.

"What do you have for us?" I asked Jaffe, hoping to change the subject.

"Well," Jaffe said, speaking for the first time since I'd entered the room. He was a small, nervous man, with thinning ash blond hair and wide-spaced hazel eyes. Those eyes always darted left and right, as if trying to judge his escape route. He was damn good with numbers and patterns. "There's no obvious MO for the killer. There were two weeks between the first two abductions, but the third was taken only three days later. And eight days passed between the third and fourth."

"Keep searching," Jack commanded. "You're missing something. Even chaos can form a pattern." He turned his attention to Mandalay. "What about the victim's body?"

"Unfortunately," Mandalay responded, "there was no blood evidence. Nor was there anything under his fingernails. No fibers—alien or human—to indicate where he was held or how he was transported. The voice recorders around the area have no alien recordings at any time on the day of the murder."

"What about Rianne Harte's home?" Jack asked. "What was found there?"

Mandalay shook her head, sending red curls flying. "Nothing, sir."

"Wonderful. Just fucking wonderful. I expected better than this." Jack shoved to his feet and strode to the side table. He poured himself a cup of coffee, then drained the steamy liquid in one gulp. He turned back to us. "We're no closer to finding the victims than we were yesterday. Pressure is rising, people, and will continue to do so until we're successful or we lose our jobs."

"Let's go back to this Kyrin character," Ghost said. "He was seen with victim number one the night before the abduction. He was also dating Harte. There's a possibility he knew the others and had some sort of contact with them. So my question is, who's going to hunt him?"

"Let me take care that," I said, hoping I didn't sound too eager.

"You're finding Atlanna, remember?" Jack said.

I spread my arms wide. "And I can't do both?"

"You're not Super Woman," Kittie remarked with a grin.

"No," Ghost said with a grin of his own. "She's Super Bitch."

Laughter rippled through the room, the kind of rough, biting laughter that came from people who encountered depravity on a daily basis. Jaxon tried to hold his amusement back, but soon gave up and burst into guffaws. Even I lost my scowl and had to smile. I *was* a super bitch.

"Fine," Jack said. "Kyrin's yours."

Those words affected me on a deep, primal level. Mine, I thought. All mine.

Jack slapped his hands against the table surface. "All

right, people. You know what you're supposed to do. So get it done."

I accompanied Jaxon down the long, winding corridor that led to A.I.R. sector five. Our ID cards allowed us to bypass the motion detectors, the heat sensors, and the weight-sensitive floor tiles without a single pause.

Jack had dismissed us five minutes ago, and I'd already called Dallas's doctor twice. The first time, he put me on hold. The second, he didn't make the same mistake. I learned Dallas's tissues were indeed rejuvenating. Dr. Hannah had discovered a foreign chemical in Dallas's blood, a substance he'd never encountered before, and he'd treated both aliens and humans.

I knew the chemical came from Kyrin.

The good doctor was running more tests, but as of now, Dallas was stable. Still, I couldn't help but hear a countdown in my head. Three more days until Kyrin reappeared, demanding his sister—unless I found him first.

"You ready for this?" Jaxon asked. He gazed down at me, his features tight with concentration.

"More than you know." I forced Dallas and Kyrin to the back of my mind. I had to concentrate on the here and now.

When we reached the end of the hallway, we waited at the metal security station doors.

"After you, Jaxon," I said.

He positioned his head in front of the blinking blue retinal scan. The computer said, "Scanning now," and flashed the light over his entire face. "Thank you, Jaxon Tramain."

Jaxon straightened his shoulders and flicked me a glance. "Your turn."

God, I hated these things. I rested my chin in the recession plate, and the metal monster clamped onto my head for a full optical scan. If one of the antiquated lasers ever received a power surge, I'd be sentenced to permanent medical leave and given an SGA, a sightseeing guidance automaton.

"Thank you, Mia Snow," the computer said, releasing me.

Now that our identities were verified, we endured a simultaneous palm scan and the doors buzzed open. We entered a long white hallway. To both our left and right sides were sealed entrances, each leading to private cells.

These rooms were rarely occupied for long. Otherworlders brought in were usually interrogated within hours. Then they were either set free if exonerated, or executed if guilty. It was that simple.

I passed Lilla's cell. Thirty-two. And kept my gaze straight ahead. I'd worry about her later.

Cell 66, our destination, was Hudson's location—which lacked one more six to be accurate, to my way of thinking. He was human, yes, but he was involved in an alien investigation, so here he stayed. The bastard would be treated with the rights of an earth-born citizen, but he sure as hell didn't deserve it.

When we arrived at our destination, Jaxon placed his hand on scanner 66A, and I placed my hand on scanner 66B. A yellow light enveloped our fingertips.

"Don't believe anything I say, okay?" Jaxon said. "You know I have to tell him what he wants to hear if I hope to get any information."

"I know."

"Just don't kill me afterward."

"Hey, do me a favor and ask Hudson about his daughter. Ask him why he claimed an alien as his own."

"Alien?" Jaxon blinked. "You think Isabel was alien? Which species?"

"I don't know. Ask him that, too."

He nodded just as the lock above each door buzzed, allowing our entrance.

Wiping all expression from his face, Jaxon stepped inside Hudson's cell.

I entered Observation. From the two-way, I saw that Hudson lay on his cot. A bandage covered his nose, and his eyes were swollen and ringed with bruises. As if to the beat of a drum, he moaned every other second.

Jaxon strode to the edge of the cot, squatted, and peered at the injured man. "You okay, George?" he asked. "You in pain?"

Hudson blinked, but didn't move. "Do I look like

I'm in pain?" His voice was nasal and pinched. "Asshole," he muttered.

As if he wasn't laughing smugly on the inside, Jaxon uttered a sympathetic sigh. "Want some meds?"

"What I want is for you to get the hell out."

Jaxon's features softened. "I can't do that. You're in trouble, George, and we both know it. Let me help you."

I knew Jaxon was deliberately using his first name. Made him seem friendlier, more personable. But Hudson didn't take the bait. Hell, he'd had the same training we'd had.

"Help me?" he squeaked out, turning his head and riveting his eyes on Jaxon. He would have shouted if his nose hadn't been packed full of gauze. "You don't give a shit about me."

"You're an agent. Of course I care," Jaxon said, as if that explained everything. His expression was so compassionate, *I* almost believed him. "Besides, we have something in common."

"What's that?"

He leaned forward, like he was sharing a great secret. "We both hate Mia Snow," he whispered.

That seemed to defuse Hudson's anger.

Jaxon, you are so good, I thought.

"I thought everyone here worshipped that bitch."

"Not me. She took my promotion. I should have become squad leader, but she slept with Pagosa, and he gave it to her."

"No shit?" Hudson's ears perked, and his lips cocked. He propped himself on his elbows. "I always figured she was blowing Pagosa to get ahead."

Jaxon flicked a glance to the mirror. To me. His eyes were sparkling with mischief, but his tone was dead serious. "She's a girl. That's the *only* way she can get ahead."

If anyone else had uttered those words, I would have burst into that cell and pounded some ass. But Jaxon's comment had worked. Hudson now considered him a freaking genius.

"Damn right," Hudson said, slamming his fist onto the cot. "I could eat that bitch for breakfast, then make her beg for more."

Maintaining his friendly, casual tone, Jaxon said, "Mia thinks you killed Steele."

"That's bullshit." Hudson jerked to a sitting position, grimaced, then sank back onto the bed. "That's bullshit," he repeated. "I didn't have anything to do with that."

"That's exactly what I told her. He's innocent, I said. Know what she did after that?"

"What?"

"She laughed in my face."

"Dumb bitch," he grumbled. "I swear, I'd like five minutes alone with her. I'd teach her a few things about men. Real men. Not those pussy-assed losers she works with."

Jaxon nodded his agreement, and didn't point out

that he himself worked with me. "You have to help me here, George. I need some information so I can prove your innocence and tell Queen Bitch to go to hell."

"What do you need to know?" he asked, his tone dripping resignation.

"Why don't you tell me about Lilla," Jaxon said. "Sherry says you were jealous of her relationship with Steele."

"Sherry doesn't know shit."

"Dumb as a box of rocks, is she?"

Hudson chuckled. "I like that. Dumb as a box of rocks. Describes her perfectly."

"Sherry says Lilla paid her to sleep with you. That Lilla wanted her to have your baby."

"Didn't take me long to figure out that's what was going on. Use my condom, Sherry said, as if I couldn't see a hole the size of a goddamn crater in the middle of it."

"What'd you do?"

"I confronted her. She told me about Lilla paying her, so I confronted Lilla too. Lilla said she couldn't have children of her own, but she wanted a baby. I think she was going to give the brat to Steele, maybe entice him away from his wife."

"I bet that made you mad."

"Mad? Hell, I went ballistic."

"What'd you do to punish the women?"

"I slapped Sherry around a little—women need that every now and again to keep them in line. Then I arrested Lilla for prostitution. Scared the shit out of her, too," he said on a laugh.

"What happened after that?"

"Lilla begged me to let her out. I thought she'd see me as her hero, you know, but the bitch took off with Steele the moment I freed her."

"Is that why you moved Sherry into your house? So you could get back at Lilla?"

He shrugged. "I'm a man. I have needs. She's easy, and she had no place to go."

"Don't you worry about her trying to trick you into getting her pregnant?"

He laughed, a sound full of evil enjoyment. "I had a vasectomy right after Isabel was born. Neither woman ever suspected."

Jaxon muttered, "Smart man," and I could tell he wanted to choke the life out of Hudson. The lines around his mouth were taut. His eyes were slightly narrowed. "How badly did you want Steele out of the picture?"

"Bad. Real bad. But not enough to kill him," Hudson added quickly. "I just told his wife he was screwing around on her. That put a stop to things real quick. Steele wanted nothing to do with Lilla after that."

"I can just imagine how Lilla took the rejection."

"Beat the shit out of him. He deserved it, so I wasn't too upset with her about it."

"Women." Jaxon shook his head. He paused for effect. "Out of curiosity, do you know anything about a group of exiled Arcadians? I'm trying to prove they're responsible."

I loved how Jaxon so expertly wove his questions with his sympathy and his desire to "help," luring his unsuspecting victim deeper into his web of false comfort.

"Yeah, I know them," Hudson answered. "They're led by a female. Atlanna."

"Do you know where I can find her?"

"No. I've only seen her once, and she didn't stay around to chat. She's real secretive. Looks like Lilla, but taller. And she's got a God complex like you wouldn't believe. Like Mia, she thinks she controls the fate of the world, and she's a real bitch, if you know what I mean."

"Oh, I know exactly what you mean." Maintaining his good-natured expression, Jaxon massaged the back of his neck. "Did Lilla ever mention a man named Kyrin?"

"Yeah, he's her brother."

"Good guy?"

"Freaky." Hudson's voice was growing softer, as if he were suddenly having trouble keeping himself awake. "When he looks at you, it feels like he's looking into your soul. He's strong, too. The man could probably crush us all with one swipe of his hand." His mouth opened wide in a yawn.

"I can tell you're tired, George. I just have a few more questions, and then I'll let you get some rest. Was Isabel really your daughter, or was she alien?"

"What the hell kind of dumb-ass question is that? Of course she was my daughter."

"There was no chance—"

"I told you, she was mine," Hudson said sleepily.

"Thanks, man. That's all I needed to know." Jaxon left the cell and peeked around the observation door. "Is it safe to come in?" he asked me, his cheeks red with a blush.

"It's safe. He was lying about Isabel, he had to be." She was the alien in my vision. I just didn't know why Hudson would lie about something like that. I let it go, though. For now.

Jaxon entered fully, then closed the door behind him with a click. "What a bastard," he said, his tone sickened and disgusted as he repeated my thoughts. "That man deserves pain. Lots and lots of pain."

"At least we've confirmed Atlanna's existence."

"And Kyrin's, as well. What if he, Lilla, and Atlanna are working together?"

"Maybe. I mean, I can see that for Steele—Lilla wanted Steele, he rejected her, so the brother and Atlanna get angry—but what about the other abductions? No motive." I sighed. "I'll question Lilla again tomorrow and see what I can learn. Tonight—" I clamped my mouth shut the moment I realized I was about to tell him my plans to search for Kyrin.

Yet, that quickly, I came to another realization. I couldn't do this on my own. I couldn't search for Kyrin, search for Atlanna, read case files, study crime scene photos, endure another interrogation with Lilla, *and* find the missing men—all in three days.

I needed someone I trusted to assist me.

Who better than Jaxon? I studied his face. Despite his scar, he was a sensually handsome man. His eyes were more silver than blue, his nose slightly crooked from being broken one too many times. Soft lips, strong chin. He wore his dark, slightly curly hair shaggy so it always looked windblown.

He was regarding me with kindness and concern.

"Tonight," I continued, after dragging in and pushing out a deep breath, "I need your help."

He didn't even pause. "Whatever I can do, I will. You know that."

"I'll hold you to that, Jaxon. I'll hold you to that."

CHAPTER
11

I drove Jaxon to Trollie's, a café and bar situated a few miles from headquarters and the only restaurant open twenty-four hours. On any given day and at any given time, the place was packed from end to end with A.I.R. agents, both on and off duty. The food was mediocre, but the atmosphere was exceptional—dimmed lighting, soft, relaxing music, and raunchy agents cracking dirty jokes. A five-star meal couldn't compare to that.

During the drive, I filled Jaxon in on Kyrin, Dallas, and Lilla. I left out nothing. Jaxon never once interrupted me. When I had finished, I waited for some type of response from him.

Only silence greeted me, and several minutes ticked away.

"So," I said, flicking him a quick glance, "do you still want to help me?"

He stared out the passenger window. "Give me some time to digest this. That's a lot to throw at a man."

Time was the only thing I *didn't* have. "You've got until we're seated at Trollie's. If you won't help me, I'll have to find someone else."

He hissed out a breath between his teeth, filling the car with a soft whistle. "Are you always this impatient?"

"Always."

"I bet you drove Dallas crazy."

"You could make a fortune on that bet."

We made the rest of the drive in silence. A few minutes later, we eased onto a gravel drive and parked in front of a cheap orange boxcar, elongated for space.

Outside, the air was cold and quiet, scented with car exhaust. When I pulled open the brass-handled door, a volley of drunken chatter spilled out. We cut through a thick haze of cigarette smoke—like we were going to arrest each other for smoking—and meandering bodies. As usual, the place was jammed. We had to shoot the shit with several agents we knew before snagging a back corner booth.

Dallas and I had spent many evenings here. Neither of us liked to cook. I tried, but the end result was always burned slop. We'd laughed in here, relaxed in here. He deserved more nights like that.

We punched our order into the wall unit, and soon Molly, a cute blond, brought our drinks and scampered away. Jaxon, the consummate health nut, had requested water with a lemon twist. Me? I wanted the strongest, blackest coffee they had, laced with a shot of pure, undiluted caffeine. I'm sure injecting crude oil into my veins would have been easier on my body, but I didn't care. I downed the burning liquid, then signaled for a refill. I was like a boozehound with a brand-new bottle of tequila.

"My God, Mia, you trying to kill yourself there?" Jaxon asked with a laugh.

"Just trying to survive."

"Is that how you stay so slim? Living on caffeine?"

I shrugged and watched him through the thick shield of my lashes. I'd had enough pleasantries; I wanted to get down to business. "So are you in or out?"

Jaxon understood what I was asking and stared at me across the speckled yellow tabletop. "Let me see if I have this straight." Shadows and light played across his features as the lamp above us swayed, illuminating his scar, giving him a menacing quality. "Kyrin—"

"No names," I interrupted, giving a pointed nod to the other agents present.

"The brother can save our friend's life. In return, he wants the sister released. And he's given you four days to free her, or our friend dies."

"Only three days left, now. But otherwise, that's right."

"And no agent—"

"But me."

"Can search for him, or he'll disappear."

"Right again."

"So you're planning to find our victims—and the brother—within these next three days?"

"That's right. Now are you in or out?" I asked again.

"In, of course."

Of course, he said now, as if he hadn't made me sweat the last ten minutes of his indecision. On the black vinyl seat beside me, I'd tucked my briefcase filled with the stolen case files. I'd already covered the Confidential sticker with a plain casing. I withdrew two and handed them to Jaxon. "We need to go over these. Study every detail."

He clasped the offered files and then, to my astonishment, set them aside. "I can't concentrate without food. Let's eat. Then study."

My impatience reared its head. The sooner we worked, the sooner we found answers. Still, I wasn't going to push my luck, so I forced myself to agree.

Our food arrived fifteen minutes later and was arranged in front of us. Jaxon dove into his turkey-on-wheat sandwich. No mayo. I managed a few bites of my double bacon cheeseburger and extra crispy chili cheese fries. Normally, I would have cleaned my plate and requested dessert. Dallas always made fun of my junk food addiction and constantly complained that if he ate like that, he wouldn't fit inside the car. Me? I had uncommon metabolism. Couldn't keep the fat on me. Which was good. I had no intention of changing my eating habits now.

Tonight, however, my stomach was simply too unsettled to allow me to indulge.

"You going to eat that?" Jaxon asked, eyeing my burger with distaste.

"There's not enough grease to suit me," I said.

"Fine." He rolled his eyes and threw his napkin on the tabletop. "Let's see what we've got here," he said, opening one of the files, "since you're not going to relax until we do."

Only moments later, he glanced at me, his features blank. "On the outside, this looks like a nonrestricted file. This *should* be a nonrestricted file. Yet what did I find when I took a glance at the inside? This is confidential material, Mia. What's it doing outside of A.I.R.?"

I shrugged and said, "I'll return everything when we're done."

"My God." He shook his head, but I detected a hint of admiration in his expression. "You are some piece of work."

While he read on, I grabbed a file and poured over every photo, every sentence. I had just reached the third page when I paused, reread, blinked. Blinked again. A thought jumped to life in my mind.

"Check this out," I said to Jaxon and handed him

the folder. "This wasn't mentioned in *our* file. Steele and his wife had just had a baby, right? Turns out they conceived through artificial insemination. Didn't Hudson say that Lilla paid Sherry to try and get pregnant by him? And now I discover that Sullivan Bay made frequent deposits at his local sperm bank." I shook my head. "Who are you working on?"

"Raymond Palmer."

"Check for—"

I didn't have to finish my sentence. Jaxon glanced up at me. "Mr. Palmer made regular deposits at Kilmer, Peterman, and Nate, too. Same place Rianne Harte worked. Why wouldn't they give us that information?"

I didn't know, but a thrill of success tingled through me. I had a common thread. Fertility. I turned my attention back to the photos and papers in front of me. A few minutes later, I was shaking my head in disbelief. "Look what else I found," I said. "Check out the fourth paragraph."

He glanced at the paper, looked back at his own file, then glanced again at mine. "Guess what? Mine says the same thing, except the name isn't mentioned. Just the description."

"Please tell me you're joking."

"I wish I could," he said gravely. "What do you want to bet the others say the same thing?"

I fought back a groan. "Let's pray they don't." We knew there was a particular person connected to two of the cases, but if all of them were connected to—I sliced that thought to a halt, not wanting to borrow trouble. Still, I fought a sense of impending doom as I withdrew the two remaining folders from my briefcase, handed one to Jaxon, then opened the other myself. Only two minutes had passed before we were staring over the table at each other.

"Glad you didn't take my bet?" Jaxon asked.

Damn it. Kyrin was mentioned in every file as a "tall Arcadian male." Twice by name. Not only had he dated Rianne Harte, he'd had dinner or some type of contact with every fucking man the night before they were abducted. The very night.

This was not the kind of information an agent could ethically withhold from a commander. If we told Jack, however, twenty agents would immediately be assigned to hunt and kill Kyrin. They might even write off the missing men as casualties, not stopping to question Kyrin about their whereabouts, just killing him in their fury.

I couldn't allow that. Because I didn't doubt for a moment that Kyrin would act on the threat he'd made to me. If he discovered other agents were hunting him, he would vanish, and Dallas would die.

Unbidden, Kyrin's image formed in my mind. White hair. Enigmatic lavender eyes. Taut sinew and rigidly muscled body. The way he moved with such grace and fluidity; his long strides of self-assurance. The way strength radiated from him.

"What do you want to do about Kyrin?" Jaxon asked.

"I don't know. God, I don't know."

Jaxon rubbed his jaw with two fingers. "We could split the search. You take one half of the city, and I'll take the other. Or . . ." He tapped his fingers against the tabletop. "Or we could bring Kyrin to us."

Intrigued, I tilted my chin and studied him. "How so?"

"He loves his sister and wants to save her, right?"

"That's right."

A man strode by our table, followed by another. Jaxon waited until the two were out of range before continuing. "What if someone alerted the media about Lilla's execution?"

"Execution? We aren't killing her yet. We need— Oh. Ooohhh." I smiled slowly. My heart kicked into overtime. "A false tip. I like that."

"Everyone at headquarters will be shocked when protesters storm the doors."

"Which will allow Kyrin entrance. And when the sea of reporters burst inside, every exit will be sealed, trapping everyone inside."

Jaxon nodded. "Think we should tell Jack and the others what's going on? They'll be able to give us more cover, and we'll have a better chance of capturing our guy."

"No." I pinched the bridge of my nose. "I'm not taking a chance on a trigger-happy agent who doesn't care if Kyrin lives or dies."

"Okay. I'll make the call at eleven tomorrow night and say Lilla's being executed at midnight. That'll give the press one hour to spread the word, yet won't give Jack enough time to deny it."

"Perfect. If he somehow finds out what we've done, though, I'm taking full responsibility."

"I don't need you to cover for me. I'll take the consequences."

"Sorry. No." I gave him my grittiest won't-take-no-for-an-answer glare, which he of course ignored. The male ego was not going to make me change my mind. "I won't let you go down. I asked you to help me, not the other way around."

"Too bad." The lines around his mouth firmed. "Dallas is my friend too. Now, do you want my help or not?"

I paused. "Fine. If we're caught, I'll tattle on you like a whiny girl. How's that?"

"That's good." He grinned. "Real good."

"Go home, get some rest," I told him. "You'll need it. I'll meet you here for dinner at seven."

Maybe I should have taken my own advice and gone home to rest. I didn't want to sleep, though, didn't want to dream. I ended up making the twenty-minute drive to Kilmer, Peterman, and Nate Pharmaceuticals.

I spent two hours inside, questioning employee after employee—but it was wasted time. Mostly they confirmed what I already knew. That several of the abducted men had voluntarily submitted sperm samples for payment. That Rianne had worked here.

The only new piece of information I received was that each male donor had had a very healthy sperm count.

I was feeling frustrated—until I stepped outside. A wave of familiar energy hit me square in the chest. I froze. Heart hammering against my rib cage, I darted my gaze in every direction, searching for Kyrin. And then I found him. He stood off to the side, his back to me. He was facing a young, dark-haired couple.

Damn, I loved this new energy-sensing gift of mine.

I slowly reached for my new pyre-gun and moved toward the group. I held the weapon at my side, not wanting the couple to see it and give Kyrin warning.

"Do not come here again," I heard Kyrin tell the couple. "Do not let your names be entered into their database. People in that database are dying."

"You're crazy, ET," the guy said. "Something like that would be all over the news. Now, for the last time, get out of my way." He dragged the pale-faced female along as he pushed past Kyrin and strode into the building.

I waited until they passed me before taking aim, yet Kyrin's words echoed in my mind, giving me pause. *Do not come here again. Do not come here again.* He'd risked implicating himself by coming here. He'd tried to warn potential victims away. Neither was something a bad guy would do.

That knowledge almost kept me from squeezing the trigger. Almost.

I had lucked out by finding him so quickly and unexpectedly, and I wouldn't spit in the face of that luck. I was going to stun him, take what blood I needed, then lock him up and question him.

Zeroed in on him, I squeezed the trigger.

Nothing happened. My mouth dropped open, and I squeezed again. And again. And again. Still nothing. Frustrated and growing more furious by the second, I glanced at the weapon. The crystal had somehow been knocked out of range. Shit. Shit! Had I tested the damn thing before I signed it out of A.I.R.? No, goddamn it, I realized. I hadn't.

Kyrin's shoulders stiffened. He spun around, giving me a glimpse of tense features and haunting shadows under his eyes. "Mia."

I didn't panic. I kept my weapon steady. He didn't know my new gun wasn't working properly. I'd use it to keep him docile, then find some other way to knock him out. "I've been looking for you," I said, holding my ground. "We've got unfinished business."

He opened his mouth to reply, but a blue beam of pyre-fire suddenly lit a path just behind him—and it wasn't mine—silencing his words. Someone screamed. Footsteps pounded. I caught a glimpse of a lithe, white-haired female as Kyrin shouted, "Get down!" and jolted forward, slamming into me and knocking me down.

The moment we hit, I lost my breath, and sharp rocks dug into my back. Kyrin rolled off me and crouched to his knees. I followed suit, and we scrambled to a car, using it as a shield as another beam flew at us.

Kyrin peeked over the hood. "Where is she?"

I set my gun to kill and prayed *that* setting would work. He ducked as another beam shot past him, hitting the ground just beyond his feet. Dirt and gravel spewed in every direction.

"Want to tell me why that woman's trying to kill you?" I said, rising slightly and firing. *Click. Click.* "Damn it," I cursed as I sank down. The gun wouldn't work on kill either.

"Perhaps she doesn't like that I wish to atone for past sins."

I slid my old kill-only gun from my ankle holster, popped up, and fired. I hit a dark blue vehicle and shattered the front window. "Yeah, what kind of past sins?"

"The bad kind."

"Your sarcasm sucks." I flicked him a glance, but he kept his profile to me. "Don't worry. I won't let her hurt you. If anyone gets your blood, it's me."

"I suddenly feel warm and giddy inside." His tone was as dry as the air. "Are you trying to make me fall in love with you?"

I snorted.

He removed a pyre-gun from the waist of his pants. My old gun, I noticed.

"How appropriate," I said.

He grinned, kissed the barrel with a mocking wink, lifted it, and fired over the car. "Who would have thought Mia Snow would be working with me instead of against me?" A fourth shot whizzed past him, this one nearly singeing his shoulder.

Just then, I felt something . . . swirl inside me. Tingling inside my veins, pulsing through my entire body. I don't know what it was, or what caused it. I blinked in confusion. As I watched with wide eyes, the world around me began to slow down.

A fly entered my line of vision, its wings moving so leisurely I could see every flutter, see even the ripple of air. I had to be hallucinating, but . . . Frowning, I reached out and plucked the insect from the air. No, no hallucination. I could feel him. What the hell was happening to me?

Three more shots soared over our car, and as I released the fly, I watched the fire meander toward Kyrin, watched him leap out of the way, moving inch by inch. I watched that fire slam into the ground behind us. I could have danced around those rays, they moved so slowly.

"Fire, Mia," he shouted, the sound deep, almost distorted, and as slow as his motions.

I popped up, my every action fast. Too fast. My gaze blazed over the parking lot. The shooter was in mid-duck, her white hair floating above her head, her delicate features fixed in place. She moved like Kyrin, by gradual degrees. I took in her lavender eyes, which were radiating intense fury, her dainty nose, and her startling familiar high cheekbones. I'd seen her before. I knew I had, I just didn't know where.

And then, just as suddenly as the odd swirl had hit me, it abandoned me. The tingling abandoned my veins, the pulsing left my body. Everything leaped into high gear, and for a split second, my gaze locked with the female Arcadian's and surprise darkened her face before she disappeared behind the car.

Gasping, I hunched down and eyed Kyrin. "Holy shit."

He was watching me with a strange, unreadable expression. I shook my head, suddenly tired, hoping an explanation for what just happened would slide into place. Nope, didn't work. Then another blast soared past us, claiming my attention. "Do you know that woman?"

"Atlanna en Arr."

Atlanna. The hairs on the back of my neck rose, and I grinned, pushing the weird slowdown thing out of my mind. I loved when suspects made my job easy.

I couldn't wait to get my hands on that woman.

She could have waited until Kyrin left this area and tried to kill him in private, where there was less chance of capture. But no, she did it here, an action that screamed "Look at me, look what I can do." That type of behavior fit the profile of Steele's killer. Perfectly.

I was going to have to trust Kyrin right now if I hoped to get close to Atlanna, and while that knowledge didn't settle well inside me, I knew I had no other choice. "She was behind the green Lexus, six cars away, straight down the middle, but she's probably running now. You go left. I'll go right. Let's find the bitch."

I didn't wait for his reply, didn't wait to see if he followed orders. I jolted into motion. Gravel cut past my pants and into my knees, and I wished to God I could rise up and walk, but I had to stay low. Atlanna might have come to kill Kyrin, but I'm sure she wouldn't have minded getting rid of me, too.

"Damn it!" I heard Kyrin curse. "I found her."

I jumped up and rounded a van as quickly as my feet would carry me, gun aimed straight in front of me. The female was running, and Kyrin was reaching out. He latched on to the long strands of her hair, but they pulled free without slowing her.

Then she disappeared completely.

I stopped and blinked, staring at the empty air where she'd been. She'd gotten away. She'd fucking gotten away. "How the hell did she disappear like that?"

He released the strands of white hair, and they floated away on the breeze. His hands dropped to his sides. "She's been practicing her molecular transportation, is my guess."

"That's not poss—" I cut my words off. More and more I was learning that I didn't really know shit about these aliens. I searched the parking lot for any sign of her and scowled. She really had transported herself away. I cursed under my breath.

"It's painful," Kyrin said, "and Atlanna hates pain, so I'm surprised she did it."

"Do you know where she went?"

"Do you think I would be here if I did?"

Damn it! "Well, I'm not going home a failure." I returned my gaze to Kyrin. I'd missed a perfect opportunity to catch Atlanna, but I wouldn't miss this opportunity to catch him. "Just stay where you are, and I won't have to hurt you." I aimed my gun at his heart, very aware the weapon did not possess stun capacity. Easy on the trigger, I mentally chanted.

A part of me hated to do this. We'd just worked as a team. He'd just helped me.

But it had to be done.

"I'll give you two choices, Kyrin. You can willingly go to the hospital to help Dallas, then the station house, where you'll answer my questions. You've got a lot of explaining to do. Or I can shoot you here and now."

"You're not going to shoot me. You need me alive."

I lowered the barrel to his leg. "Then I'll simply incapacitate you."

He gave me a languid grin. "As if a puny wound to the leg would even slow me. You've seen how quickly I heal. And do you really want to waste my blood?"

He stepped toward me.

"Stay where you are," I shouted. I didn't fire. Damn him, he was right. I wouldn't shoot him. Why had I even threatened?

Slowly and leisurely, he closed the rest of the distance between us, and I let him come. Yes, I lowered my weapon and let him come. He stood in front of me for several seconds—an eternity, perhaps—without touching me. My breath became ragged as his energy surrounded me; my skin heated. I licked my lips. I knew what he planned to do. "What are you waiting for?" I growled. "Do it. I can't stop you."

"You don't want to stop me." His arms wound around me, and his mouth remained a whisper away. "Thank you for your help," he said.

"You're welcome," I replied grudgingly.

His lips crushed mine, and his tongue swept inside my mouth. Our teeth scraped together with the force of his invasion. I welcomed him completely. I hated myself, but welcome him I did. As he'd walked toward me, need had grown inside me. Strong and hot—undeniable. He tasted of heat and passion. I pressed more deeply into him.

But I forced my hands to stay at my sides. I might enjoy his kiss, might crave it, but I wouldn't allow myself to participate any more than I already was. Remaining still was the hardest thing I'd ever done. I hated him. I liked him. Hated. Liked.

He tore his mouth away and we stared at each other. "You risked your life, staying with me."

"Yes, I did. For my reward I want you to tell me everything you know about Atlanna." The words emerged breathlessly, I was ashamed to realize.

"You taste better than I dreamed, Tai la Mar." Kyrin trailed feather-light kisses around my jaw. "Until next time."

He, too, vanished.

I stood in shocked silence, trying to catch my breath and staring at the empty space where he'd been. I traced a finger over my lips and frowned. Obviously, he could transfer molecularly like Atlanna. The bastard. So why had he stayed at all? He could have left this scene any-time. Had he been trying to protect me?

I holstered my gun and shook my head. Would I ever understand these aliens?

The blare of sirens registered in my ears, and I sighed. I'd be here a while, explaining to New Chicago PD what had happened. Shit.

I didn't allow myself to think about losing Atlanna or kissing *and* losing Kyrin as I drove home hours later. I didn't allow myself to think about the strange . . . *thing* that had come over me and slowed down the world around me for those brief seconds. Thinking about it brought fear, waves and waves of fear because that kind of ability was unnatural.

Fear made a person weak. Made her lose focus.

I trudged inside my apartment and checked my messages. There were six from my dad.

"Where are you?" he asked in the first message. His voice was pleasant, almost like I remember it being when I'd been a little girl.

"Why aren't you here?" he said in the second.

"Is this how you treat family?" he said in the third.

Pushing a series of buttons on the wall, I skipped the other messages, yet I couldn't halt the deep pangs of regret already working their way through me. I shouldn't care what he thought about me. He was an old, pathetic man, and I was a grown woman. I'd been on my own since the age of sixteen.

A small part of me, however, a part I despised, desperately craved his approval. Always had. I wanted the kind of approval he'd given Kane. The kind of approval he might have given Dare, if my brother had survived. The kind of approval I'd once had from him, but lost for some reason I'd never understood.

He liked to toss me a bone every now and then when I killed an other-worlder, but that was about it. Even then I only received a weak smile and an unemotional, "You did okay."

"You need your head examined, Mia," I muttered to myself as I picked up the earpiece. "Dad," I told the speaker and listened as the systematic ringing began.

My stomach churned with dread as I placed the small, fitted receptor in my ear. I could face a group of treacherous aliens and smile. Sometimes I even anticipated a fight. But I could not face my father without becoming a little girl again: nervous, desperate. Sad.

On the seventh ring, he barked a gruff hello.

"Hey, Dad. It's me." I winced at the neediness in my tone.

"Where have you been?" he asked, his unemotional self.

"I had an emergency at work."

"You disrespected your brother by not attending his memorial. You know that, don't you?"

"I know, but I'm trying to hunt down an alien serial killer."

He paused. "Any leads?"

I couldn't discuss the case with him, so I said, "Not yet."

"Then we have nothing left to talk about, do we?"

Abruptly, the connection severed, and the dial tone buzzed in my ear. I held the small black earpiece in front of me for a prolonged, silent moment, blinking down at it. I shrugged off my hurt. Overall, not a bad conversation. He'd taken it better than I could have hoped. Pushing out a breath, I replaced the receptor back on its wall hook.

I padded a perfectly straight course to the kitchen. No obstacles slowed my progress. Instead of a couch, I had a desk in the middle of my living room, cluttered high with papers and books. And in the far left corner perched a small screen, always displaying the local news. Two barstools and a snack bar in the kitchen completed the ensemble. All brown, all bland.

And that was the extent of my furnishings.

I was rarely here, and besides, the only thing I did here was sleep and work, so why spend the time and money required to make the place cozy? This modest one-bedroom apartment had never felt like home, anyway—as if I even knew what home felt like. I'd never belonged as a young girl, had always been an outsider.

I readied my coffeemaker and set the automatic timer for three hours from now. I'd have a beer, catch some sleep, and when I awoke the coffee would be hot and waiting for me. I opened my fridge, and a list of needed groceries instantly printed from the side.

"I know. I know," I muttered. I hadn't had time to shop in a while. Yawning, I reached for a beer—but it slid across the distance and came to me instead.

Startled, I let go, and the glass shattered on the ground. I blinked down at the broken shards, liquid swimming in every direction. What the hell? First the slowdown at the shootout, and now this.

No, no. This had not just happened. I'd imagined it. I was tired, that was all. The bottle had not come to me. I hurriedly cleaned up the mess, not allowing myself to think about it anymore, and strode into my bedroom.

A vivid sapphire and emerald comforter topped the bed, and a three-tiered bureau was pushed against the north wall. The comforter was my only splurge. I stripped to my panties and fell onto the mattress.

When sleep claimed me, so did my dreams.

One moment my mind's eye saw nothing; the next I saw a brilliant kaleidoscope of images. A woman's face flashed before me—my face, I realized seconds later, though my hair continually changed colors. Red, white, yellow, brown. I was like a chameleon, and I didn't understand the reason for the changes. Each time I almost grasped the answer, my ever-changing image floated away.

Then I saw my hero, Dare. His arms were outstretched as I ran to him for a hug. I was only six years old. He was ten. He caught me in his arms, and we both uttered carefree giggles as we toppled onto a cushion of bright green summer leaves. On impact, they propelled high in the air, then floated down around us, a multitude of colors.

"I love you, goose," he said in that nurturing voice of his.

"I love you, too, Dare." Anticipatory and smiling, I wiggled from his embrace and pushed to my chubby legs. "Find me, Dare. Find me." My laughter trailing behind me, I raced into the nearby woods.

Though we'd played hide-and-seek a thousand times before, I always hid behind our towering oak, which boasted swaying branches and chirping birds.

I glanced over my shoulder as he skipped after me. He had just about reached me, had just about shouted, "Gotcha!" when the leaves scattered, disappeared, and my dream shifted. I was suddenly fifteen years old and being dragged down a dark stairwell, then a dirty hallway, by my dad. I was crying, screaming, "Please don't do this, Daddy. Please don't."

"You need to learn respect, Mia." His features

remained indifferent as he jerked open the basement door and shoved me into the dark.

"I'll be good," I whimpered. "I promise."

"This is the only way to learn," he said. "You'll thank me one day." He slammed the door, cutting off all light. The click of the lock resounded in my ears.

So cold. So dark. Both consumed me almost instantly, and my chest suddenly felt too tight. I couldn't draw in a breath. My heart was pounding frantically, near bursting from the strain. "I'll be good," I cried to the door. "I'll be so good."

I sank to my knees, the cold wall at my back. Tears froze on my cheeks, and the stale, dusty air stung my nostrils. I wished my mom were here, or Dare, but they were both gone. They'd both abandoned me, though in different ways. Right now my only companion was a single rickety chair, visible for the few seconds the door had remained open. I was going to die here, my mind screamed; the darkness was going to swallow me whole.

As my body shook with terror, the room's only exit suddenly twisted, and my dream shifted again.

In the next instant, I was sixteen and holding an overnight bag. I stood over Dare's grave. The moon was high, the air warm. Fireflies flickered overhead, and crickets sang a chorus of hosannas around the headstone. Colorful faux flowers bloomed all around my feet, in direct contrast to my mood.

"I will avenge your death, Dare," I vowed. "I'll avenge your death and make Dad proud. You'll see."

I slowly cracked open my eyes, only to realize I was panting, sucking in breath after breath as if I couldn't get enough oxygen. Sweat soaked my body, causing the blankets to stick to my skin.

Dreams usually had that effect on me, and I hated it.

With a conscious effort, I forced my breathing to slow and my bones to relax. I cast a glance at my wall clock. The numbers flashed 5:39 P.M. I had time to clean up and do a little research before my dinner with Jaxon.

I lumbered from the bed and only tripped twice on my way to the bathroom. I brushed my teeth, showered, the dry spray doing nothing to wake me.

When I emerged, the scent of freshly brewed synthetic coffee filled my nostrils, strong and intense. I donned the same type of clothing as yesterday—well-fitted black slacks, black button-up shirt, boots, and a black leather jacket. My pants possessed a Velcro strip down the outer seam, allowing easy access to the weapons strapped to my thighs. Of course, I also had guns and knives strategically tethered to the rest of my body.

I twisted my hair in a ponytail, frowned when several locks slipped free, then retied the band with a scowl. Sometimes I yearned to hack off every freaking strand, but I always stopped myself before actually applying the scissors. It was the one feminine aspect of my life, and I just didn't want to give it up.

Dressed now, I trod into the kitchen and quickly drained two mugs of coffee. I poured myself a third cup and carried the steaming liquid to my desk. I logged on to my computer by voice recognition and fingerprint ID. Mandalay had mentioned that neither Kyrin nor Atlanna were in a database, but I checked again anyway.

When I typed in Atlanna's name, information about the lost city of Atlantis filled the screen instead. Atlanna's namesake, perhaps? I scrolled, found the most intriguing articles, and uttered a single command: "Print."

Holding the papers in my hand, I read, "At the beginning of history, Zeus, the god of gods, granted his brother, Poseidon, the city of Atlantis. This island lay outside the pillars of Hercules, a meeting point of all the worlds' oceans. For many generations, Atlanteans flourished in wisdom and riches, and the lands overflowed with food and wine. Yet these great warriors and scientists did not remain content with what they had, and greed soon grew in their hearts. They began to invade other lands, hoping to enslave foreign citizens. War reigned supreme. Zeus was angered by the constant battling, and rightly blamed the Alanteans. He hurled a great lightning bolt from the sky into the heart of the city. The land rumbled and shook, and in minutes, the ocean swallowed every rock, hollow, and denizen."

Brow furrowed, I placed the article beside my coffee mug and frowned. Was Atlanna like these Atlanteans? Was she greedy for slaves? If so, where did the babies come in? Did she want to raise them and make her own army?

That sounded so far-fetched.

To sell them, perhaps? I sat up straighter. Now that made sense.

"Fertility," I said to the computer, recalling that that had been a common thread in all of the cases. Seconds later, several sites popped onscreen. I printed each page and discovered that Rianne Harte, the lab tech, had been trying to gain government support for fertility drugs to help increase the number of children alien women could bear. Alien women, not human.

That was interesting, but it didn't help my case. I was dealing with human men, which meant Atlanna had to breed them with human women. Our scientists had tried splicing alien and human DNA to create halflings, but it simply couldn't be done. Something about the different cell types being foreign and trying to kill each other.

I read the rest of Harte's article and stilled when I came across the name A. en Arr, who was helping fund the research. A. en Arr. Atlanna en Arr. So, she wanted her aliens to be able to have more babies. So what did she need with the human men? They couldn't help her with that.

I typed my notes and thoughts into a new base titled "Fertility Murders and Abductions." I worked for the next half hour, relieved that I had one answer, at least. Without a doubt, Atlanna was the killer.

When I finished, I muttered, "Save and close," and my computer shut down. I stood. It was time to meet Jaxon for dinner. I could barely wait to tell him what I'd learned.

Just then my phone unit erupted in a high-pitched wail. My dad, was my guess, so I purposely didn't answer as I gathered the rest of my guns and knives. I didn't have time to deal with him. A few moments later, my cell unit erupted in a series of beeps. Caller ID revealed the station house.

I immediately answered.

"We found Rianne Harte," Jack said. "She's dead."

I stood in the middle of the crime scene, cataloging the details. Unlike William Steele, Rianne Harte had not been posed to look seductive. She'd been posed to look brutalized. Of course, she *had* been brutalized. Her eyes were still wide with terror; she lay inside a coffin, her legs and arms painfully akimbo.

We had the casket completely open, giving us an unobstructed view inside. Naked as she was, I was able to catalog the welts, scratches, bite marks, and bruises that marred her entire body. The hair atop her head had been hacked off completely. Her nails were ragged and broken.

She was barely recognizable as the smiling woman I'd seen in ID photos, yet a blood sample had revealed this was indeed Miss Harte. She'd been locked inside the stifling black coffin with some sort of snake or lizard, only it was bright red and obviously not from this planet. Mandalay had found her here in Whore's Corner, in the same woods where we'd discovered Steele.

"Damn shame," Mandalay muttered before striding to her car.

"Lilla couldn't have done this," Jaxon said beside me. His voice carried on the winter breeze. He stared down at the body, shaking his head. "Not enough time."

"You're wrong. She had plenty of time. This body isn't fresh, and Lilla hasn't been in custody long. To be honest, though," I added, "I don't think she did it. Again, this crime is too methodical. Too precise. Every detail complete."

I paused as a thought occurred to me. "Was Harte, or is she, pregnant?"

"I don't know."

"You," I called to one of the agents nearby. "Do a pregnancy test on her blood, pronto."

Five minutes later, I discovered she was not and had not been pregnant recently.

"Ghost found two strands of hair," Jaxon said. "Arcadian."

"Of course."

"They were located on the same branch as before.

It's highly doubtful the killer would snag their hair twice in the same spot. Either they were planted and we're on the wrong path, or the killer is taunting us."

"We're being taunted." Yes, Atlanna was taunting us. I told him what I'd found out about fertility, Harte, and the deadly Atlanna. "She's cocky as hell and assured of success. That much we already knew. But why not pose Harte as prettily as she posed Steele?"

"Could be we're getting too close to the truth, and we're pissing her off. Could be Harte betrayed her. Or could be Steele was a gift to us, but Harte is a warning."

All of those made sense. Atlanna had seen me in the parking lot. I'd shot at her, tried to catch her. That had to have pissed her off. "Only one way to find out for sure," I said.

"By catching our gal," Jaxon finished for me.

I nodded. Easier said than done.

CHAPTER
12

*W*hen homicide arrived, Jaxon and I gathered our notes and vacated the scene. We had all the information we needed, anyway.

"Let's visit Dallas," I told him. "Then we'll do dinner and talk." I hadn't seen him in a while, and I suddenly needed to assure myself that he was okay, that he hadn't slipped closer to death.

Jaxon must have sensed my desperation, because he opened his mouth to protest, then snapped his lips closed. "Good idea," he finally said.

He drove to County without another word. I rested my head on the back of my seat and emptied my mind. Minutes or perhaps hours later, we arrived, and I found myself striding down the twisted, bland hospital hallways. Visiting hours were over in ICU, but the staff was smart enough to let us pass.

While Jaxon waited in the corridor, I stepped into Dallas's room, drew in a cleansing breath, and perched myself at his bedside. I read his chart. His condition was still considered stable, though there had been no new improvement. I held his cold, limp hand. His complexion had faded slightly; his breathing was not as strong as before.

I fought back a wave of fear, wishing to God I could cling to life for him.

"Listen up," I told him. "You're going to recover. Do you hear me? You're going to recover. I've got a plan." And I proceeded to tell him every detail. "Jaxon is going to help me. He doesn't have your flare for drama, but I think he'll provide some entertainment."

Once, Dallas actually squeezed my hand, as if he heard every word I uttered.

When I left, I felt revived, more willing to conquer the day's events.

"You hungry?" I asked Jaxon.

"Always."

I sped down the highway and parked at the front of Trollie's, in a no parking zone.

Jaxon and I ate a quick, silent meal, both lost in our own thoughts. I had the special, club sandwich, fries, and a bowl of steaming beef soup. Jaxon had wheat toast, plain chicken breast, and a large orange juice.

"How do you survive on so little?" I asked him.

"By eating more meals than the average person." When he finished, he wadded up his napkin and tossed the crinkled paper onto the tabletop. "Something you should consider."

The time for relaxation had ended.

A hard gleam entered Jaxon's eyes, and I knew the same gleam was reflected in mine. Time for business. I leaned back in my seat. "The most important thing is to find Atlanna, but we have no leads on her. There are two people who seem to know the most about her— Kyrin and Lilla. Lilla's in lockup, and I'll question her again, but we need Kyrin too. We can play them off each other."

"If we're going to have any hope of catching him, we need to talk with Lilla's boyfriend, St. John, ASAP," he said. "Get our ball moving, so to speak, for the big event."

Ah, yes. The fake execution. "Let's go."

Half an hour later, I found myself standing inside St. John's office.

This was nothing like the sparsely decorated enclosure Lilla had occupied. Here, plush burgundy carpet layered the floor. The desk was composed of high-gloss Moroccan wood, expensive and rare. The chairs were padded with altar cloth and mated with matching, perfectly rounded footrests. Murals of cavorting, naked religious figures covered the walls, their mocking expressions so richly detailed that they almost appeared alive.

St. John was seated behind the desk, his freckled face cold and hard. His fingers were laced in front of him. At least he was dressed, and his hands weren't filled with breasts. I noticed he didn't ask us to take a seat. I didn't want to anyway.

A tall, muscular Ell-Rollis, though it wasn't Bob, I noticed, stepped inside the room. He was wearing a shiny purple suit. "You okay, boss?" he asked, eyeing us like we were ice cold mugs of water and he'd been trapped in the desert for at least a year.

"I'm fine," St. John said. "You may go."

The other-worlder gave a quick nod, turned, and snapped the double French doors shut behind him.

I crossed my arms over my chest and waited.

"I want you to know my lawyers are working diligently on Lilla's case," he said through clenched teeth. "She'll be released before you can snap your fingers."

Just for the hell of it, I snapped my fingers, then glanced over each of my shoulders. "Think she's been released?"

Beside me, Jaxon grinned.

St. John's nostrils flared, and he leapt to his feet. His chair skidded behind him, blending with the sound of his hissing breath. I heard the *tick, tock* of the wall clock as St. John glared at me with hatred in his eyes, but he visibly reined in his temper. He eased back into his seat.

"What can I do for you, Agent Snow?" he asked,

his tone all that was polite, though I caught a hint of fury in the undercurrents.

"What were you doing February second between the hours of nine and twelve P.M.?" I asked.

He laughed with genuine amusement, completely abandoning his anger for the moment. He even lifted a cigar from a small humidor on the corner of his desktop and ran the length through his fingers, practically daring me to arrest him for the illegal possession. "You're not going to implicate me in this murder."

I arched a brow. "Answer my question."

Still grinning, he shrugged. "I was here, working. A thousand people can verify that."

"So you weren't at the murder scene," I said, unfolding my arms and planting my fists near the weapons strapped to my waist. "That doesn't mean you weren't involved in the actual killing."

Just like that, in the space of a heartbeat, he lost his good humor. He bared his teeth in a scowl. "What's that supposed to mean?"

"You were jealous of Steele, weren't you?"

"No, I wasn't."

I ignored his reply. "What's the cost to make a hit these days? One thousand? Two? That's pocket change to you."

Silence thickened the air.

Then, "Your desperation is showing, Agent Snow," St. John stated quietly, menacingly. "I'm not involved."

I gave him a slow, smug smile. I really liked this

part of my job. "Maybe. Maybe not. I think it might be fun to try and prove you were."

"Be careful." His eyes glowed with menacing fire. "You don't want to push me. I have many, many influential friends."

I rested my foot on the edge of the closest chair and swept back my coat to display my gun. I hadn't yet had time to replace my pyre-gun, and this one was set to kill. "Well, I have a temper, Mr. St. John, and I don't always follow the rules. I highly doubt you want to push *me*."

When he caught my meaning, he paled. His fingers were shaky as he reached for his phone unit to punch for security.

Jaxon stopped him with a quickly uttered, "I think you've gotten the wrong idea here, Mr. St. John." He kept his tone affable. "We know you're not responsible for Steele's death. It's simply standard procedure to question everyone familiar with him."

The man's finger stilled over the button, and his eyes narrowed. "Is it standard procedure to accuse and intimidate?"

"No, sir," Jaxon said. "I apologize if we've offended you."

My lips pressed tightly together, preventing me from shouting obscenities. I refused to apologize to this dirty little weasel, but I wasn't going to undermine Jaxon's efforts either.

St. John gave his blue silk lapels a tug, his expression somewhat mollified. "I'm certainly glad someone isn't blind to the truth. Now, if you're done with your questions, you may see yourself out."

Yeah, like I'd leave that easily.

"There's one more thing," I said. "I'm suspending Ecstasy's license of operation until further notice. Not only do you have illegal substances in plain view, you were harboring a predatory alien, and charges could be brought against you." Watching him, I sauntered to his desk, leaned over, and straightened his tie. "Think about that while you decide if there's any more information you have for us."

In a seething explosion of fury, he once again jolted to his feet. "Who do you think you are? You can't suspend me. You have no right."

"I have every right." I waved my index finger in a sugary-sweet good-bye. "Have a nice day, Mr. St. John."

"Why, you bit—"

I closed the office door with a snap and smiled up at Jaxon. "I think it's safe to say we got his attention. Call your contacts at every media outlet in the area. I'm ready to deal with Kyrin."

He held my gaze, nodded. "Thank God you're not my enemy," he said with a slow grin.

11:43 P.M.

Our plan began perfectly.

I'd almost panicked the moment I pictured Kyrin molecularly transporting himself and his sister out of the building. I calmed down, however, when I realized that wasn't something he could do.

He would have done so already.

My guess was he couldn't transport inside a building. Still, I wasn't taking any chances; I planned to erect a force field at the proper time. That could hold anything.

I'd spent the last hour interrogating Lilla again and got nowhere. Afterward, I had replaced my defunct pyre-gun with one that actually worked, and now I sat in Jack's office with Jaxon. Waiting. Pretending to listen to my boss as he instructed me on the night's mission.

And then, thankfully, it happened.

Tumultuous and chanting, press and protesters stormed into A.I.R. headquarters, their signs bobbing up and down like dinghies in a tidal wave. Thankfully, checkpoint guards and unsuspecting hunters—who were prepared for almost anything—loitered in the lobby and were able to halt any civilian progress into the actual offices or cells. Inside A.I.R.'s white walls, the boisterous crowd was a sea of colors and shapes, like a misshapen rainbow that had fallen from the sky.

Jack halted mid-sentence when the call came in. "Pagosa," he barked into the phone. His eyes went wide, and his lips dipped into a scowl. "What the hell do they have to protest about?"

This was it, I thought, flicking Jaxon a glance. Our gaze locked for a split second before we faced Jack and waited.

"We'll be right there," Jack said, slamming the phone in its unit and blinking over at us with unparalleled shock. His cheeks beamed bright red. "We've been invaded," he gasped out.

"What?" Jaxon said in mock surprise.

"How did this happen?" I asked. God, I needed an award.

He gave us a brief, "I have no idea. Let's go."

We jumped to our feet and rushed into the hallway, weapons drawn. The alarm suddenly screeched at high volume, blending with the constant wail of code blue. Red lights buzzed on the walls.

Before we even reached the lobby, a chant of "Kill hunters, not aliens" rang in my ears. My fingers tightened on my gun as a wave of anger hit me. These people needed a good dose of reality. Kill hunters? Please. They saw only the good aliens, the ones who now worked steady jobs and lived in their pristine neighborhoods. They didn't see the evil ones, the ones who enjoyed mutilating humans, beating and raping them. They didn't know some aliens could control their thoughts, change the weather, and transport into their homes undetected.

If they did, they'd get down on their knees and thank us for what we did. But we never told them what could happen. Panic would spread, and our government preferred not to have panic. They'd rather have ignorance.

We reached our destination. People paced every

square inch of space; signs waved in every direction. "Save Lilla," they all proclaimed. We pushed through the throng. I fought another crest of anger and forced myself to think only of the matter at hand: Kyrin.

"How did the goddamn press get the idea we were executing Lilla tonight?" Jack demanded over the noise.

"I wish I knew," I said, dragging in a breath and scanning the crowd for Kyrin's tall, handsome form.

"The damn bastard who told that lie needs to be kicked into next week," Jaxon said.

Jack nodded. "Damn right."

My lips twitched as I continued to gaze around, but a scowl quickly followed the action. Damn it. Where the hell was Kyrin?

Had he recruited someone else to come here in his stead? Someone we wouldn't recognize? Maybe, I thought, then shook my head. No. I'd only been in his presence a short while, but I knew he possessed a hero's mentality. He would want to save his sister himself. As arrogant as he was, he wouldn't trust someone else to see to the job.

He'll be here, I assured myself. All I had to do was wait. When he entered the room, I would know it. I would feel his vibrations, just as I felt him when he'd entered Dallas's hospital room. Just as I'd felt the hum of his energy in the alleyway, and when we'd worked together against Atlanna—and when we kissed.

The memories made me shiver. So many emotions

skittered through my mind. Anticipation. Dread.
Uncertainty.

Desire.

As if I'd conjured him, a spark of awareness pricked
and sizzled along my nerve endings. Soon after, the
sweet scent of Onadyn filled my nostrils. Every muscle
in my body tensed. My shoulders straightened, and I
went on instant alert.

He was here.

I reached in my pocket and withdrew a small black
box. On the inside was a single button. I pressed it,
knowing a force field was erected outside.

"Don't let anyone past these doors," Jack commanded me. "I'm calling in reinforcements." With
that, he stormed away.

I leveled a glance at Jaxon and mouthed, "Kyrin's
here."

He, too, straightened. "Where? Do you see him?"

"No. But I will." I shoved my way through the
crowd and waltzed upstairs, checking twice to make
sure I wasn't followed. I endured an ID scan, then
stepped into the main observation room. Two guards
were seated in front of monitors, eyeing me warily.
"Shut off the alarm, lock every door to every room,
then broadcast me all over the building."

The guards glanced up at me in surprise. We'd
trained for a hypothetical situation requiring a lock-
down, but this was the first practical application.

"Do it," I barked.

One of the men pushed a series of buttons. "Doors locked and systems ready for broadcast," he said.

Speaking into a mouthpiece, I said, "Agents, arrest every citizen present."

"These protesters are humans," one of the guards said. "We can't arrest them unless they aid an alien in a crime."

"That's an order," I snapped into the mouthpiece.

11:55 P.M.

Waiting for the unknown was hell for someone like me. Impatient and anxious, tense and ready, I wanted this night over with, the victory mine.

Jaxon and I stood at the edge of the foyer, watching as hunters continued to round up and band each and every protester and reporter present. A few men and women raced to the doors in a futile attempt to escape. Others fought. But every damn one of them kept chanting, "Kill hunters, not aliens." Blah, blah, blah, that's what I heard.

The protesters outside the building were being arrested as well. They'd thrown bricks at our metal-shielded windows and had tried to bust down our doors. And by God, they were going to pay for it.

Intermediately, the press launched questions at me. "Why are you murdering Lilla en Arr?" "How many murders does this make for you? Two hundred? Three?" "Do you possess a heart, Agent Snow?" "How are you able to sleep at night?"

I ignored them all. Yeah, I'd killed a lot of aliens over the years, and I wasn't sorry. I did what I had to do for human safety.

One of the reporters, who had yet to be banded, had his voice recorder pointed in my direction. "Some have begun to call you and your men the Angels of Death. How does it feel to actually live up to your name?"

"Shut the fuck up," I said, then paused. Kyrin, too, had called me the Angel of Death. I had to wonder if this man had heard it from him. "Lock this one up separately from the others," I told one of the agents. "I want to talk with him privately."

I stepped up onto the dais, straining to see Kyrin. I still felt his presence, but I had yet to catch a glimpse of him.

12:21 P.M.

The crowd had been subdued, banded, and ushered into a straight line against the wall. I did a head count. There were over eighty men and women here.

Kyrin wasn't among them.

Where the hell was he? I shifted from one boot to the other. Had he fled? No, no. His energy still purred inside me. He was here; he had to be here.

I pinched the bridge of my nose. God, I was at a loss. I didn't know what to do next. I couldn't very well broadcast his name over the speaker and ask if he'd like to meet me for coffee in sector twelve.

Then . . . the second alarm erupted at high volume, a staccato wail of disharmony. "Breach in sector five," a computerized female voice calmly acknowledged. "Unknown alien entry."

I froze. The blood drained from my head. Shit. Shit, shit, shit.

Somehow Kyrin had bypassed our defenses and actually made it into cell check-in.

CHAPTER
13

"Stay here," I shouted to the hunters trying to subdue the increasingly frightened protesters. "Keep them calm."

To Jaxon, I said, "It's him." We leapt into action. As we raced through the building, we remained side by side, our arms pumping in unison. The walls beside us became a white blur, an ever-constant sea of motion. A bead of sweat trickled between my shoulder blades, and the scent of fear rocked me.

The fear was my own.

Kyrin was smart. I knew that. There was also a distinct possibility that he was immortal. Yet even still, I doubted he was able to walk through metal-braced walls. So how had he slipped past security? How had he bypassed locks, motion detectors, fingerprint IDs, heat sensors, eye scanners, and weight-sensitive floor tiles? Molecular transportation? Then why not take Lilla and go?

If he actually rescued Lilla . . .

Only the bolts and eye scanners slowed Jaxon's and my progress. When we at last passed them, I quickened my step, flying past agents who diligently hastened toward sector five. I had to get there first.

"If he nabs Lilla," Jaxon said, putting voice to my fears, "we're in deep shit."

"God, I know."

We reached our destination, the only entrance to the cells, and endured another retinal scan. The door buzzed consent, and we shoved our way inside . . . only to discover the thick metal entryway to the cells closed and secured, the cell guard asleep at his post. Asleep? With this noise? Not hardly.

Jaxon had the same idea and nodded. "I've got your back."

I checked the slumped man's pulse. Too rapid for restful slumber. Definitely not a natural sleep. Either drug-induced, or the man was under mind control.

"Kyrin's been here," I said.

Jaxon cursed under his breath.

A sense of foreboding swept through my veins. "I don't like this," I muttered. "Let's get inside and guard Lilla's door."

I reached out, just about to press my palm against

the print scan to release the locks. Then I paused, hand suspended midair. My skin tingled. Another wave of foreboding, this one stronger, more intense, crashed inside me.

I needed to open the entrance, but . . .

Jaxon watched me expectantly.

Do it. Open the door echoed in my mind, the words spoken by that same rich male voice that always made me shiver with both dread and heat. *Open the door.*

I remained motionless. Was it possible . . . could Kyrin make himself invisible? Was he here, now, waiting for me to escort him inside?

"Mia," Jaxon shouted over the alarm. "What's wrong? We need to guard Lilla. He might already be inside."

I jerked my hand back. "How could he have opened this door?"

Jaxon shifted impatiently on his feet. "I don't know. It doesn't matter. We need to get inside. This conversation can wait."

No. No, it couldn't. A slight breeze caressed my neck, a breeze that held the subtle fragrance of Onadyn. I spun to my left. Saw nothing amiss. I spun to my right. Again, saw nothing amiss. Yet I knew, *knew,* Kyrin was inside this room with me.

"Mia, damn it," Jaxon said. "Let's do this." He stepped forward, reaching out, waiting for me. We had to do the fingerprint scan together, or the door wouldn't open.

Just before his palm hit the sensor, I closed the distance between us and grabbed his wrist. "Kyrin is inside this room. I don't know how, but he's here."

"What are you talking about? He's not here. He's—"

"There's no way he could have opened this door. I think—" Another breeze, this one so close I felt a wave of heat brush my cheek. I didn't finish my sentence as I released Jaxon's hand and pivoted on my heel. I pressed my back against the cold steel door, dialed my weapon to stun, then pointed the barrel straight ahead.

Jaxon finally caught the truth of my words. Without another protest, he moved out of my way and stood beside me, his weapon trained, as well.

Open the door, Kyrin said, the words whispered next to my ear like a lover's entreaty. His voice was low, a menacing growl. Strangely, I wanted to obey, though I did not feel phantom fingers inside my mind trying to bend me to his will. The most feminine part of me simply wanted to help him.

"Do you hear that?" I asked Jaxon, keeping my eyes straight ahead.

"The alarm?"

"The voice."

He shook his head.

I forced my ears to block the screech of the alarm and my head to block the seductive rhythm of Kyrin's timbre. I willed my breathing to slow and concentrated on the movement my physical senses could not detect.

Up ahead, a lightning swift rustle blurred my

vision, and in that instant, a tingle of languid awareness rippled through me. Another blur, this one to the right. Then another, this one to the left.

"I'm not opening the door," I said to the air in front of me.

I felt Jaxon's silver gaze level on me.

Maybe I was wrong. Maybe Kyrin had already slipped past this door, and I was an idiot for not storming into the cells and stopping him. But I believed in trusting my instincts, and to do that, I was willing to take a chance.

"I don't care how long the alarm blasts or what happens beyond this room," I said. "I'm not moving from this spot."

In the glass panel of the far entrance, I watched as Jack and several other agents sprinted toward the enclosure. Damn, I didn't need their interference right now.

I had to stop their progress. They might unintentionally—or intentionally—ruin everything I was struggling to do.

"Lock the entrance," I told Jaxon.

After only a slight hesitation, he darted across the small area and disabled the wires that allowed passage in and out. When Jack reached the portal, he hit the steel beams with a thud. I watched his mouth move swiftly in a stream of curses as he attempted to pry open the door with a solid kick, then with a punt of his shoulder. No luck. He shook a fist at us, his hand arcing wildly through the air in an attempt to wave me over and threaten at the same time.

I gave one swift shake of my head.

"Reveal yourself," I shouted to Kyrin.

He didn't, of course.

"Stay alert," I told Jaxon. He didn't appreciate the warning, but I offered it anyway. He hadn't seen Kyrin slash a knife down one palm, hadn't seen the wound mysteriously close as if it had never existed. He hadn't seen the way Kyrin could move, so swiftly the human eye was unable to detect it. Hadn't felt his unnatural strength. "Keep your pyre-gun on stun."

Jack disappeared for several long heartbeats, and when he returned, he and several other agents held a battering ram. How soon before they beat their way inside?

"Reveal yourself, Kyrin," I shouted again. "I'll help you leave this place unscathed. Let's help each other, like we did before."

Again, he ignored me. I saw a hint of a shadow dancing close to me, then misting away before I could fire. How could he move like that? Frustration ate at me as I floundered to lock on him.

"I'm your only hope of escape," I said.

A whoosh of air rippled. Before I could even react, Jaxon's features contorted in pain. He grunted, then collapsed onto the hard blue tile, his chest continuing to rise and fall as he drew in oxygen. Shocked, I stood frozen for a single tick of time, staring down at him.

In the next instant, my gun was swiped from my hand. I watched, horrified, as the firearm sailed through the air, only to thud next to the far wall. Fury acted as kindling in my blood, heating quickly and lethally, ready to explode.

I had managed a single step toward the wall when four feet in front of me, the air began to liquefy, becoming a dappled, upright pool of majestic azure. Mist swirled and curled like a dainty ribbon, prancing up to the ceiling. I blinked, only a sweep of my lashes, but when I refocused, Kyrin was there. Completely visible, a looming tower of danger. His scent wafted all around me, warm and exotic, with a hint of Onadyn thrown into the blend.

Black leather pants and a black shirt, much like the clothes of a hunter, hugged the thick muscles of his thighs and chest. His white hair fell loose about his shoulders, with two braids framed against his temples. War braids? I wondered. That only added to his appeal, the infuriating bastard.

"How did you do that?" I demanded. Whatever he'd done, he hadn't used his molecular transport ability. Had he?

His violet gaze pierced me with purposeful intent. "Do you truly plan to kill her?"

I raised my chin a notch and remained closed-mouthed, refusing to answer. If I said yes, he might resent me for lying about her death in the first place. If I said no, I would lose any advantage I might have gained.

The alarm screeched to a halt; someone must have switched the code to silent. My ears continued to ring, and my gaze remained cinched on Kyrin's.

"You know and I know that I need you alive," I said, tempering my voice to match the abrupt quiet, though all I wanted to do was scream. How could my plan have backfired so quickly? "Leave with me. Help me, and I help you. It's that simple."

"I am as safe here as anywhere," was his only reply.

I arched my brows. My attention flicked toward the door, toward Jack and the agents clamoring beside and behind him. "If those hunters break past that barrier, they will not stop to ask you for an introduction. They will kill you. They do not know who you are, that we need you for our case or that I need you for Dallas. They only know you are an alien, and you are in a restricted area."

His lips edged up in a slow, decadent smile. "To kill me, they would have to catch me. And as you have found, that is impossible." Steps precise and carefully measured, he moved slowly toward me. "You never answered my question, Tai la Mar. Do you plan to murder my sister?"

"An alien execution isn't considered murder. We at A.I.R. like to consider it a public service."

A muscle jumped to life in his temple, and he ran his tongue over his teeth. "Does Dallas mean so little to you, that you are willing to destroy your only bargaining power?"

I softened my tone—for Dallas, I assured myself, not because I hated to see this man troubled. "Your sister can help our case; she can help us save human lives. She is safe enough for the moment."

"I could force you to open her cell," he said softly.

"Two agents are required, Kyrin. Two. I doubt you could subdue me and prop up Jaxon at the same time."

"I cannot allow you to hurt her, Mia. Do you understand that?"

"Then let's work something out. Tell me what you know about Atlanna and the abductions. Tell me where to find her. I know you're not the killer, but I also know you're involved somehow."

He stilled, surprise darkening his features. "What exactly do you know about me?"

"That you had contact with each of the victims. That you were dating Rianne Harte." I paused. Very carefully, I flicked a glance toward my gun. Ten steps, and I'd have it. I'd stun him and force him to my will. Simple. Easy. Yeah, right. I inched to my right, trying to appear casual. "I know that fertility is at the heart of the matter. Is Atlanna trying to make babies and sell them?"

He tangled a hand in his hair and blinked up at the ceiling.

I took another step.

His gaze swung back to me, colliding with mine. His expression was unreadable. Silence wrapped around us like a blanket, thick, heavy, and oppressive.

From the corner of my eye, I saw an agent hand Jack some sort of tool. Jack crouched, and I heard the grind of steel against steel. He was going to dismantle the hinges. Desperation struck me.

Another step. Another. "Kyrin—," I said.

He waved me to silence. "I refuse to cooperate with A.I.R.," he said, and before I could utter another word, he disappeared again. There was no warning, no flash of light or mist. He simply vanished from my line of vision.

Something . . . tart burned in my nose. I flinched from it. Tried to wave the smell away. Grew dizzy. Inky fog drifted through my mind, breaking my thoughts apart. I fought against the mist's heaviness, but a strange lethargy seeped into my bones, and I floated down, down, down.

But I never hit the cold tile. Strong, comforting arms surrounded me and scooped me into a warm, male embrace. I should have been afraid. I wasn't. I should have tried to protest. I didn't.

"Sleep, angel," Kyrin whispered, his sweet, heated breath fanning my cheek.

And I did.

CHAPTER
14

I awoke tied to a bed.

My wrists and ankles were bound to mahogany bedposts by thick straps of pink silk. My weapons were gone; I didn't feel their weight. My clothing felt too airy, but I knew some sort of material draped me. Slivers of light seeped into the room, yet somehow that slight bit of luminescence only increased the darkness, giving way to more shadows.

My heart tripped inside my chest, and fear sank sharp claws inside my stomach. I struggled against my bonds, trying to kick my legs, trying to loosen my hands. I only managed to tighten the restraints, and with each movement, the buttery soft silk sliced deep into my skin. Oh, God, I couldn't escape. With the knowledge came panic. Consuming panic.

A sob bubbled to life in my throat.

Air became ashes inside my lungs, burning. Couldn't . . . breathe. I couldn't breathe. My throat swelled, constricted with terror. A cold sweat trickled between my breasts and shoulder blades.

Childhood memories of dark closets and horrifying aloneness spilled into my mind. I squeezed my eyes tightly shut, trying to block the electrifying terror. Please, I tried to scream. Someone please help me.

Had I been left here to die?

Death did not frighten me; but I did not want to die this way. Not here. Not alone. I *would* fight my way out. I screamed as I bucked against the bonds.

My heart was beating so rapidly, I feared the pathetic organ would soon explode past my ribs. Even though my eyes were closed, I felt the room tilt and spin. Faster and faster. Shallow pants I recognized as my own echoed in my ears. My struggles increased, frantic. So frantic.

"Be at peace, Mia," a man whispered.

Kyrin.

Kyrin was here.

Have to breathe, I thought desperately. Another scream tried to burst from my mouth, a scream so deep and intense my vocal cords strained together, raw from exertion.

"You are unharmed," he said in that ever-calm voice.

"Fuck you," I snarled, my voice hoarse and broken. "Cut the bonds. Cut the fucking bonds."

"You are unharmed," he repeated, caressing his fingertips over my fevered brow, my cheeks, and my chin. His touch was gentle, like pure, liquid heat and sensation, and somehow, the simple feel of him penetrated my panic.

I was at last able to suck in a great gulp of precious air. Once, twice. As I breathed, I smelled a gentle rain—Onadyn. The fragrance invaded my senses. *I'm not a child. I'm not imprisoned inside a small, dank closet.* My heartbeat slowed gradually, and my terror ebbed as realization settled inside my mind. I was inside a bedroom, and Kyrin was here beside me.

Little by little, I ceased my struggles. I opened my eyes. Kyrin loomed over me, his gaze boring into mine. His eyes were a lighter shade of violet than ever before, and they swirled with a life all their own. Concern etched the lines around his frowning mouth.

Our fingers were intertwined, I noticed, our palms flat against each other. The skin on his hands was not smooth but rough and callused, the bones thick and strong. Heat and energy flowed through me, calming me even further. Sunlight dappled through brilliant sapphire curtains covering the large window on the far wall.

"Light," I said raggedly. "I need more light."

"Three shades lighter," Kyrin said. Instantly glowing bulbs dripped like crystal tears from an overhead source, brightly illuminating the spacious room. My gaze circled my surroundings. I lay atop a large, decadent four-poster bed, a crimson velvet canopy cascading around each edge.

Ebony-framed mirrors with gold-plated boundaries hung at each midsection of the wall. Bright pillows of turquoise, emerald, and ruby were scattered across a plump lounging dais, and thick floral carpet draped the polished cherry wood floors. Beside the window, a cobbled hearth devoid of any embers glistened, clean and inviting.

A place of depth and blatant sensuality, most assuredly, but at the moment, it was merely a prison.

I glared up at Kyrin through the haze of my lashes. "Release me," I snarled. My teeth were clenched so tightly, I feared my jaw might snap. Now that my fear had abandoned me, fury bubbled white-hot in my blood.

Watching me, Kyrin grinned languidly and released my hands from his grip. He eased back on his elbow and traced a fingertip over my thigh. "There. I am no longer holding you."

"That's not what I meant." Bastard. "Cut the ties."

Still grinning, he shook his head. "Not just yet, I think. Too much do I like you where you are. In my bed. Awaiting my pleasure."

"I await only your demise."

He chuckled. "What an amusement you are, little Mia. Where is the passionate woman I kissed?" His finger continued to dance atop my skin. "Do you still lie to yourself about your desires, or just to me?"

I trembled again, unable to halt the motion, then tried to mask my growing arousal and awareness of him with heated words. "Get your hands off of me before I cut them off."

The wide expanse of his shoulders lifted in a shrug. But he didn't remove his hand. "I meant only to give you pleasure."

Or perhaps he meant only to make me scream, I realized. Perhaps he hoped to break my spirit. Well, I would not allow that to happen. Glowering, I jerked up my knee, dislodging his fingers. "You want to pleasure me? Let me go."

His head angled to the right; his gaze never wavered. "Why does being bound upset you so? Some women have found it quite exciting."

"Well, those women are idiots." I tried once again to tug myself free from the restraints, ignoring throbs of pain as the silk cut deeper into my skin. A trickle of blood slithered down my arm, warm against my chilled skin, then dripped off my bare elbow and onto the sheet.

"Be still," he chided. "You have hurt yourself."

His face strained with intense concentration as he opened his palms and circled them around my ankles. Warm, tingling heat arced up my calves, then slowly cooled to relaxing perfection.

I hated to admit it, but I didn't want him to stop.

The sensations were too entrancing. Too . . . right. They were creating a deep hum of carnality within me. I wanted to spread my legs and invite those magic fingers inside. I wanted his mouth on the heat of me, lost in my essence.

"What are you doing?" I questioned, nearly breathless. My back arched.

"Shh," was all he said.

He caressed his hands up my thighs, over my belly, and to my wrists. I bit back a moan. God, he felt good. He paused a moment to study the tattoo on my wrist. He traced his finger over the black scythe and smiled slowly. "How appropriate." He deviated to the scar on my inner arm—a little present I'd received from a crazed Mec. He placed a light kiss over the raised, jagged flesh. Our eyes met. His lips were inches from mine. So close, in fact, I felt the sweetness of his breath on my nose. I melted in response. Soon the same drugging warmth settled in my arms, cooling all too quickly.

When Kyrin eased himself away, my wrists and ankles no longer ached. But my body did—it ached for the return of his weight.

I gulped, then asked, "Why did you bring me here?" My traitorous body might yearn for him, but my mind knew better.

His features became a mask of resignation. "I brought you here because we have much to discuss. Uninterrupted. Without your pyre-gun at the ready."

"What makes you think I'll talk to you here, hmm?"

He gave another chuckle, that rich, rumbling chuckle that washed all over me, as intimate and inviting as the sweetest kiss. "As if you could resist."

I released a frustrated growl. He was right. "Just fucking release me!"

"Were I to do that, you would lash out, and we would spend our time together fighting instead of talking."

I chewed on my bottom lip and remained silent. I couldn't deny his charge without lying, and while I didn't mind lying to this man, I knew he'd know the truth, so what was the use?

"A.I.R. will come for you. They'll trace you by your voice."

"One, I am not in your database. And two, there are no amplifiers here. No recorders. Even if there were, my home was constructed of soundproof walls. I doubt A.I.R. even knows this place exists."

I shifted my hips atop the comforter, away from him . . . and for the first time saw what I wore. I was dressed in a white gauzy froth of a gown. Pleats gathered in a low circle at my neck, then split down the middle to cover my breasts, yet bare my stomach. The soft material gathered again at my waist, riding low on my hips, then draped me from leg to ankle with a thin see-through veil.

A bejeweled armband circled my bicep. Mesmerizing purple stones, too light to be amethysts and too luminescent to be of this earth, formed an intricate pattern around the base. My nails dug into my palms.

How dare he undress me, then redress me so scantily?

"Where are my weapons? My pants and boots?"

Unconcerned with my questions, Kyrin lifted a strand of my hair. The dark lock proved an erotic contrast to the paleness of his skin. "I like your hair this way," he said. "Unbound. Like a black thundercloud around your face." Next he trailed a finger over my breast, causing my nipple to pebble and my breath to hitch.

I quelled the urge to dissolve into his touch. When had I become so eager for a man? So needy?

When had I become such a slave to my senses?

"I want my clothes back," I said, purposefully making my tone harsh.

His gaze traveled the length of my body. "Do you not like this gown?"

"What do you think?"

He smiled slowly.

"Tell me, Kyrin. Did you enjoy yourself? Undressing a helpless, unconscious woman?"

With exaggerated movements, he leaned into me until our faces were inches apart. "I doubt you have ever been helpless, Tai la Mar."

I lifted my head, closing even more distance. My

nose brushed the tip of his. "You have one minute to return every article of clothing, every weapon that you stole from me. Or I'll—or I'll—"

His brows curved with insolence. "Or you'll what?"

God, I didn't know. My head flopped onto the pillow, and I screeched.

He didn't hesitate, didn't even seem concerned when he admitted, "I have already destroyed your clothing and your weapons."

"You fucking bastard."

"Do not be angry I have dressed you so. I wanted to see you in the attire of my homeland." His voice lacked any hint of remorse, held only a husky resonance of desire. "And I must tell you, dark angel, that garbed as you are, you look like sex. Rare, carnal sex. You are more beautiful than I had imagined . . ." He leaned closer with every word, closing the distance between us again as if he didn't like to be separated. "And imagine you I did. Naked, under me, over me, taking me inside your body and—"

"Shut up," I said on a wispy catch of breath. Moisture pooled between my legs.

Don't soften. He's strapped you to his bed.

His gaze fastened on my lips, then moved to my eyes. I held his stare, the air around us thickened with sexual tension. Abruptly he shook his head. "No. Not yet."

Breaking the strange spell he possessed on my senses, he jolted up and stalked to the window. Keeping his back to me, he said, "I want to kiss you again, but I will not until I have explained some things to you." Here he drew in a sharp breath. "You cannot leave this house, Mia. The armband will see to that."

I blinked in confusion. "I don't understand."

"Do you stray outside of this home, a shock will begin at the band and travel the length of your entire body. The pain, intense and consuming as it will be, will only cease when you reenter my home."

"You're lying."

"I tell you this not to anger or scare you," he said, "but to warn you what an attempted escape will bring. You will remain here as my guest until our business is concluded."

The husky timbre of his voice was so finite, so res-olute.

My God, he really was telling the truth. He thought to trap me like an animal, to take away my freedom and rights. My toes curled with the force of my distress. "Did you abduct Rianne Harte and tie her this way?"

He pivoted and faced me, his eyes tortured. "I tried to protect Rianne."

"The same way your sister tried to protect William Steele?" I sneered.

A muscle ticked in his jaw; he didn't answer.

"This is not the way to woo a woman into your arms."

His brows lifted. "Is it not?" He eased beside me

again, his hip pressed against mine, and lifted another tendril of my hair. He shifted the glossy strands through his fingers, watched them fall, then recaptured them, desire growing in his expression. "Perhaps I should try and prove you wrong."

The knowledge of my imprisonment warred with my still-swirling desire. Keep talking, I told myself. "You never told me what type of business we have, what was worth risking your life to abduct me from my own workplace."

"At first I thought to trade you for my sister," he admitted, caressing my hair against his cheek. His eyes closed in surrender, just as my scalp tingled with heady sensation.

I jerked my head to the side, quickly and efficiently tugging the inky locks from his hands. "An agent's creed is duty before emotion. A.I.R. will not negotiate for my release."

"Your colleges would sentence you to death?" he inquired.

"In a heartbeat," I answered. No, that wasn't true. They would hunt him down and fight for me, just like I'd do for them.

Kyrin's chin edged to the side, his eyes lit with curiosity. "And this does not upset you?"

I understood A.I.R.'s policies. I'd even helped make them. "Why set a killer free to save one life? The killer will then take many more."

"This conversation is moot," he said with a wave of

his hand. "Before you woke, I had already decided not to trade you."

Dread unfurled inside me. "Then what do you plan to do with me? How long do you hope to keep me here?"

He deliberated a moment, before answering evasively, "I will keep you only as long as needed to gain your trust."

Trust? Was he serious? I snorted.

"You trusted me once, to help you catch Atlanna."

"You've got me tied to a bed. How can I ever trust you again?" I trusted so few, anyway, and those I did were human. "I did not think you a foolish man until just now."

"We shall see," was his only reply.

He eased to his feet and stepped toward the door.

A small ember of panic sparked to life. I wrenched again at my bonds. "Where are you going?" I cried. "Don't leave me here."

He paused, faced me. I collapsed against the soft mattress. I had to say something, anything, to keep him here. I didn't want to be alone again. "Why are you so secretive about Atlanna?" I asked. "Are you helping her? Is keeping me here a plan you've concocted together?"

That tortured gleam returned to his eyes. "No. I'd rather die than aid her."

"Then let me go and help me find her."

"I *will* help you, Mia. You. Not A.I.R. I detest all hunters."

"I *am* a hunter." Our gazes clashed, and I was helpless to glance away.

"You," he said, "I am willing to rethink." He pushed out a breath. "Are you hungry?"

My stomach knotted in protest, but I said, "Yes." Food always relaxed people. Made them more willing to talk.

"We shall eat."

"You'll have to untie me," I said, making a conscious effort not to beg.

He nodded. "I had thought to bring you food in here, but I have decided to trust you the way I hope you'll trust me. You must give me your word that you will not fight me."

"I vow I will not murder you until after our meal. How's that?"

Grinning, he said, "After we eat, I will simply retie you. How is that?" He approached me, slipped a small, thin blade from his pocket, and gently cut the silk that bound me.

Once freed, I reacted on instinct. Sitting up and jerking back my elbow in one fluid motion, I made a fist and punched him. My knuckles connected with the top portion of his cheekbone. His head whipped to the side.

When I made no other move to attack him, he

slowly turned back to face me. He fingered the now reddened skin.

"I said I wouldn't kill you, and I haven't. I said nothing about beating the shit out of you."

"My mistake," he said.

"Don't ever tie me up again," I growled. "Now, let's eat."

CHAPTER
15

Guilt wound through me as I sat at Kyrin's dining table, feasting on rosemary salad and shrimp scampi. Dallas lay in the hospital, fighting for his life. Hunters were probably scouring the city limits for me. Yet here I lounged atop a high-backed gold satin chair, stuffing my face with delicacies.

Worse, I was actually enjoying myself.

Kyrin and I had formed a sort of truce. For now, this moment, we were simply a man and a woman, enjoying a delicious meal. A hand-carved Egyptian tabletop separated us, but our legs were close enough to touch, and touch me he did, caressing his thigh against mine. The softness of his pants and the thinness of my veil created an unignorable friction.

I found myself breathlessly awaiting his next touch.

"Would you care for dessert?" he asked, easing back on the brocade bench.

My mouth watered. "Yes," I said, the cool air wafting along the walls and tormenting my bare skin. "Thank you."

One of his servants, who refused to meet my gaze, arranged a porcelain platter of chocolate eclairs and blackberry truffles directly in front of me. I almost purred in sheer joy.

Since the near annihilation of the cocoa plant, chocolate was considered a rare treasure. Only the most wealthy and influential of people were able to acquire it. Before he'd decided he didn't like me, my father had given me a chocolate treat. I still remembered how wonderful it had been. How I'd begged for more, but he'd had only the one.

With shaky fingers, I placed one gently in my mouth and . . . my taste buds burst. Oh, my God. My eyes closed of their own accord as pure surrender dissolved in my mouth. That's what chocolate tasted like. Pure surrender.

Kill me now, I thought, because I've finally entered the gates of paradise.

When able, I opened my eyes. Kyrin was watching me, molten fire in his eyes. I held his stare for a protracted minute. "Are all Arcadians as . . . sexual as you?"

He grinned sheepishly. "We are a highly sexual race, yes."

I forced my gaze away from him and watched the flickering vanilla- and cinnamon-scented candles. Shadows and light frolicked along the rose-tinted floral-painted walls, dancing with the flames. Those same shadows had danced across Kyrin's face, giving his cheekbones a stark, almost harsh appearance.

My attention veered to the surrounding furniture. A sea of vivid colors and textures, eclectic all, filled his home. Fresh flowers overflowed from end tables, and the edges of a finely woven rug were fringed with those same flower petals. Elegant ivory chairs offset a silver-flecked wall.

Such wealth amazed me.

"How did you acquire all of this?" I asked.

He lifted his shoulders in a shrug. "Arcadia is rich in the rocks your world holds dear. Diamonds, gold, sapphires, and many more. When I came through the interworld portal, I simply brought those things with me."

The more he spoke, the more intrigued I was. "Tell me about Arcadia."

"It's much smaller than this world and much more crowded, with barely room to breathe. Our people live so long that the population is never evened out." He fingered the rim of his wineglass. "We enacted a law years ago forbidding women to have more than one child, but many have them in secret."

"You are obviously more technically advanced than us, which explains your ability to molecularly transport outside."

"We've yet to master indoor transportation without seriously damaging ourselves. Whoever tries ends up with pieces of the wall or furniture inside them, and dies soon after."

"Since you're determined to stay here, perhaps you should be working with our scientists to help advance this world."

"Or perhaps," he said, meeting my stare dead on, "technological advancement does more harm than good."

My brow furrowed. "Explain."

Glancing down at his food, he gave another shrug. He couldn't hide or mask the haunted pall that settled over his features. "Innocent people die during experimentation. Sometimes they die horrible deaths."

I leaned back in my seat, keeping my gaze on him. "I'm beginning to figure you out, Kyrin. You've done some things you're ashamed of. Don't try to deny it," I said when he opened his mouth to speak. "Figuring people out is part of my job. You performed experiments, didn't you? Those experiments killed people. At the shootout with Atlanna, you mentioned atoning for past sins."

He didn't reply.

"Listen, you can rest easy. If people volunteer for the job, they willingly accept the risk. I don't see the problem."

"And if they do not volunteer?"

All right, so he obviously hadn't had permission for

whatever experiments he'd done. I didn't know what to say to that. Was the scientist a monster for trying to advance society, no matter the cost? Did the end negate the means? As a paid killer, I'd often thought so.

"Did you work for Atlanna at one time?" I asked him. She'd funded Rianne Hart's research, so the woman had her fingers in science.

Kyrin scooted his plate away. "Dinner is finished."

Bingo. "What did you help her do?"

"I did not help her abduct or kill any of the men, I assure you." His voice was strained. "Now, dinner is finished."

Fine—I let it go. For now. Because, well, I believed him. He hadn't killed the men, hadn't helped.

I blinked at my plate, only just then realizing that I'd eaten every bite and nibbled every crumb of chocolate. I sighed. "Yes, dinner is over."

"Will you force me to bind you now?" he asked, folding his arms over his chest, "or will you behave?"

My teeth ground together. "I'm not a child."

His gaze raked over me, and he said, "You most definitely are not a child."

"What makes you think I'll allow you to tie me a second time?"

"You live for challenge, and I like that about you. It makes me feel alive. I never feel so alive as when I'm with you."

The same could be said of me.

The realization hit me, and I almost made a play

for the nearest exit. It was scary, the way he affected me. I forced myself to stay seated. I had Kyrin exactly where Jaxon and I had wanted him—readily available to probe for information. Of course, I had three disadvantages to being here instead of the station house. One, none of my weapons were in my possession. Two, this was Kyrin's turf, not mine. And three, I was practically naked. This damn gown was made for enticement, not war.

Well, I thought in the next instant, I could actually use the gown to my benefit.

I sipped my wine and reclined in the satin-cushioned chair, eyeing him expectantly. "Before we end our truce, I have some more questions for you."

"Ask," he said.

So I did. "You didn't use molecular transfer at the station house. So how exactly were you able to appear and disappear so quickly?"

"I did not disappear. Not really. I simply moved faster than your eye could see."

"You could have sped away like that before our little tussle in the hospital parking lot."

"True." The gleam in his eyes became wicked. "If I had, though, I never would have had full body contact with you."

I tried to hide a grin. How like a man. "Not all Arcadians can do that," I said. "Move so quickly, I mean."

"Very few can," he said, pride lacing his tone.

As I regarded him, curiosity filled me. Not just about the Arcadians, but about this one particularly. "Why is it *you* can?"

"Quite simply, it is an ability I was born with. All Arcadians are blessed with certain abilities. Lilla, for example, has a great capacity for mind control."

"And you do not?" I asked, realizing he'd never tried to dictate my actions with his mind. One point in his favor.

"I am telepathic, able to speak my thoughts inside others' heads, but dominating that person's actions is not an ability I possess. Nor one I care to."

"Why use mind control when you can use force, right?" I patted the armband.

"What I do, I do for the greater good. Isn't that how you do your job?"

I jolted upright, leveling him with a frown. "What are you trying to say?"

He sighed. "What other questions do you have for me?"

"I want to know if I'm right. I want to know if Atlanna is making babies."

"Yes," he answered simply. Carefully.

A piece of the puzzle clicked firmly in place. I'd been right. Fertility. Babies. The bitch planned to create as many children as she could and sell them for profit. What kind of sick woman did that? And why the hell was she abducting *human* men? Did she have human followers and was mating them?

"What's your involvement? You had dinner with William Steele the night before his abduction. Why?"

His expression became leery. "I befriended William not to hurt him, but to help him."

My brows arched. "And did you? Did you actually help him?"

A muscle ticked in his jaw. "I am well aware that my aid did him no good. I do not need your reminder."

His accent was growing thicker, more pronounced, with each word he spoke. I'd hit a nerve. "I know you warned the men in hopes of atonement, but that makes me wonder how you knew they were in danger in the first place."

"How can I trust you with the truth, Mia Snow?"

"If you want me to learn to trust you, you must also learn to trust me."

He lifted his crystal flute to his lips and drained the rich burgundy contents. "You haven't asked what Atlanna is doing with the children," he said, taking the focus off himself. His chin tilted to the side. "Why is that?"

"She plans to sell them. I could guess that much."

"Some of them, yes."

"And the rest?"

"She's a scientist at heart. The others, well, she's using them in experiments."

I stiffened. "You make it sound like the children have been born, but there hasn't been time. William and the others were taken recently."

"William and the others weren't the first. They are only the ones you know about. Many children have already been born."

My God. Revulsion for this woman's crimes and pity for the innocent babies being sold to the highest bidder, or worse, filled me. "What kind of experiments?" As I spoke, hatred—pure, undiluted hatred—sparked to life inside me. I wanted Atlanna dead. I wanted her to suffer. And I wanted to be the one who made her suffer.

Kyrin pressed his lips together and set his glass aside.

"You won't tell me," I said, a statement, not a question. I bit my tongue to keep from spewing a mouthful of curses.

"That is correct. Not yet, at least."

"I want to know." I slammed my fist against the table. *"Now!"*

"You are not ready for the truth."

I gripped my fork so tightly, color drained from my knuckles. "You know I will hunt her and kill her. You know I will do my best to save those babies. That is what matters here. Nothing else. Or do you want Atlanna alive?"

"No. I want her dead, just as you, but there is more to this situation than you understand."

"Explain it to me. I'm here. I'm willing to listen."

Hair swaying at his temples, he shook his head. "I told you. You are not yet ready for the truth, Mia."

Before I could respond to that, he added, "Would you like to discuss your friend Dallas?"

My shoulders straightened. I leaned forward and rested my elbows on the table, letting the subject of Atlanna be temporarily shelved. "You will heal him?"

"Perhaps."

I vaulted to my feet, my gown swirling at my ankles. My chair skidded behind me, then landed on its back with a loud thump. "I have had enough of your half-ass answers and you-are-not-ready-to-know-the-truth shit. Our truce is over."

Slowly he stood, disappointment deepening the lines around his mouth. "Let us work together, like before. Weren't those your words to me?"

"I'm willing to do that, you're not. If you won't answer my questions, you're not interested in working with me."

"There is so much you don't know."

"So tell me."

"I can't."

"Why?"

"I just—can't. Come. I will escort you back to the room."

"I meant what I said. You'll have to fight me."

"If that is your wish. You will merely end up tied to the bed again."

"Think it will be that easy, do you?" I laughed, the sound completely devoid of humor. "If you come near me right now, I'll drain your blood into a bowl and let you die here." I said it so calmly, so assuredly, my words left a cold pallor in the room.

He pursed his lips, looking as casual and at ease as if he were selecting which pastry to consume for breakfast, the cocky bastard. "You'll understand if I defend myself?"

"Of course. I'd be disappointed if you didn't. Will your servants interfere?"

"Absolutely not. They will not disturb us"—his eyes shimmered with depraved anticipation—"no matter what sounds you make."

"Very well, then. One ass-kicking, coming up."

I moved around the table with deliberate slowness, heading straight for him. He stepped in the opposite direction. We circled each other, and impatience thrummed through me. I stopped and cocked a finger at him. "Come here. If you have the courage."

He smiled. "I happen to like where I stand."

He was going to use his lightning-quick abilities. I could see it in his eyes, and I couldn't allow him that advantage. Before he could take his next breath, I grabbed the bowl of rosemary vinaigrette and tossed the contents in his face, porcelain and all. The liquid splashed into his eyes and mouth as the bowl thumped against his forehead.

He grunted, then he howled. I guess vinaigrette burns. Ha! I controlled the urge to grin. I leaped atop the dark, glossy table surface—and almost toppled to the floor when my foot caught the hem of my skirt.

My amusement faded as I righted myself. I pitched three more platters at him in quick succession. As he rubbed his eyes, he tried to dodge each missile. He only managed to bump into his chair and trip on the edge of the carpet.

While he lay there, unable to see, I paused to admire my handiwork. Noodles and vegetables dripped from his saturated clothing. My alien salad, I thought smugly.

But it wasn't enough. He'd abducted me, held me captive, stripped me, and forced me to wear this flimsy porn costume. He deserved more. He refused to give me all of the answers I needed, and thought *perhaps* he *might* help Dallas. Well, that wasn't good enough. I'd originally hoped to force him to my will by imprisoning him, and that plan hadn't changed. He'd just changed the location of his capture.

Determined, I jumped onto the carpet and punched him with every ounce of strength I possessed. His chin swung to the side, and he rolled onto the expensive rug I'd just ruined with food. He tried to stabilize himself, tried to work his way to his knees, but I kicked his stomach. His breath jolted from his lungs. I shoved his shoulder, spinning him to his back. Then I jumped on him, straddled his waist, and pinned him where he lay.

"Abduct me, will you?" I ground my fist into his left eye.

"Tie me to a bed, will you?" I smashed my fist into his right eye.

"Refuse to answer me, will—"

My words sliced to a halt when his hands grabbed my hips and jerked me down to his chest. Hardness to softness. One of his sticky palms twisted in my hair and yanked me close, until only a breath of air separated us. He smelled of rosemary.

"I'm going to kiss you," he warned. "Not the sweet, lingering kisses of your earth men, not like last time, but the hard, thorough kiss of the Arcadians."

"Do it, and I'll bite your tongue off," I told him heatedly, but I made no move to pull away. No, I sank more snugly into him, and my nerve endings burst with sensation. "I'm not done kicking your ass," I said, this time without any ire at all in my tone, but breathless.

I shouldn't want him like this.

I know I'd told myself that before, and I'd probably have to give myself the reminder a thousand times more. The man was forbidden to me. Perhaps that was his allure. Like the time my mother told me not to eat that box of cookies. The moment she'd spoken the words, those damn cookies had suddenly become more delicious looking. I'd had to have them.

I'd eaten them, of course, and earned myself a roaring stomachache.

The hand on my hip traveled down, cupping my ass. Fire simmered underneath my skin, the flames licking over me, deep and dark. My growing hunger for him was nearly as seductive as the man himself.

"If you can't be honest with me," he said, "at least be honest with yourself. You want me. We've kissed before, you know how good it can be."

"Yes." The word held a wealth of meaning.

He jerked me closer until nothing separated us. My lips parted, ready. And then he ravaged my mouth there on his dining room floor. Over and over he teased his tongue past my teeth, stroking inside, taking. Demanding.

Devouring.

My hands glided under his shirt. My fingertips kneaded his muscles, pinched his nipples, and he groaned. Such strength. Such heat. His energy hummed inside me, a potent vibrancy that ignited my blood and made every inch of me sing. I uttered a low, needy moan of my own.

"Mia," he said harshly.

The sound slammed into me, fueling my passion. His ragged breath fanned my nose and cheek as our tongues danced and sparred. The sheer desperation in his kiss filled my head, invaded and consumed my senses.

"You taste so good," I breathed. "Better than chocolate."

"I've been desperate to taste you again," he whispered hotly. He tried to tell me something else, but switched to a language I didn't understand.

He gripped my ass more tightly, fitting me snugly against the thickness of his erection. I ground into him, mimicking the motions of sex, all the while loathing our clothing. My tongue moved against his in sync with the movements of our bodies. I shook with the force of my need, oh, how I shook. My control teetered on the brink of elimination. I'd never experienced anything like this, never experienced anything so intense, as if I needed him to survive.

What the hell was wrong with me? I couldn't allow this. I had to regain command of myself.

I shoved away from him, but he just rolled me to my back and fit himself more snugly against me. The apex of my thighs cradled his erection. Before I could utter a single protest, his lips once again took possession of mine. The softness of his lips . . . the lingering wine on his tongue . . . I almost caved. Almost.

I jostled him to *his* back.

"Enough," I said, knowing hunger still glittered in my eyes.

His eyelids were at half-mast, and his features glowed, actually glowed, with ardor. He was elemental and raw, and the hard length of his body pressed against me, demanding attention. Duty and desire and fear warred within me.

Ultimately, duty and fear won.

I hated myself for what I was about to do, but even as I inwardly cursed myself, I reached out with my fingertips and latched on to a nearby porcelain bowl. Sometime during our kiss, I'd lost my anger, and I didn't want to actually hurt him.

"I need to leave now," I said. And then I smashed the dish against his temple.

His eyes went wide, then closed. His body jerked, then stilled.

I stayed where I was for a long moment, just watching him. A bump grew on his forehead, only to quickly disappear. His color remained good. With a shaky hand, I reached out and placed my palm over his heart. A gentle *thump, thump* greeted me.

Guilt wound through me.

"I'm sorry," I said. I leaned down and kissed him softly on the lips. I stood. I didn't know what part of the city I was now in. I wasn't even wearing shoes, and I was 99 percent sure I looked like a porn star. Still, if I had to, I was going to drag this rock-solid alien outside and flag down a car. And if I couldn't find a car, I would drag him all the way to the station house on foot. There I'd stun him, then haul him to the hospital. After that, I'd lock him up until he gave me all the information I needed to find Atlanna. No more evasions.

I made a quick search for a phone unit. Didn't find one. However, I did find a Road Kill special, an antique that used bullets instead of fire, and confiscated it. I strapped the barrel to my waist.

I stepped behind my captive and locked my arms around his chest, propping his back against my chest. Slowly I dragged him to the front door, each backward step I took requiring every ounce of my strength. The man weighed more than Dallas. Thankfully, the servants remained out of sight, just as Kyrin had promised.

Inside the foyer, I eased Kyrin to the marble floor. I turned the knob with my free hand and shoved open the front door. A cold wind immediately blustered around me, and a shiver raked my spine. Damn. I'd forgotten about the snow. If I had to, I could go without a coat, but I desperately needed shoes. Kneeling in front of Kyrin, I removed his boots and socks, then fit both on my own feet. They were too big, way too big, but they would have to work.

Thankfully the closet beside me boasted an assortment of men's coats, so I wouldn't have to go without one. I tore the one nearest me from its hanger and secured the heavy wool around my shoulders, then did the same for Kyrin.

That done, I once more gathered my burden and hauled him outside.

The moment I stepped beyond the threshold, a sharp, piercing ache began at my left bicep, exactly where the armband rested, then traveled and grew in intensity throughout the rest of my body. I was able to ignore the pain at first, but that soon proved impossible. Too much pain. Sharp, prickling. Everywhere. Surely my head would burst. I doubled over and dropped to my knees, barely feeling the ice as nausea churned inside my stomach.

"Did I not warn you of this?" Kyrin sighed beside me.

I gasped. "Why . . . aren't . . . you . . . unconscious?"

"I heal quickly, remember?" He trudged to his feet.

The torrent of agony continued to beat at me, hammering, eroding my determination with the savage intensity of a tempest. I smashed my lips together to keep from screaming. I didn't even think to protest when he draped his arm around my shoulders, helped me stand, and led me back toward the house. Along the way, he confiscated the gun I'd found. I couldn't summon the energy to care.

When we eased inside, my pain instantly vanished. My head cleared. I drew in several shaky breaths. Kyrin positioned himself in front of me, and I pulled my gaze from his bare feet up his black trousers, and glared into his amused gaze.

"Take this damn thing off me." I attempted to rip the cold metal away, yet it remained firmly in place, snaked around my arm.

"We still have much to discuss, so you will remain my guest. This I have already explained."

"It's you who refuses to finish our conversation." My hands clenched into fists. "You will remove this band, or I will—"

"What?" He grinned. His hair was plastered to his head and gleamed with oil. There was a noodle stuck to his neck. "Try again to render me unconscious with a bowl of food?"

A muscle ticked below my eye. This situation was

not amusing to me. "Don't you ever kiss me again. Do you hear me?"

Grin slowly fading to a frown, he reached out and caressed a fingertip across my cheek. "We must find common ground or many of your people will die."

I grabbed his jacket lapels and jerked him closer. "Is that a threat?"

"It is reality."

"Why do you even care? You're an other-worlder. Why do you care about human lives?"

"I live on this world, Mia. It is my home. I want peace with your people, and that will never be achieved when we are blamed for every crime."

I pushed out a sigh, losing the darkest heat of my rage. "I'm willing to work with you, okay, but you have to compromise with me."

"Compromise? All of your *compromises* aid you, no one else. You wish me to save your friend, yet remain unwilling to set my sister free."

We stared at each other, both considering the other's words.

Finally, he rubbed a weary hand down his face. "We are getting nowhere with this conversation," he said, his voice turning deep, rhythmic, hypnotic. "You will sleep."

That tart, cloying fragrance I was coming to loathe engulfed me. I fought against what I knew was coming, but darkness propelled me into sweet oblivion.

CHAPTER
16

My dreams were erotic.

Kyrin slowly peeled away my clothing, and I did the same to him. His breath was hot on my skin as he licked my neck, nipped at my chin. His muscles were hard and taut, and I knew he fought for control. That he wanted to take me, *claim* me.

"Don't stop," I said on a moan, arching into him. Only now, in this dream world, could I admit my deepest desires. "Don't stop."

"Always you command," he said on a ragged laugh, his voice heavily accented, "but worry not. I will never stop. Promise me you will never leave me," he said. "I need you too badly. I crave you too fiercely."

He kissed me, and I welcomed his tongue. He

always tasted so good, like a forbidden drug I shouldn't have but couldn't resist. I whispered his name.

The sound awakened me.

My eyelids popped open. My heartbeat was thundering in my chest, and my breathing was ragged.

When I calmed long moments later—though I didn't think my heartbeat would ever slow—I scanned my surroundings. I was in Kyrin's bed. Alone. Sweat soaked my gown to my skin, but at least my wrists and ankles were free.

Had Kyrin experienced a similar dream? I wondered. That dream had been more vivid than any of the others, almost as if he truly had been there with me. I didn't know what to think of that.

I stumbled from the warmth and softness of the mattress and padded to the window. The carpet plumped beneath my feet. My shoes were missing; well, the shoes I'd stolen from Kyrin. I rubbed the sleep from my eyes and swept aside the velvety curtains. Moonlight spilled across the night, painting the snow-covered forest with muted gold and silver. Leafless trees sprang from the earth in a wide arch, almost kissing the heavens.

"Where am I?" I muttered. I'd never seen so many trees or so much uncultivated land.

A lone figure caught and held my gaze as it emerged from the house. A man. He was tall, his white hair blending with the snow as he disappeared inside a two-story brick garage. Kyrin. I sucked in a breath. A moment later, a black Jag sped from the garage and onto a gravel road.

Where was he going? I lifted my hand to the window, and the chilly glass against my over-warm skin made me gasp. What was he planning to do?

For the moment, the answers didn't matter, so I wasn't going to worry about them. He was gone, and I could use that to my advantage, could hopefully find some sort of outside communication device.

Servants milled around all the rooms, going about their duties. No one said a word to me while I explored the entire house. An hour later, I still had not found a single phone unit or computer. I approached a servant, intent on questioning her, but her eyes widened in horror and she raced away. The others soon followed.

"I give up," I said, throwing my hands in the air. Damn, damn, damn. I stomped back into Kyrin's bedroom and plopped onto the bench beside the hearth. I used the time alone to work at the armband, trying to somehow unwind it. The metal remained firm and unyielding.

While I was distracted, a female servant emerged from her hiding place and rushed to the door, a haze of white hair and violet froth. She slammed the heavy wood, then clicked the lock in place.

"I need to talk to you," I called, already on my feet.

Racing footsteps greeted my ears. I dropped back into my seat.

Two hours passed. Two miserable hours.

I wrote down every experiment I could think of that could be performed on babies. By the time I got to number six, I wanted to vomit. My hatred for Atlanna increased. My desire to kill her increased.

I had to find her. Stop her. Destroy her.

Why wouldn't Kyrin tell me more about her and her experiments? Was he afraid of her? No, the man didn't seem to be afraid of anything. Not even me. I sighed. How the hell was I going to find her?

Hinges squeaked as someone slowly opened the bedroom door. I jolted to my feet.

"Do not hurt me," an Arcadian woman said, peeking inside. "I come bearing food and drink. I mean you no harm."

My shoulders sagged with disappointment. Had it been Kyrin, I could have beat out some of my frustrations. "Enter," I said.

She did so wearily. She wore the same type of open, feminine gown that I wore, only hers was light purple, just like her eyes. She radiated youth and vibrancy, even while she trembled with fear.

"Do you have a moment?" I asked, keeping my voice gentle. "I'd like to ask you some questions."

Without a word and without a glance in my direction, she placed a tray piled high with fruits and wine atop the desk, the sweet scent of melon wafting all around her, then sprinted from the room.

"Merla," I heard her say, and the bolts slid in place once again. Obviously the word meant lock.

"I guess not," I muttered.

Just to prove how ridiculous locks were, I snatched up a small, solid sculpture and stalked to the door. I intended to slam the thick metal into the door's hinges, but before I reached it, I felt my eyes heat—actually heat as I glared—and the hinges shattered of their own accord, raining like broken glass onto the silver rug. The entrance fell open. I heard the woman yelp and watched her back disappear as she scampered down the hall, putting as much distance between us as she could.

Horrified, I dropped the sculpture to the floor and heard the heavy *thump, thump* of dismantled pieces. I rubbed my eyes, but they had already cooled.

What the goddamn hell was wrong with me? How was I doing things like that? I knew I was different, but these things were *too* different. These things were freaky different.

A tremor raced down my limbs. I'd pretended the slow-down thing hadn't happened. I'd pretended the beer incident hadn't happened, and neither had happened again. This wouldn't happen again either. Like the others, I'd pretend it had never happened.

Determined, I walked back to the desk and sat. Work. I needed to work. I spent twenty minutes constructing a chart about Kyrin. If anything could consume my thoughts, it was that man.

He wanted my trust, and honestly, despite everything, I was well on my way to giving it. He desired his sister's release. That showed loyalty. He hadn't hurt me physically, even though I'd knocked him around. That showed discipline. He'd even helped me through my panic at being tied. That showed compassion. He wanted to atone for past sins, and saw killing Atlanna as a way to do that. That showed remorse.

He operated on his own scale of justice and righteousness. He was a law unto himself. But Kyrin wouldn't kill an innocent. He'd had numerous chances to kill me, and I was far from innocent. He'd always been careful not to hurt me.

I was ready to talk to him again. I *needed* to talk to him again. But the wall clock continued to tick away the midnight hours without his return.

CHAPTER
17

$\mathcal{I}$ spent several hours prowling through the house, this time searching for clues about Kyrin, about Atlanna. I learned Kyrin had expensive tastes—in everything. Even underwear. He was meticulous and didn't like clutter, and he left nothing personal out in the open. He was a guarded man. And very smart.

Where the hell was he?

I spent the next hour running up and down the staircase for exercise. Toward the end, my arms grew shaky and my legs burned. Sweat ran down my back, and air singed my lungs. I managed to exhaust myself . . . and fuel my anger with Kyrin. How dare he leave me here like this, with this damn unremovable armband.

I trudged into the bathroom. The floor tile boasted burgundy and cerulean porcelain, the wall gold-plated marble. The winding, double-hinged faucet cost more than I made in a year. Had I not been a prisoner, I might have enjoyed the extravagance.

After programming the wall unit, I stepped into the shower. I yelped when water, actual hot, steaming water, burst from the pipes. I almost jumped out of my skin, in fact. But as the water continued to rain upon me, I relaxed. It felt so . . . good. Odd, but good. Soothing. No wonder people used to bathe this way.

When I emerged, I was deliciously wet, my muscles unknotted. A new gown was waiting for me upon the bed, this one crisscrossed pink and creamy white. Pink, for the love of God. Scowling, I slithered my moist body into the ultra-soft material and sank onto the bed. I stared up at the vaulted ceiling. Why me?

Usually I didn't sleep at night, since I had to be on the street, prowling for predators. I slept during the day. Yet, as I listened to the wind howl outside the window, and heard the branches scratch against the glass, my eyelids began to feel heavy. The mattress was soft . . . so soft.

Sleep soon claimed me.

Dreams instantly overtook my mind. This time, I saw Dare, only he wasn't a child. He appeared eighteen, yet his eyes held a fountain of worldly, seedy knowledge that had never been there before. I ran to him. He didn't open his arms. He turned away from me.

I ground to a halt, my stare boring into his back. Why had he done that? Why had he turned away? He'd never done that before.

His form twisted, and suddenly I was chasing an alien through a shopping mall. A Mec. His skin pulsed green with his fear as he looked over his shoulder at me. He shoved humans aside in his haste to escape. I had my gun drawn and finally had a clear shot. I fired.

Bull's-eye.

He tumbled down, taking a human female with him. She screamed. And then all went silent. I raced to the body and kicked him aside, intending to free the woman. Her features were frozen. The Mec had stabbed her on the way down.

I dropped to my knees in horror.

"Arise, Mia," someone in the crowd said, a lyrical vibration in the undercurrents of their voice. "Kyrin returns soon."

I awoke with a gasp, my fingers gripping the sheet.

My gaze darted left and right. I was alone. Yet the words *Kyrin returns soon* still rang in my ears. Confusion consumed me as my dreams replayed in my mind. First, Dare rejected me. Then my vision spoke directly to me. Both were new occurrences, and I didn't know what to make of either of them.

At least, if Dream Mia was to be believed, Kyrin was alive and well and due here at any moment.

I shoved my way from the bed, dislodging my

limbs from the tangle of linens. When my feet hit the carpet, I glanced down and frowned with distaste. I still wore the pink gown; the flimsy thing hadn't magically disappeared. Turning in every direction, I blinked at my image in the wall mirror. I looked too feminine, like I was weak and incapable and needed a big strong man to take care of me. I much preferred my huntress slacks and top. And boots. God, I loved my boots. Ass-kicking wasn't much fun in anything else.

I sailed past the bedroom entrance, down the polished staircase, and into the kitchen, where the sweet scent of caffeine greeted me. Several Arcadian servants, both male and female, flittered about with morning chores. All but one sped from the room after spotting me.

"Coffee," I said to the remaining woman. I plopped onto a waiting barstool. "I need coffee."

"I get. I get for you," she said. She possessed the white hair and purple eyes common to her kind, yet she lacked the grace and facial beauty I'd seen in the others. She offered me a soft smile. "You like sugar?"

"You have real sugar?"

"Yes."

I usually took it as thick as motor oil, but I couldn't resist real sugar. "Make it half and half, then. Half coffee. Half sugar."

She nodded her approval and dried her hands on her gauzy apron. "Glennie like hers that way, too."

Pensive, I tilted my chin and watched her bustle

about, shuffling through cabinets, lifting a crystal pitcher. My ears perked as she hummed a song under her breath. Here was an alien who didn't cower in fear at my very presence. She appeared calm, relaxed even. Unconcerned.

"Mind if I ask you a few questions, Glennie?"

"Ask, ask," she said. "I glad to answer."

"How long have you known Kyrin?"

"Oh, I do not know," she said, steam wafting around her as she poured my drink into a plain black mug. "Long time. By your standards, at least."

When she handed me the fragrant liquid, I gratefully laced my fingers around the offering. I allowed myself a tentative sip. Perfect, and so deliciously sweet. Not too hot, not too cold. I sucked down the rest. If I'd been alone, I would have licked the cup clean.

"Exactly how long?" I probed.

Turning back to her duties, she lifted her strong shoulders in a shrug. "Fifty years, I guess."

I nearly choked from fluid inhalation and pushed my cup aside. "You're kidding, right?"

"No, no. I never kidding."

I'd known the Arcadians stopped aging physically after a certain point in their lives, but actually hearing the words *fifty years* associated with the virile-looking Kyrin astounded my mind. The man who had kissed me so passionately was . . . what? Eighty years old? Ninety?

"How old is he?" I asked.

Again, the servant shrugged. "Three hundred Earth years would be my guess."

My jaw dropped. Three hundred fucking years old. I was attracted to a man, had kissed a man, who should have needed diapers and calcium supplements.

Why was I even surprised? I wondered next. Of course I'd fall for a guy like that. I'd never lived a normal life. Why start now?

"Does he treat you well?" I asked.

Slivers of awareness stroked the back of my neck, and tingles prickled along my spine. A low heat kindled deep in my belly. A palpable surge of relief and desire swept me. The coffee mug shook in my hands as I resisted the urge to spin around.

Kyrin had returned.

How could I long to kiss him and choke him at the same time?

Unaware, or unconcerned, Glennie kept her back to me, to Kyrin. She clasped a rag in her hand and continued to scrub the counter clean. "He is a true Arcadian," she answered. "Proud, honorable. Courageous. He treat me very well."

"Of course," I said, gauging her reaction through my lashes, "you could be saying that because he's your boss."

"Bah." Facing me, she leaned against the gleaming silver surface. "He bring us here when he no have to. He could have leave us in Arcadia, slave to

Atlanna." She shuddered, her expression tight with fear. "Yet he fight for us, and bring us through the world-portals."

While I, the Angel of Death, caused not a spark of worry in this servant, the thought of Atlanna had her trembling. "Was *he* a slave to the mighty Atlanna?" He was royalty according to Lilla, but could have been under Atlanna's spell.

"That is enough," Kyrin said, his voice as warm and rich as I remembered. Glennie hustled back to her duties.

Slowly, I turned. His hair fell in tangled disarray about his shoulders, and his clothing was dirty and wrinkled. I'd never seen him so disheveled. I . . . liked it. Made him sexy and raw. Made me want to make him dirtier.

"Where were you?" I said, punctuating each word.

He crossed his arms over his chest. "What did you do while I was gone? Were you a good girl?"

"Listen, Grandpa," I said, pointing a finger in his direction. "You don't want to irritate me today. After leaving me here without telling me where you were going or what you were doing, you're at the top of my shit list."

"Among other things, I visited Dallas," he said.

"I—" My lips clamped together, and I shook my head. Surely I had misheard. "What did you say?"

"I visited Dallas."

I shot to my feet and raced toward him. "What

happened? How is he?" The words snagged in my throat, emerging broken and unsure.

He clasped my hand in his, his palm warm and soothing. "Close your eyes and let me show you."

I didn't question him. This was too important. I simply obeyed.

The moment darkness folded over my eyes, images flashed through my mind.

Kyrin strode down a long, narrow hallway. There were nurses about, but no one paid him any heed. They couldn't see him. He moved too quickly, like a human bullet. He slipped inside Dallas's room and removed the oxygen mask from Dallas's face. He made a deep incision in his own wrist and placed the torn, bleeding flesh over the dying man's mouth. At first, Dallas did nothing. Then, like a hungry infant, he sucked greedily, drinking Kyrin's blood. With each second that passed, Dallas's color deepened.

Kyrin released my hand, and my mind went blank.

My eyelids slowly lifted, and my focus snagged Kyrin's. Sweat beaded his brow, then tiny rivulets trickled down his temples. Almost too afraid to hope, I rolled away the cuff of his shirt before he could withdraw from me. My eyes widened. A long, jagged scar bubbled the skin of his wrist, matching my own. An hour, maybe two, and his injury would fade completely.

Amazed by what he'd done, I blinked up at him. He'd done it. He'd saved Dallas.

I didn't know what to think. Didn't know what to say. My relief and joy were too great. Dallas would live. *Dallas would live!* My knees weakened, and I almost crashed to the floor in a boneless heap. I grasped Kyrin's arm and held myself steady, drawing from his strength.

"I—" I gulped. He'd done what he'd sworn he would never do. He'd given me something without receiving Lilla in return. "I don't know what to say. Thank you doesn't seem good enough."

"Do not thank me yet. Your friend now bears my blood. Arcadian blood. When he awakens, he will not be the same man he was before."

I didn't care. He would be alive, and that was all that mattered. "I do thank you, Kyrin. I thank you with all of my heart."

He drew in a steady breath. "Then I accept your thanks."

Biting my lip, I stroked my fingertips up the smoothness of his forearm, over the ridged swelling of the scar. "Why do you still bear the mark?"

"The deeper the incision, the longer the healing requires."

"Why?" I asked softly. "Why did you save him?"

"For you," he said simply. "We need each other, and it was time I did my part."

Those words . . . I didn't know how to respond. A lump formed in my throat. He had decided to trust me completely. I saw the knowledge in his eyes, and it scared me. Was I worthy of that kind of trust? If I had to betray him to close my case, I would. Only the job mattered. Didn't it?

His long lashes dipped in a seductive blink, casting shadows over his cheekbones. "Come. There is something I wish to show you."

He extended his hand. I faltered briefly—I don't know why—then placed my palm in his. As with every time we touched, an electric tingle raced up my arm. I expected it this time, yet was still surprised by its intensity. He led me into the dining room. There he laid his free hand flat against one of the panels and said, "Begin scan." A yellow glow pulsed between each of his fingers before a single panel split down the middle, revealing a downward staircase.

"This is voice and alien flesh activated," he said. "You will not be able to enter without me. Even my servants cannot enter."

I was too astonished to comment. We descended the dark flight of stairs, the air clean and welcoming.

"A hidden room," I muttered. "I should have known."

He squeezed my hand gently in response.

When we reached the end of the steps, he halted. "This," he said, "is my lair."

Bookshelves towered from floor to ceiling, and a huge flat-screen television occupied the center, emitting a spring of colors and shapes. His desk separated the room into two halves. One half boasted shiny oak floorboards, and the other half was softened by a thick faux fur rug.

Kyrin released my hand, and I flexed my empty fingers, suddenly feeling cold and alone—like I'd felt most of my life.

If I weren't careful, I would come to depend on this man.

"Why did you bring me here?" I asked, changing the focus of my thoughts.

"You will see," was all he said. Without a glance in my direction, he rooted atop his massive, half-circle desk, separating and stacking papers. "I need but a moment. I did not plan to bring you here so soon."

While I waited, I strolled through the chamber and studied the wall hangings. Lilla smiled from all of them, her features perfectly stitched. He'd taken great pains to hang these in order of age. His love for his sister was commendable, his need to protect her admirable. A ripple of longing drifted beneath that knowledge. Lord, I missed Dare, his laughter. His love.

Sighing, I eased onto a plush emerald chaise in front of the haloscreen TV.

"This Atlanna," I said, reclining. "I did a computer search on her name, and the only information I discovered was about the mythical island of Atlantis. Are you familiar with that story?"

He didn't give me his direct attention, but offered casually, "Yes. I am."

"Any link between the two?"

"You could probably say so, yes. Your Atlantis was a

world of perfect people. They were strong, intelligent, and beautiful. Atlanna wants that, too."

I blinked over at him. "She thinks to make babies that can conquer the world?"

"No, nothing like that. Her desires run toward creating a perfect race of children she can sell. She does not have money like I do. Perfection always gains top dollar, does it not?" With a satisfied nod, he lifted the fresh stack of paper and eased beside me on the couch. Our knees brushed, causing that ever-present hunger to renew, white-hot and intense.

His eyes lifted, beseeching mine. "Are you ready for the entire truth?"

"Of course."

"When you learn what I know, you will be faced with a decision. A decision I am not sure you are prepared to make."

"I'm stronger than I look," I said. I doubted whatever it was I needed to decide would be difficult. "You know that firsthand."

A smile played at the corner of his mouth. The very mouth that had kissed and tormented me—in reality and in my dreams.

"That I do," he said.

"I will always fight for what is good and right."

"Do you swear this?"

"Do not question my honor, Kyrin. I said I will and I will."

He uttered a resolved sigh. "Very well. I only pray

you recall those words," he said, handing me a newspaper clipping.

The headline read:

LOCAL WOMAN FOUND DEAD

I read the story and frowned. A human New Britain woman had been discovered dead in an abandoned house. She'd recently had a baby, though the infant had never been found. Suspected cause of death: poison.

I glanced at the picture of her in the top right corner. A picture of how she'd looked before her death. She'd been very pretty, with short dark hair and wide brown eyes. A young woman, probably no more than twenty-five, who looked like she had many years of happiness ahead of her.

"Notice the date," Kyrin instructed.

I did, and my lips pursed. March 17. But this was dated twenty-nine years ago.

Kyrin handed me another clipping. Same story. Different woman. Different day. Same year.

He handed me yet another.

And another.

And another.

All of the women had disappeared within the same year, all possessed dark, glossy hair and brown eyes, and all were killed by some sort of poison and found nine to thirteen months later, their bodies still distended from recent pregnancy. Not a single baby had been found.

The similarities between these cases and the current cases were staggering. Yes, my victims were men—well, other than Rianne Harte—but each male had dealt with some aspect of fertility. "Did Atlanna kill these women, too?" As the three-hundred-year-old Kyrin proved, Arcadians aged at a much slower rate than humans.

He nodded.

"We might have never learned about her activities if she'd just hidden the bodies. Instead, she places them outside like gifts."

"I don't know why she wanted these women to be found. I only know she used William Steele to draw A.I.R.'s attention."

My brow crinkled, and I fought through a haze of confusion. "Why would she want our attention?"

"I'll get to that in a moment. Rianne was helping Atlanna, giving her names of the men who fit their needs. When I realized this, I went to Rianne and paid her to stop. That's why she was doing it, for the money, so she was more than willing to take mine instead."

I jerked a hand through my hair. "I'm sure Atlanna could have made more money by selling Arcadian children to humans. I don't understand why she used humans."

He paused. "The babies were half of each race, Mia."

I blinked, shook my head. I hadn't expected such an answer. "It's not possible to merge alien and human DNA. Our scientists have tried. Many times. They never succeeded."

"It *is* possible," he said darkly. "Atlanna discovered a way. For these women, though," he said, lifting the newspaper articles, "the process was not yet perfected, and they died as a result."

"And the babies?" I asked, my throat filling with a hard knot.

Sadness and shame flickered across his features. He turned away from me. "They died, as well. When they emerged from the birth canal, their bodies craved both Onadyn and oxygen. The two worked against each other."

I clasped his jaw in my hands and forced him to face me completely. My hands were trembling. "Tell me how you know this."

His shame cresting, he reached up and curled his fingers around my hands, holding me there. He tugged my wrists to his mouth, kissed the soft inner flesh, lingering over my tattoo.

"I was there," he said, a torrent of remorse in his voice. "I helped her."

I gave no outward reaction. A part of me had been prepared for such a response from him. I'd known he was involved somehow, that he needed to atone for something, but I hadn't truly expected to hear he'd helped Atlanna.

"Why?" Had he said anything else, I would have told him to get over himself. To stop acting like a martyr. He'd killed. So what? "Why would you do that?"

"I thought I was doing such a wonderful thing. Something miraculous for both our worlds, something that would bring complete harmony between our people. Halflings would be accepted by earthlings. I never meant to hurt those women. Never meant for the babies to suffer. When I realized the babies couldn't survive, I fought Atlanna every step of the way."

"Please don't tell me you hoped to sell the kids too."

"No. I would die before I sold a child. Any child. What I did, I did for my people." He squeezed his eyes shut. "I have to make this right. Atlanna has to be destroyed."

I agreed 100 percent. "The experiments failed. So why would she now abduct dark-haired, dark-eyed male humans?"

"Such coloring is the opposite of the Arcadians and revered by our kind. That is what Atlanna deems perfect. That is what Arcadians would pay the most to possess since she's trying again to make the halflings."

"I want hard evidence of her culpability," I said. "Evidence I can take to my superiors. That way we can devote all our manpower to finding and killing her."

Grim, he shoved to his feet and stalked to the hearth. There, he lit a fire, and the flames soon crackled and grew, filling the room with the crisp essence of pine. I waited, silent, not pushing for a response. He was struggling inside himself, so for once I showed patience.

"I have what you need," he said, as if he hadn't kept me at the edge of the chaise in suspense. "I have proof of her actions."

At his words, a sense of foreboding claimed me—sank razor-sharp talons into me. I swallowed hard, knowing what he was going to say, and it didn't require psychic abilities.

Perhaps I had always known.

I prayed that my instincts were wrong. But they never were.

Slowly, he turned and faced me. "You, Mia. You are the proof. You are a halfling, not quite human, not fully alien either."

CHAPTER
18

*T*calmly rose from my seat, my face devoid of emotion as I walked to Kyrin. One moment I didn't know what I was going to do, the next I was raising my hand and slapping him with all the strength I possessed.

His head whipped to the side, and he rubbed at his lip with his fingers. "Did you do that because you know I'm right, or because you hope to make me withdraw the truth?"

My eyes narrowed to tiny slits. "You're contradicting yourself, Kyrin. A few minutes ago, you said all the babies died."

"No, I said none of the babies born to the *human* women survived."

I hit him again, using my fist this time and cutting his skin. The wound quickly healed. Violence churned inside me every time he opened his mouth. My ears rang as blood rushed to my head.

"The man you know as your father truly is your father. But the woman you knew as your mother is no blood relation at all. You are one of Atlanna's experiments, born to an Arcadian female. This experiment worked only once. We did not understand at the time how we achieved success with you; we only knew that your birth destroyed the woman's womb, and she was unable to conceive again." He gripped my shoulders, forcing me to hold his gaze, to face the truth. "Until now, that is. She has found a way to duplicate the procedure, and she is using human men to impregnate her Arcadian women."

"Halflings do not exist, therefore I am not a halfling. I—"

"You have psychic abilities," he said, cutting off my words. A steely determination reflected within the darkening purple luminance of his gaze.

"Many humans do," I countered.

"You are able to track and kill aliens other hunters never find."

"I work hard." My awkward attempt to convince myself of the impossibility of this seemed like nothing more than wasted breath.

"I saw the way you moved that day, when Atlanna attacked us." He growled low in his throat, a sound of deep frustration, and shook me once, twice. "What will it take to prove your origins?"

I had no answer for him. I didn't know what would convince me when I didn't really want to be convinced. I'd spent so many years of my life hating other-worlders. Hunting them. Killing them. To be one of them . . . to be all that my father hated . . .

But what else explained how I'd slowed down the world as I myself had sped up? What else explained how I'd drawn that beer bottle to me without touching it? What else explained how I had shattered those door hinges with merely a gaze?

I pressed my lips together as another thought swept through me. In my vision about Dallas, I'd seen one alien and one human. I'd thought Isabel was the alien and I the human. I'd thought— Bile rose in my throat. Oh my God.

Kyrin covered his face with his hands. "I tried to defeat Atlanna myself, all those years ago," he said. "I tried. And I failed. Her power for mind control sur-passes even Lilla's. I've known since the first man disap-peared that I cannot face her alone, so I've done little things to hinder her. I spoke to the men, befriended them. Warned them. That didn't slow her down. I knew I needed you. *You* can defeat her. Power churns inside you, churns as deeply and aggressively as an ocean storm, and you have only to reach inside yourself to find it."

My teeth ground together. "How do you know this?"

"I sense it. Just as you sense my power whenever I walk into a room. But more than that, you . . . you are Atlanna's daughter."

"You lying fucking bastard," I spat. Maybe I could accept being a halfling. Maybe. What I could *not* accept was being related to a monster like Atlanna. How dare he even utter those words.

He grabbed hold of my wrists, preventing me from striking him. "You are Atlanna's daughter," he repeated. "Your powers are as numerous and great as hers."

"Shut up. Just shut the fuck up."

"I do not know how you came to live with your father when Atlanna meant to raise you. I only know that Atlanna followed you here. And so, too, did I."

Violently I shook my head in denial. "No—"

"Yes. Your father knows this to be true. You have only to ask him."

Hate the aliens, Mia, my dad always said. *Despise them. They are responsible for all our troubles.*

"No!" I shouted.

"Deep inside, you know the truth." His voice was so gentle yet held the dangerous power of a whirlwind.

He strode to a locked safe where he murmured a single command, the word unfamiliar to me. The safe door creaked open, and he withdrew a silver chain and locket. "Every Arcadian possesses one of these. A *kalandra*, we call them. Inside the center, they showcase a beloved moment in our lives. Sometimes the moment has happened, sometimes it has yet to happen. Here is yours."

Mine? The color drained from my face as he approached me. Dangling the chain from his finger, he reached toward me. I pinched it between my fingers and held it from view. I wasn't ready to look. I kept my gaze on him. "How did you get this?" I asked.

"You have seen how quickly I move." He gave me a wry smile. "Need I say more?"

"No." I shook my head. "No."

I continued to hold the necklace away from me. I sat there, gathering my courage, battling a twisted mountain of turmoil. I blinked, gulped. *Just do it.*

With a deep breath in, I dragged my gaze from Kyrin, from the far bookshelf, to my fingers. I focused on the locket—and almost sighed in relief. The locket was round and appeared to be nothing more than a small, clear ball. My lips were edging in a mocking smile when I realized something was moving inside. I intensified my study.

I gasped. In holographic detail, I watched a woman with braided white hair gently rock a bundled infant in her arms. Humming softly—I could actually hear her—she faced the baby. Her profile was the image of mine. Slightly sloped nose, high cheekbones. Full lips.

"Mia," she said to the infant, her voice lyrical and soothing. "You are my perfect angel."

I'd seen her before. In my dreams . . . at the parking lot shootout.

"That woman is Atlanna," Kyrin told me, "and she is holding you."

My fingers tightened around the locket, blocking the image. That didn't keep the woman's voice from fading from my ears. *You are my perfect angel.* With my free hand, I covered my mouth.

Atlanna.

My mother.

Color drained from my face, and a rush of dizziness swept inside my head.

Kyrin sat down and wrapped his arms around me. He drew me close, and I willingly burrowed my face into the hollow of his neck. "Accept what you are, Mia. For your sake. For mine. And for the innocent."

"I can't."

"You can," Kyrin said. His warm breath fanned the top of my head. "An Arcadian can do anything."

When he said that, my origins seemed so . . . affirmed, and my desperation grew. Of their own accord, my fingers curled around his shirt collar. "Everything I know is crumbling," I said. "Help me understand."

He caressed his hands down my spine, massaged my lower back, then traced his fingers up to my shoulders. He continued the comforting motions as he spoke. "Your father was married to Kane and Dare's mother when he and Atlanna had an affair. It lasted over a year. Then something happened between them, and your father disappeared, taking you with him. For a while, she abandoned her research in her quest to find you."

I allowed his words to flow through me. "If I accept what you say," I said, "I will have to accept that my entire life is a lie."

"You can now live a life of truth," he said, tightening his hold.

Could I, though? If A.I.R. heard any of this, I'd be out a job. Aliens were not accepted in that line of work. I might lose the only friends I had. And just what would I do if I lost my job and my friends? They were all I had.

"I need to call my dad, Kyrin. I need to talk to him."

He released me immediately and strode to his desk. Expression resigned, he unearthed a phone and placed the small unit in my hand.

I spoke my dad's name, hating the way my voice shook.

He answered on the fourth ring. "Yeah?"

"Dad, it's me, Mia."

"Yeah," he said again. "What do you want?"

"Is Atlanna en Arr my mother?" The words emerged as nothing more than a ragged whisper. I squared my shoulders, forced my throat to obey, and repeated my question. "Is Atlanna en Arr my mother?"

His breath crackled over the line. I pictured him casually smoking a cigar. "Why are you asking me this?"

"Is she?"

"This is not a subject up for discussion, little girl."

"Is she?" I screamed.

Another crackling breath. "Yes. She is," he stated. "Happy now?"

I pressed my lips together as the truth hit me. Fully hit me. I *was* a halfling. Atlanna *was* my mother. "Is that why you stopped loving me?"

"Yes," he answered without hesitation, not even trying to deny it. "You began to look just like her."

"I'm half yours, Dad. Doesn't that mean anything?"

"Maybe once." His tone remained indifferent. "Not anymore."

"I've done everything you ever wanted. I've killed aliens. I've hated aliens. I could have destroyed them all, and that wouldn't have made a difference to you, would it?"

He said nothing. He didn't have to.

"Why did you take me from Atlanna? Why didn't you just leave me with her?"

"She seduced Kane," he growled, showing his first emotion. "I found them together, and she laughed. Laughed!" Now *he* laughed, a cruel sound. "I killed Kane and managed to injure her. And you know what? That wasn't enough. She wanted you so badly, I took you from her." He chuckled again. "I made you hate your own kind. I—"

I didn't let him finish. I said, "End," and let the earpiece drop into Kyrin's waiting hand.

My shoulders squared, I pushed to my feet and consciously placed one foot in front of the other until I stood beside the bookshelf. I am a halfling, and Atlanna en Arr is my mother. The knowledge tore me apart inside, slicing deep, leaving raw, open wounds.

Obviously top brass hadn't wanted us to know halflings could, indeed, be created. That explained why they'd removed all mention of fertility from the A.I.R. files.

My eyelids squeezed firmly shut, and a painful knot grew in my throat. The future I'd imagined for myself was now shrouded in uncertainty.

"Atlanna is more powerful than I have ever been," Kyrin said, and I knew he hoped to distract me from my inner turmoil. "But you . . . you have the greatest of her strengths coursing through your veins. Once you tap into that power, you can kill her."

"Kill my own mother?" I screamed. He actually wanted me to execute my own mother—the woman who sang so sweetly and had called me her greatest treasure?

Kyrin cursed under his breath. "I feared this would happen. I feared you would do this. Bad people are bad people, Mia, and it is your job to kill them."

"Shut up." My voice cracked. I was quickly reaching my breaking point, and I suddenly wanted to be alone. I hooked the necklace around my neck. What I was going to do with it, I didn't know. "Give me some time," I said, shoving past him.

I know he saw my shattered spirit in my eyes, but he pushed to his feet with every intention of stopping me. "Two other men were found dead last night. Raymond Palmer and Anton Stokenberg. If we do not act, the others will soon follow."

I halted mid-step, then spun, glaring up at him. Through clenched teeth, I said, "How do you know that?"

"I am a hunter, just as you are, though I seek a different kind of prey. You stalk aliens. I stalk Atlanna. I followed her, and watched her dispose of them."

Fury conquered all of my other emotions. While I had been here sleeping and eating like a queen, two more men had been found dead. Perhaps I could have saved them, perhaps not. Either way, I hadn't been on the streets, searching for them. No, I'd practically embraced this mini-vacation.

I had to get out of here. Scowling, I jerked at the armband on my forearm. I jerked until my skin was bruised black and blue from the strain. The thick alloy stubbornly remained in place. My bones were stiff, my muscles achy, when I finally allowed my hands to fall to my sides.

"Take this damn thing off me."

"No," he said, determined. "Not until you calm down. Not until you realize Atlanna might be your mother, but she is still a monster."

"Damn you," I seethed. "I'm leaving now, this

moment, and your actions dictate whether I leave in peace or in pain."

He crossed his arms over his chest.

"Very well, then." I strode from the office and to the front door. Without a single interruption in my step, I emerged into the afternoon sun.

CHAPTER
19

*P*ain clawed from my arm to my head and slashed down all the way to my toes. I kept walking. Dizziness mingled with the ache in my head, both nearly felling me. My steps slowed, became agonizing, and I stumbled. But I didn't stop.

Keep moving. I had to keep moving.

The snow froze my bare feet, the needle-sharp pricks of cold almost unbearable, and the farther away I moved from Kyrin's home, the sharper my suffering became. Hurt. Hurt so desperately. Anguished screams were lodged in my throat by the time I reached the shade tree in his garden.

Footsteps echoed in my ears, and then suddenly I was propelled toward the ground by a force greater than myself. Strong arms wrapped around me. Kyrin, I realized. He hoped to stop me. I fought against him as he turned me midair, taking the brunt of the impact upon himself when we hit. We rolled several feet.

When we stopped, I sat astride him. I shoved against his chest, but he clasped my arm, and with a wave of his fingers, the armband dropped away.

"You are free," he ground out. "Free."

His words penetrated my mind, and I realized then that my pain was already gone, that he'd actually removed my shackle. Shock beat through me, as cold and real as the snow around me. I met Kyrin's stare, his words echoing through my mind. *You are free.*

"I—" I stopped. I would not say thank you when he never should have imprisoned me to begin with.

"There is nothing you can do right now that A.I.R. isn't already doing. You're upset, and you need me. Just like I need you."

Yes, I did need him. Just like I needed to forget, if only for a moment. The air sparked between us, tiny pinpoints of white-hot lightning and heat. Heat that was always present between us.

I studied him. His eyes were heavy-lidded, and his teeth were parted on a groan, as if he was in deep pain. His arousal strained between my legs, hard and potent. He didn't ask my permission, he simply tangled his hands in my hair and jerked my mouth to his. I didn't protest. No, I thrust my tongue into his mouth and met him stroke for stroke. I savored the sweetness of his taste, like summer rain and carnal desires. I'd hoped to nip the—Thought scattered.

Right then nothing mattered except the feel, the touch, the pleasure of this man. Not my parents. Not the past. Not my job. My fingers tore at the middle of his shirt, ripping the black material down the middle, sending those stubborn buttons flying through the air with a pop.

He rolled me on my back, and the snow made me gasp. So cold. Yet my skin felt so hot. I arched up against him, my legs twining around his. I wanted more. Needed more. I pushed him over, straddled him again, and scraped my nails over the solid wall of his chest. Several ice crystals had melted against the heat of his skin. I licked away every drop.

He moaned. Kissed me. Then tore his mouth away. I growled at the loss. He rolled me over a second time and jumped to his feet, violet fire blazing in his eyes.

"This way," he said. He scooped me up into his arms.

"Not this way. I want you here. Now. In the daylight. In the snow." I didn't want to wait until we reached the inside of his house. I didn't want him in a soft bed, nice and cozy. I wanted him in a place that matched my desire. Some place untamed. Wild. Wicked.

Some place raw.

"Here," I said.

"Here," he agreed. He carried me into a hidden

cove shadowed by towering naked branches. The walls were man-made and warmed to the touch. Hot, just like my blood.

Kyrin eased me to my feet. We stood there, and our eyes met and held. Only a whisper separated us. I reached between our bodies, unfastened his pants, and shoved them down his legs. He kicked out of them and was suddenly naked. Unabashedly aroused. God, he was beautiful. Like a sculpture. Pale and hard, tall and majestic, with dark tattoos scattered across his abdomen. My tongue descended and followed the designs, and his heady flavor, a mix of desire and man, fueled my need.

"What do they mean?" I asked, licking each symbol.

His arms circled my shoulders, and his fingers brushed my neck. "The light shall overpower the darkness."

"That fits," I muttered. And it did. My palms slid across his chest. My fingertips circled around his small, puckered nipples. He was so solid. So rippled with sinew. I had pure, unadulterated power at my fingertips, and I liked it. I liked him.

This man challenged me in a way I'd never been challenged. At times he irritated the hell out of me, and he never bowed to my dictates. Perhaps I was insane, but I admired those qualities in him.

"I have wanted you," he said, his words intermixed with nipping kisses on my jaw and neck, his breath labored, "since the first moment I saw you."

"Shut up and kiss me."

He uttered a warm, husky chuckle, then crushed his lips to mine. Arousal pounded through me, frantic for release as his tongue dove into my mouth. His hands tunneled beneath the silky material of my crisscrossed top. And his fingertips traced the edge of my nipples. I shivered.

Desire pooled between my legs. I was wet. I was ready. Ready for him and only him. I needed the hard, thick length of him inside me. Pounding in and out. Maybe slow at first, but growing in speed.

"See," I beseeched. "See what you do to me." Eyes closed in surrender, I guided one of his hands under the froth of my skirt, up my inner thigh and onto the edge of my panties.

"Here?" he muttered huskily, then slipped past the fragile silk barrier.

"There. Right—yes! There." Unable to stop myself, I arched into his touch, creating more pressure, more friction. "Do you feel how much I need you?"

"You are liquid fire," he praised. He dropped to his knees in front of me, keeping one hand on my panties. The other caressed a path under my skirt and up my feet, calves, and thighs. "I want more. So much more." Reverence dripped from his words.

"Then take it," I said, my hips writhing as he touched me.

"I will," he said. "I will take everything you have to give, and then I will take even more."

He slipped the pink panties from my legs and tossed them to the ground. With a flick of his wrist, he parted the folds of my skirt. He didn't have to spread my legs; I did so eagerly, willingly, and in the next heartbeat, he was kissing the wetness between my thighs. At the first flick of his tongue, I exploded. Fire, joy, pleasure, all seared me, and my head reeled. My knees shook. I gripped his head, losing touch of where I was, who I was, only feeling an incredible shiver race through me again and again.

And just when I thought I might die from it, Kyrin kissed my heat again until I could only gasp his name. He tasted me, sucked me, made me want him all over again.

My head arched back as delight ripped across my nerve endings. I moaned and cried out, the sounds escaping on ragged catches of breath. My eyelids closed, and I chewed at my bottom lip.

"Don't stop," I told him, panting. "Don't stop."

He uttered another chuckle, and the vibrations tickled my thighs. "Always the commander," he said.

Only when I screamed his name again did he stand. He propped his arms on the wall behind me, trapping me in his embrace. "You are beautiful when you come."

"I want to see you that way," I said. I curled my fingers around his penis. He sucked in a hiss of breath and muttered something in a language I didn't understand. "I want to see you when you come."

"Not yet," he said brokenly. "I will savor the rest of you first." A heartbeat passed, a mere whisper of time, before his lips touched mine. His tongue moved over my mouth with heady slowness, exotic and consuming. I tasted myself, and it excited me, reminding me of where he'd been and what he'd done. I moved my hand up and down his length, stroking.

"Do you know," he said, his voice growing more hoarse with every word, watching me through the thick shield of his lashes, "that you are the most passionate woman I've ever encountered."

"You make me that way."

"I am glad." His hands slid languidly up my sides and cupped my jaw. He planted breathy little kisses and nips over my nose, my eyes, my chin.

Warmth skidded along my spine. "I wasn't glad at first. I was pissed." I palmed the heavy weight of his testicles.

A bead of sweat ran down his temple, and his words seemed even more labored. "If this is the way you channel your anger, I'll strive to infuriate you more often."

I chuckled huskily. He tugged me to my tiptoes for another kiss. While his tongue worked magic, he shifted his hands under my butt and urged my legs around his waist. I spread my thighs and hooked my ankles at his back until I straddled him and cradled his erection without actual penetration.

One of his hands flattened against the base of my

throat, so warm, so inviting, a heartbeat away from dipping inside my shirt and cupping my breast. But that strong, masculine hand remained in place, teasing, taunting. Tormenting.

As one expectant minute ticked by and then another, my nipples hardened painfully. The rosy peaks anticipated his touch and strained against the silkiness of my top. I shouldn't have been this excited. I'd already come twice.

"Kyrin . . ."

"Mia." With his eyes squeezed tightly shut, he traced a path down my sternum. He traced the seam back up again, never once deviating from that path. "I told you I want to savor you. Memorize you and brand you. Later is the time for wild and rushed."

"I want wild now."

He only uttered a soft but strained chuckle. "In this I will have my way."

"We'll just see how long you can hold out." I'd long since lost control over my body where he was concerned, and strangely, I didn't mourn the loss.

He pressed his erection against me, and I gasped. I rubbed my chest against his, urging him on. He moaned, bit my collarbone. His hands were everywhere, all over me. Every so often he paused to simply look at me, or to whisper erotic promises in my ear, but always he left me aching for more.

"You feel so good against me, angel. I have to touch more of you."

"Yes, yes," I groaned, then, "No, no," when he did. I was on fire for him.

"Did you ever imagine that a human and an alien would feel so perfect together?" he asked. His tongue licked and sucked my exposed neck and chest. He kneaded my butt. I writhed; I melted into him; I tried to force his hands where I needed them most, but he always thwarted my efforts by drawing his palms a safe distance away.

"Damn you, Kyrin. Let's finish this."

His laugh was a taut, desperate purr. His hands dipped inside my gown. But instead of cupping and squeezing as I so ravenously craved, he teased a fingertip around my nipple. The action only increased my frustration, my need. How was he doing this to me? Making me want, need more?

Then he grazed the tip of my waiting nipple with his teeth.

My hips jerked, and I almost came again. "Yes, there. Right there! Do that again."

He gave my other nipple the same treatment—a light grazing, followed quickly by the heat of his tongue. My lower body arched into him. Just one more touch. One more.

"Where else do you need me?" he demanded, all touches ceased.

"Everywhere, damn it." I reached between our bodies and wrapped my hand around the hardness of his cock. Watching his face intently, I led his hand to the juncture between my legs and guided his fingers through my dark curls. Then I rocked forward.

Contact. I moaned. His hand darted away. I growled and followed. In the next instant, I heard fabric rip, felt cool air. I was suddenly completely naked and flat on my back. Kyrin stood over me, his chest heaving, his cock ready. His hair seemed lighter than a ray of sunshine, and his eyes . . . his eyes were blazing with passion, bright and crystalline. He gazed down at my body, at my spread legs and wet arousal.

"You amaze me," he said. Muscles bunching, he knelt and crawled over me. We both gasped as skin met skin. "I'd hoped to prolong this, to prolong our pleasure, but you are driving me crazy with your little moans and your bold caresses." He rocked himself against me, careful not to enter me.

"Just like that," I gasped. "Do that again."

He did, gliding back and forth in the slick V of my thighs while I rubbed myself against him. He kissed my breasts, dragged his teeth over my nipples, and positioned himself for penetration. He poised himself at the precipice, not actually pushing inside.

His teeth clenched. "Once I take you, you are mine. My woman. No other man can have you."

"Yours," I agreed on a moan, not caring about the consequences of such a vow.

He plunged inside me.

We both cried out at the perfection of it, the exquisite rightness. My nails scored his back as his lips crushed into mine, taking, giving. For the first time in my life, everything felt completely right.

He was so big and thick inside me, sliding in and out. He filled me completely. Passion uncurled with his every movement, seeking total satisfaction. I used the strength of my legs and rolled him to his back so I could ride him, so I could command the depth of his penetration, the swiftness of our pace. I moved up him, then down, increasing the delicious friction.

He maneuvered me to my back.

And I immediately switched our positions again. "Kyrin—"

"Mia," he said. My name was like a reverent prayer on his lips, and he allowed me dominance this time. His hands slid from my hips to grasp my ass and jerk me tighter against him. We began moving faster. Faster still.

I'd never felt so alive. So free. I wanted this feeling to last forever. I didn't want reality to intrude.

"Harder, Kyrin. Deeper."

He ground against me, hard. Perfectly. Deeply.

He reached between our bodies and circled my clitoris with his thumb. I gasped, cried out. My inner walls tightened and spasmed against him, and he moved faster. Harder. Deeper. Just like I needed. Almost instantly, another orgasm catapulted me to the stars, this one stronger than the last. Only when he heard his name rip from my throat did he spill inside me.

When the last pulse subsided, he thrust me to my

back and collapsed on top of me. A long while passed before the hazy sexual fog lifted from my mind.

When I opened my eyes, Kyrin was gazing down at me, his lips soft with tenderness. "I have waited for you my entire life," he said. "Give me the rest of this day. Tomorrow we can deal with the outside world."

Immediately I opened my mouth to tell him no. There was so much I needed to do. Call Jack. Search for Atlanna. Visit Dallas. I had a case to wrap, but after everything I'd learned today, I needed a bit of normalcy in my life. More pressing than any of those, however, was my need to be with this man.

"I . . . would like that," I said.

He grinned and gave me a swift kiss. We didn't bother with clothing. We didn't need it. I allowed him to carry me inside his house—into his bedroom.

CHAPTER
20

*L*ater that night, I awoke in a dirty alley behind an abandoned grocery store. Crickets chirped a lazy tune while I oriented myself. Cold, pungent air. Hard ground. Moonlight. I blinked. This didn't make sense. I'd been in a bed. A soft, warm bed with Kyrin.

He'd climaxed.

I'd climaxed.

Then . . . What?

I'd fallen asleep, obviously. But how the hell had I'd gotten here? I shifted my gaze in every direction. The night sky winked above me, discarded papers and food cartons whirling on the concrete.

Why wasn't I shivering? I wondered, looking

down at my body. A thick coat draped across my shoulders. I wore thick socks and heavy boots, and leather pants hugged my legs. I didn't recall getting dressed, which meant Kyrin had done it for me.

Where the hell was that lover of mine?

As if sensing my thoughts, he appeared beside me and crouched down. I sat up, noticing that we were hidden behind a stack of reeking garbage. My nose wrinkled in distaste. No one was nearby, and neither was there any noise. Kyrin didn't spare me a glance, but kept his attention directly in front of him. "I hope you do not mind, but I transported us here."

I would have loved to watch the whole transportation thing, but let it slide. "What are we doing here?" I whispered.

"Waiting," he answered just as softly.

"For?" The man needed to learn I'd never settle for half-answers.

Now he leveled me with an intense gaze. "Atlanna. I want you to see firsthand that she is not the motherly woman you want her to be."

I instantly went on alert and moved beside him on my knees, staring at the dark alley he had watched moments before. Eagerness thrummed in my blood. Eagerness . . . and dread.

We waited.

"When she appears," he said, "you are to study her, nothing more. No matter what happens. Before we attack her, you must see how she utilizes some of her powers."

I almost screamed a denial. Almost. I knew studying the enemy and learning his weaknesses and strengths before jumping into action was the right way to hunt—and win. I knew that. Yet my impatience was strong. I yearned for some sort of confrontation with Atlanna.

"Give me a gun anyway." I said. "I will—"

A twig snapped.

I sliced off my words and went completely still.

At the far end of the alley, a woman suddenly appeared from the shadows. Moonlight bathed her in youth and beauty, paying nothing but tribute to her fair skin and curly mane of white hair. Black pants and a long black leather jacket draped her, showcasing her curves. She looked like a hunter. She looked like me.

Atlanna.

Kyrin stiffened.

I watched as a body floated behind the woman. She blinked, and the bulky, naked form fell unceremoniously onto the ground. Shit. Her telekinesis must be unbelievably strong to lift such weight.

As a wave of her energy hit me, she paused and frowned. Her gaze darted in every direction, searching for something—or some one.

My heart raced. I controlled the urge to stride to her. To strangle her. To hug her. Before I took my next breath, she disappeared in the shadows.

The winter wind kicked up a notch, swirling and

whistling around the alley. Keen disappointment nearly felled me, and I massaged the back of my neck.

"She sensed us," Kyrin said.

"Yes. She probably felt a hum of energy in her blood." Like I felt every time I'm near an Arcadian. I strode to the body, preparing myself for what I'd see. A male. He was naked, his body devoid of any sign of torture. The poor bastard was even smiling. I checked his pulse, just to be sure. "Dead," I muttered. "I wish to God I knew why she was leaving them out. You said William was to get A.I.R.'s attention. What about this one?"

I dropped my head into my hands. I'd always wanted a mother to love me. Hell, I'd always wanted a mother to love. But my mother had killed this man. My mother was a predatory alien, had done such evil things, and just thinking about them made me sick. I was duty bound to hunt and kill her. And yet . . .

"Amusement, probably," Kyrin said. "There was no way to save him."

"We've got to call Jack. He needs to know about—"

A familiar, pungent scent filled my nose. "Sorry, angel. You are not ready, and too much do I fear for your life."

The last thought to drift through my mind before darkness claimed me was that I was going to murder Kyrin and his damn sleeping potion.

"Bastard," I shouted as I awoke.

Sunlight streamed through the burgundy curtains,

illuminating the spacious decadence of Kyrin's bedroom. Honey oak floors gleamed, the elaborate vanity glistened, and the sconces and jasmine-scented candles glittered.

I was sick and tired of being drugged when he wanted to move me.

I searched the room for Kyrin, but he was gone.

As soon as I found him, he was going to give me his phone unit so I could call the station house and tell Jack everything I'd learned—except for the part about Atlanna being a blood relation. I didn't know if I'd ever broach that particular subject. And I'd probably leave out the part about sleeping with Kyrin, too.

I abandoned the warmth of the comforter and trekked to the bathroom. There, I brushed my teeth and hair and programmed the wall console for a shower. The water burst on, deliciously waiting for me. I was just about to step into the tub when a flash of gold caught the corner of my eye. Filled with a sense of dread, I scrubbed mist from the mirror.

That rat bastard!

My fists clenched as potent fury consumed me. If I'd had a pyre-gun, I would have found Kyrin and blasted his ass to ashes. He'd done it. He'd really done it. After every erotic thing we'd done together, after promising to trust each other, he'd returned the armband to my bicep, keeping me a goddamn prisoner here.

I jerked on the fresh blue sheath folded neatly on the sink rim. "Bastard," I growled under my breath.

"I'd thought he meant to free me permanently. But no, he meant to keep me here all along."

I stormed through the mansion, pushed my way past his servants. They scrambled out of my way. Kyrin was nowhere to be found. A low growl worked its way past my throat. On top of everything else, he still thought to play detective on his own. His death would be my greatest pleasure.

I kicked and clawed the hidden door to his office, but the stupid thing wouldn't budge. Did he think I'd be okay with this? That I would forgive him? What, give the little woman a few mind-shattering orgasms, and she'd be content to wait at home?

"Bastard," I spat again.

Whipping around, I saw I was alone. Smart of the servants to hide. In my frustration, I might have accidentally hurt them. I stalked to the kitchen and withdrew a cooking blade from a wooden sheath. Before the day ended, I was going to hack this armband from my body. Then I would await Kyrin's return. And I knew that with each second that ticked by and he remained absent, my fury would grow hotter.

"I'm going to skewer him alive," I said, slamming down on a barstool. "I'm going to rip out his heart and feast on it for days. I'll tie his intestines around his neck and choke him to death." I jabbed the tip of the knife under the band.

"Oh, and just who do you intend to torture this way?" a husky female voice asked behind me.

I quickly jumped up and spun, knife braced and ready. When I saw who stood there, my jaw dropped open. Atlanna. I hadn't sensed her presence, yet there she stood, a vision in creamy lavender cloth. My first thought was that of a hunter. I wished I had my pyre-gun. I wished I had a tape recorder.

My second thought was simply that of a daughter. I wondered what she thought of me as she examined me so intently.

Up close, her uptilted violet eyes, high cheekbones, and pixie nose were the epitome of perfection. Even the arch of her eyebrows dared not deviate from the flawlessness of her features. She resembled me, yet was so much more delicate.

Gold armlets snaked around her biceps, and bracelets adorned her wrists and ankles. Her glitter-soft white hair nearly reached the floor, and was plaited in several braids. Innocence enveloped her, glowed lovingly around her. Deceptively.

Two separate needs battled for dominance. I could run to her, accept her as my mother, and talk to her. Or I could use the blade I held in my hands and end the mess this Arcadian had created.

I did neither.

I simply stood conflicted, my heart rate increasing, my palms sweating. I was so filled with curiosity. What would my life have been like if I had remained with her as a child? Would I have known the love I'd always craved? Would I have killed innocent humans to please her?

I was supposed to hate her, and I did hate her on so many levels.

Take her into custody, the huntress in me cried. *Question her. Find the missing men, if any of them are still alive. Find the babies.* Still, I couldn't force myself to move. To act as I'd been trained.

"Why are you here?" I managed.

"To see you." Her fingers skipped down her braid. "Would you like me to leave?"

"I— No." I shook my head. No matter my needs, that wasn't an action I could allow.

She gave me a half smile, and amusement sparkled in her expression. "Holding that knife, you remind me of myself. So strong. So ready to conquer the world."

"Except we use our weapons for different reasons." There. I'd said it. It was the first step in forcing myself to think of her only as a murderer, not a mother.

"Killing is killing." Slowly her smile faded, and she leaned her hip against the kitchen doorframe. A hint of anger stiffened her chin. "Which of us do you think has more fun with our victims?"

"Life isn't always about fun."

"Then what's it about, hmm?"

"Doing the right thing."

"Is the right thing admitting to my crimes? Fine. I did it. I killed the men you found. They had served their purpose, and I learned well not to leave fathers with their babies."

I blinked at her cold confession, uttered so nonchalantly. I'd never—*never*—had an alien admit so blatantly to a crime. And yet her confession fit so perfectly with her other actions. Shocking. Uncaring. Bold.

"I'm glad I did," she said. "It brought you to me."

"You cannot mean to convince me that you killed them only to get to me. What about the babies?" I asked, keeping my tone as neutral as hers—a feat that required every ounce of strength I possessed.

She shrugged, waved a delicate arm through the air, and gave a light chuckle. "What about them?" Like a queen before her court, Atlanna strolled around the kitchen, touching and lifting certain items for her inspection, then haplessly dropping them back into place. Wrinkling her nose in distaste, she traced a fingertip over the counter. "I expected Kyrin's home to appear more . . . I do not know. Rugged?"

My teeth ground together so forcefully my jaw almost snapped. "You do realize you will be executed for your crimes, do you not?"

"Humans cannot hurt me." She faced me again, her gaze boring into mine, her eyes thoughtful. "You, though, could do great damage, I think. You are, after all, my finest creation."

Her words sent a rush of anger through me, and I scowled. "You had nothing to do with shaping me into the woman that I am."

"You are more mine than your father's. More alien than human."

"I am not like you. I will never be like you."

"No, Mia en Arr. We are the same." Her beauty glowing in the light, she approached me. "Your father hid you well. I spent years, so many wasted years, searching for you in New Britain. Then I read an article written about New Chicago's A.I.R. team. There you were, staring out at me from a computer screen. I packed my belongings and traveled here that very day. I've watched you, you know. You are everything I wanted you to be." There was a "but" in her tone.

"But I fight for the wrong team," I finished for her.

"Yes. There is that small little detail. Small"—a grin flitted across her face—"but fixable."

"How did you know I was here, in Kyrin's home?"

"I followed your trail of energy last night. That," she said, her grin becoming sheepish, too innocent for the monster hidden inside, "and I have my people watching Kyrin. The silly man thinks he is so smart, that he sneaks undetected through my home. But I know. I always know."

"So here we are," I said, trying for a casual tone.

"Yes, here we are. What better place for our first meeting? A.I.R. does not know where you are; therefore they cannot give me trouble." She moved directly in front of me, and I smelled the subtle floral fragrance that encompassed her. "I wasn't trying to hurt you that day in the parking lot. Kyrin was my target."

Do your job, I told myself. She's evil. Vile.

I had to take her down. Duty first and always.

Innocent lives rested in this Arcadian's hands, and if I didn't snatch them away, she would crush them.

"How horrid Kyrin is to keep you here, locked away. Do you plan to kill him? Of course you do."

Not giving myself time to think further, I dropped my knife and pounced. Perhaps I should have kept the weapon, but I wasn't ready to kill her. Not when she might be the only way to find the babies. Not when— I didn't allow myself to consider the other reason.

I wrapped my leg around hers and pushed. Because my action was so swift and unexpected, and delivered with expert precision, she fell backward, her expression stunned. I was on top of her in the next instant. By then she had already gained her momentum and unleashed a torrent of power so great, I dropped to my knees with a thud.

My hands covered my ears, trying to block out the loud, piercing blast of reverberating energy through my head. This was a thousand times worse than the pain I had experienced when stepping outside Kyrin's home. Wave after wave of agony rushed through me. A scream tore past my throat.

An eternity passed, or maybe minutes, but I felt a brush of fingertips across my cheek and forced my gaze open. Atlanna crouched in front of me, her features filled with anger, as well as a hint of pride. "Not many could have taken me unaware." With a simple glide of her fingers, she removed the armband from my bicep.

"You are free now, Mia. Free to kill Kyrin for locking you away."

Slowly, the ringing inside my head subsided.

"Take me to the babies and return the human men you abducted," I croaked. "Please."

"But I'm not finished with them yet," she said, rising.

I grasped her hand, meaning to keep her from leaving. When our palms touched, her image filled my mind. I saw her lying on plush carpeting, covered in blood. Whose? Hers? She didn't move, didn't utter a sound. Was she dead or alive? Who had hurt her?

I tried to manipulate the vision, hoping to reveal the answers, but the harder I tried, the more the vision faded. *No,* I almost shouted, unsure whether I spoke to the vision or to Atlanna's bleeding form. *Stay with me.* I probed the edge of my consciousness, twisted each image with a mental hand. Soon the vividness of colors and the complexity of shapes evaporated into mist, finally vanishing completely.

My eyes wide, I stared up at her. She watched me, her lips parted, her features now pale.

"What did you see?" she demanded, clutching my shoulders. "Tell me what you saw."

I shook my head. I wouldn't tell her, didn't know how to tell her she might perish in the coming days. I didn't even know how I felt about what I'd seen.

She released me, stepped two feet away. "I, too, have visions. They are never wrong."

"I know," I said sadly.

"Do you know, too, that we sometimes see distortions of the truth?"

My brows drew together. "What are you saying?" That what I'd seen might not come to pass? That what I'd seen was merely one possibility of what the future held?

"I—" She paused, whatever she'd planned to say dying a quick death. "Come to me after you have killed Kyrin. Your . . . brother would like to see you again."

With that, she strode from the house.

CHAPTER
21

*T*bolted after her, my footsteps pounding into the wood panels. Just before I reached her, Atlanna glanced over her shoulder, and for a moment of suspended time, our gazes held. "Do not make me wait too long," she said.

My head filled with the same intense ringing she'd caused before, and I squeezed my eyes shut as I dropped to the waiting ground. How many minutes passed, I didn't know. I only knew that when the sound cleared and the pain subsided, I opened my eyes and found myself alone. Atlanna had disappeared as if she'd never stepped into the house.

Her final words inside the house penetrated my now pain-free mind. *Your brother would like to see you again*. I blinked once, twice. Kane. The brother I didn't remember. The brother my father worshipped and thought he'd killed.

So Kane was with Atlanna. Was probably helping her. I should have been shocked. I wasn't. Why should anything go right for this shitty case?

I whipped to my feet, retrieved the knife I'd dropped, and sheathed the sharp blade inside the waist of my skirt. Upstairs, I confiscated a pair of Kyrin's boots and multiple pairs of socks. The socks I used as stuffing inside the boots, but even then the black leather boots proved several sizes too big and flopped on my feet. I didn't waste time with pants or a shirt. I simply tugged one of his jackets over my shoulders. The thick material sagged, and the sleeves covered my hands. It'd have to do.

Urgency hammering through me, I raced outside. No street signs. No traffic. The afternoon air breathed a frosty cover in every direction as a large expanse of trees and untamed land greeted me. How many miles stood between the city and me? I didn't know, couldn't even see New Chicago's skyline. I could begin walking, hoping someone would drive past and give me a lift, but . . . I didn't like the odds, the waiting. The time involved. Kyrin could return at any moment.

There had to be another way.

The answer entered my peripheral vision as I stepped farther away from the house.

To my right rested a four-car garage, square in shape, white trim and red brick, detached from the house. The very garage I'd watched Kyrin speed from only one night ago. I quickened my step, pumping my arms and flinging snowflakes up my calves.

The side door proved locked, and the automatic entrance too heavy for me to lift. I busted the back window with a rock and climbed inside, knowing I'd set off whatever alarm system he used. I didn't care. Warmth enveloped me as I studied three SUVs, each clean and all-terrain. And waiting for a driver.

Waiting for me.

I grinned. One space proved empty, which meant Kyrin was still using the Jag. As I considered what to do next, my smile dissolved. I didn't know how to hot-wire a car. Earthlings used fingerprint IDs to start cars. Most aliens did not have fingerprints, so they used voice recognition.

Without Kyrin . . . No. Wait. Most likely, Kyrin would have programmed a few of his servants' voices into the system, in case he needed someone to run his errands. Or he would have left a recorder with his voice commands for their uses.

Cursing, I ran back through the snow, my teeth chattering, my body shivering. Inside the house, the servants were still in hiding. As I searched for them, I also searched for a recorder. I rummaged through drawers and cabinets on the ground floor, finding nothing but a few batteries and bullets. Scowling, I pounded up the stairs to Kyrin's room, where I left no corner or hollow untouched.

I discovered a feather boa and a straw cowboy hat in his closet—but I didn't want to consider why he had those items.

Back downstairs I went. A few minutes later, I found a young woman hiding in a cubbyhole under the kitchen floor. She screamed when she saw me. I grabbed her by the upper arm and hefted her up.

"Come with me. Be good, and I won't hurt you."

Her body trembled, but she didn't try to fight me. I raced back outside, dragging her with me as I retraced my steps to the garage. Thankfully, there was no sign of Kyrin's return. I approached the far SUV, the one with chains on the tires, low mileage, and turbocharge.

"Open it," I commanded the woman.

"Op—open," she whispered.

Nothing happened. I banged my hand on the hood in frustration. "Say it again. In the right language."

"Luo," she shouted.

The door popped open.

Relief pounded through me. "Now make it start."

"Pren," she shouted, and the engine hummed instantly to life.

I released her and slid inside the car. As she sprinted away, I programmed in the coordinates to my apartment. The garage door opened automatically and the car jolted into motion. The squeal of thick tire tread filled my ears as I sped away.

I snatched the car phone and said, "Jack Pagosa, A.I.R.," into the speaker. I heard the ring, but he never answered. Shit. I'd try again when I reached my home. I drove north for half an hour, and had almost given up finding a familiar road when New Chicago's skyscrapers rose ahead, above the horizon. An hour later, I eased into my building's parking lot. I left the car running.

My steps clipped and frantic, I strode inside the building. The hallway was a broad opening into an expansive sunlit lobby that left nothing to obstruct my vision. Just as I rounded the corner, I heard a high-pitched you're-looking-good whistle. I turned sharply on the balls of my feet. My neighbor, Eddie Briggs, paled when he realized who he'd just objectified.

He was damn lucky I didn't knife him.

"Uh, hi," he said, pressing his glasses up his nose and trying not to stare at my cleavage. He wasn't doing too good a job. He stood in front of the elevator, tall, lanky, and young, probably twenty, with dark blond hair and freckled skin.

"If you want to live, don't comment on my clothes." I never slowed my step and quickly passed him. I felt his gaze on my legs.

"Uh, the police have been here looking for you," he called.

I stopped mid-step and spun to face him. "Did they question you?"

I waited. Nothing further was offered. He just continued to stare at the gown beneath the jacket, and I waved my hand in front of his face until he actually made eye contact. "What'd you tell them?"

"That I didn't know nuthin'. That I hadn't seen you in a few days."

"You did good," I told him, jumping back into stride.

Only when I reached my apartment did I stop again. I cursed. My ID unit was busted. I cautiously stepped into the foyer and scanned my living room. Nothing appeared out of place or destroyed, but . . . something didn't feel right. The air pulsed with someone else's energy. Someone, maybe A.I.R., maybe not, had searched my place. That someone might still be here.

I unsheathed my knife. A thorough search revealed an empty trash bin and a missing answering unit, but thankfully, no intruder.

I tried Jack again. After eight rings, I slammed the receiver onto the kitchen receptor, once, twice. Where the hell was he? My fingers stiff, I phoned the hospital next, only to be informed that Dr. Hannah was absent. Was everyone conspiring against me?

After locking up as best I could, I hurried through the spray-shower, changed into fitted slacks and a button-down, then ceremoniously dumped Kyrin's clothing into the corner. God, it felt good to wear my own things. Even better, I had strapped on a pyre-gun, clips, and several knives. I secured the necklace Kyrin had given me in my closet safe, where I usually kept old weapons. I didn't know what I was going to do with it yet.

Thankfully no one had stolen the SUV, so I used it to drive to the hospital. Anticipation filled me as I strode into Dallas's room; sunlight streamed through the open blinds and gleamed on the white tile and silver bed rails. I stood there, drinking in every detail.

Dallas was propped up on the bed, eating lunch and speaking with another agent. Garret Harsbro, I realized, a young recruit fresh from school.

I felt a surge of joy and relief, consuming, pure. Dallas was alive, healthy, and whole. His skin possessed a strong pink tint. His motions were slow but sure. The only evidence of his recent brush with death was his thinner cheeks and the lines of tension around his mouth.

He chuckled at something Garret said, the sound a little strained, yet I found myself laughing with him. True laughter. Uninhibited. He heard me and glanced over. I had to bite back a gasp. His eyes . . . even from this distance I could tell they were no longer the deep brown of before. They were lighter. Almost blue. Like Kyrin's.

"Mia," he said, dropping his fork and returning my smile. "Damn, but it's good to see you."

I rushed to his bedside and clasped his hand in mine. "Welcome back," I said. "Welcome back."

He gave my palm a squeeze, his grasp weak. "Glad

to be back. Dr. Hannah said I should be dead, but the gods must like me."

I blinked up at Garret. "Will you excuse us?" I asked. I didn't give a shit if I was being rude. I needed some time alone with my friend. My best friend.

Garret gave me an appreciative grin, nodded, then strode from the room.

When we were alone, I turned back to Dallas and said, "How do you feel?"

"Better every hour." Suddenly the smile fell from his lips, and he eyed me with concern. "You missed Jaxon by ten minutes. Something's going on, Mia, and it has to do with you."

I didn't want him to worry. "I've been out of touch for a few days, that's all."

He shook his head. "It's more than that, and—" He paused, like my words had only just reached him. "What do you mean you've been out of touch? You're never out of touch. Your job is your life."

"Long story, and I don't have time to explain. What did Jaxon tell you?"

"He wanted to know if I'd spoken to you since I'd come out of the coma last night. And of course I hadn't."

"That it?"

"Well, it's what he didn't say that threw me. Jack called on Jaxon's cell. Another body was found this morning. I don't know who. Jaxon wouldn't tell me. Anyway, while Jack was talking, Jaxon turned pale. He whispered your name, and at first I thought you were the one dead. But when I asked Jaxon about it, he said I'd misheard and to call him if I spoke to you."

That didn't sound good.

"Jaxon bolted after that. I called your house and your cell, but couldn't reach you. Your unit didn't even pick up."

Trying not to reveal my trepidation, I kissed his cheek. "I'll explain everything once I've spoken with Jack, okay?"

He reluctantly nodded and tugged on my hand to keep me by his side a moment longer. "Be careful."

I managed a grin. "Always."

By the time the station house came into view, my unease had grown to unimaginable proportions. I refused to be a coward, however, so I maneuvered into the parking lot. I watched the building as agents came and went. Nothing seemed unusual. Resigned but still unsure, I slipped inside the lobby.

Several agents greeted me normally with a quick "Hi" and a smile. Some rushed to my side, patted me on the shoulder, and asked how I was doing. I answered politely but sternly, "I'm fine," and kept moving. Others eyed me with leery distrust and maintained their distance.

When I reached Jack's office, I paused, hand raised midair. I'd never knocked before. Why start now? I pushed open the door. Jack was in the middle of a sentence and cut himself off abruptly when he saw me. Jaxon, Jaffee, and Mandalay were seated in front of his desk, and all turned their focus to me.

Jaxon jumped to his feet. He strode one step toward me, then stopped. "Are you okay?" he asked, concern dripping from his words.

I gave him a weak smile. "As good as can be expected."

"He didn't . . . hurt you, did he?" Jaxon asked softly.

"No. He didn't."

A moment of silence encompassed the room. Silence tight and heavy, unnatural.

Finally Jack said, "What the hell are you doing here, Mia? We've had PD and agents scouring the countryside for three days. Three damn days, and you stroll oh so pretty into my office, as if nothing ever happened."

There was no time to explain. "I know who killed Steele, Jack. And the others."

"Yeah," Jack said, easing back in his chair and popping antacids like candy. "So do we. Kyrin en Arr."

I opened my mouth to utter a determined, "You're wrong," but Ghost and Kittie rushed inside, halting my words. They flanked my sides and ground to a halt when they saw me.

"Dallas called my cell," Ghost said, dragging in breaths after every word. "He said you were on your way here." He enfolded me in his arms. "Kyrin didn't hurt you, did he?" he demanded, repeating Jaxon's question. "Because I will personally find him and kill him—if you haven't already."

"He's still alive," I answered, "and I'd like him to stay that way. He isn't violent."

"Oh, he's not, huh?" Jack threw back a few more antacids. "Then why is his voice DNA recorded at the scene? And why," he added darkly, "are your finger-prints there?"

There was something in his eyes, a gleam I'd never seen directed at me before. They knew I'd been at the scene, but did they know about my origins? Did they suspect? My attention moved to Mandalay. She hastily glanced away. Next, I focused on Jaffee. He, too, couldn't face me for long. Jaxon, Ghost, and Kittie all watched me, each with equal expressions of concern and dread.

I faced Jack. "What are you getting at?"

"Think back to the day you were taken, Mia. One minute I'm watching you have a pleasant discussion with an invading Arcadian, and the next you simply disappear. We don't hear from you for three days, and then we discover your fingerprints all over a crime scene. How does that look to you?"

I didn't answer his question, but spoke one of my own. "Do you think I'm guilty of murder? Is that what you're saying?"

Defeated, he slumped back in his chair. "No," he said firmly. "I don't. You're the best hunter I've got.

You've saved God knows how many lives, and taken God knows how many alien lives. But the top guns are out for your blood. They think you're guilty, that you've helped Kyrin every step of the way." He pushed out a sigh. "They want your badge."

Dread uncurled inside my stomach and launched a path through my blood. "Neither Kyrin nor I killed those people."

"I know *you* weren't involved, but this Kyrin—"

"Trust me. I—"

"I trust you," he interjected. "Always have. But I don't trust him. And besides that, I have to do my job. Right now I have orders to take your gun and your badge, pending investigation. You're on leave until further notice, and don't give me any shit about it. This is standard procedure. You know that. You're lucky it's not worse."

"I'm keeping my gun, Jack, and I'm staying active," I said, hand tightening around the gun in question. "Legally or not."

He blinked over at me, searching my eyes for . . . what? The strength of my determination? The lengths I'd endure to triumph? Whatever he saw deflated his intent.

"I knew you'd be difficult," he said, but there wasn't any heat to his tone. "Fine. Keep your gun. I suggest you spend your time proving your innocence and bringing me the one responsible. But by God, you were never here. Understand?"

"I didn't see her," Jaxon said.

"See who?" Ghost asked. "Mia's still missing."

"Think I'll search for her in the Northern District," Kittie said. "You know how that woman likes to shop."

"Get out of here before I change my mind," Jack commanded gruffly.

God, I loved these men. I gave each man a quick hug. When my arms wrapped around Ghost's neck, he whispered, "You need anything, you call. Understand?"

I nodded.

I also knew what I had to do next. Even though it would make me look that much more guilty.

When I stepped into the hall, I stayed in the shadows. I'd worked here so long, I knew every secret room, every place to hide. Sweat beaded on my face and hands, and my heart raced. What I was about to do was going to piss off Jack, and maybe destroy his trust in me. But this had to be done.

Kyrin had said I had powers, that I had only to reach inside myself to find them. Atlanna, too, had said I possessed powers as strong as her own. I had felt glimmers of them over the years, and especially these last couple of days. I'd had no control of them, however.

I had to try, though. I closed my eyes and mentally reached within my mind, plucking away the walls I'd erected there. One by one the stones fell, until slowly, so slowly, the entire structure crumbled. Nothing happened at first. I stood on the precipice, hovering, waiting, the force of everything I'd buried churning like a tempest.

I realized at that moment I'd been asleep my entire life and was only just now about to awaken. With a shaky arm, I stretched out a mental hand. The moment my fingers penetrated the swirling fog, energy flooded me. My knees almost buckled from the intensity. So much power. It consumed me, ate me alive.

I trembled, and my eyelids flew open.

Focus, I commanded myself. *Focus*. Everything around me—the people, insects, dust—moved in slow motion. Barely moved, in fact. Almost as if they were standing still. Just like before, in the parking lot with Kyrin. I heard the tick of a clock, yet the ticks seemed to come every other minute instead of every second. The voices around me sounded deep and dragging.

I took one step, then another, and found that I moved quickly, faster than I'd ever moved before. I flew through motion detectors and across weight-sensitive floors, then checked myself into the cell hall. I had Lilla by the hand before my presence was even announced over the computer. Lilla's expression was shocked, yet she didn't resist me as I dragged her from the building and into Kyrin's car.

Only when we were on the highway did I allow myself to relax. The moment I relaxed, all energy deserted me, and time kicked back into regular speed. Things no longer moved slowly, voices no longer dragged. I was the one dragging now.

A wave of dizziness assaulted me. My stomach

rolled. I programmed the car to a stop, tumbled out, and emptied the contents of my stomach there on the side of the road.

Lilla opened the passenger door. I thought she meant to run, that I'd have to find the energy to chase her, but she crouched beside me. "How long have you known?" she asked.

My head felt heavy, too heavy, but I managed to turn toward her. "Known what?"

"That you are like me?"

"Two days."

Something vulnerable flickered in her eyes. "Why did you free me?" she asked.

"For your brother. Now answer a question for me. Did you help Atlanna abduct those humans?"

Silence swelled around us.

Finally, "Yes," she admitted. "But when I realized she planned to kill them after we had finished with them, I asked Kyrin to help me stop her. I just—I wanted a baby of my own, and I thought that was a wonderful way to have one."

I drew in a breath. I didn't trust this woman fully, but I had to put my life in her hands. I had no other choice. "Get us to Kyrin's, okay. I need to close my eyes."

She helped me back into the car, and the last of my strength deserted me. I didn't want to sleep. I wanted to be awake when we reached Kyrin's. But the moment the car jerked into gear, my mind went blank, and a deep haze cocooned me.

CHAPTER
22

ibbons of awareness slipped into my conscious mind, incrementally prodding me to wakefulness. I blinked open my eyes. At first, I saw nothing more than black spiderwebs, making my surroundings appear hazy and unclear. When I focused, a sight more delicious than a smoldering ocean of coffee greeted me, and a smile played at the corners of my lips. I stretched like a contented kitten. Kyrin lounged beside me, propped on his elbows.

"Hello," I said, a yawn at the edge of each syllable. Then I remembered what he'd done to me, how he'd shackled me. I lost my smile and punched him.

His head whipped to the side.

"That's for trying to hold me prisoner again."

As he rubbed his jaw, he gave me a repentant sigh. "I am sorry. I only thought to protect you. I knew you would chase after Atlanna, and I didn't want you to do that alone. I never expected her to come to you."

I crossed my arms over my chest.

"You have my solemn oath that I will never, *never*, clamp you with an armband again."

Muted beams of light etched his frame, darkening the aura of disquiet around him. My brow furrowed together, and I frowned. "What time is it?" I asked.

"Nine P.M."

"How did I get here?" I asked, then paused. "Wait. My memories are a bit fuzzy, but I remember bits and pieces. Lilla drove me, right?"

"Yes, she did." He brushed his fingertips over my cheek, around my ear, then tunneled into my hair. "Thank you for freeing my sister."

"My pleasure." I relaxed into his touch.

With slow, sensual grace, he swirled a dark tendril around his finger, then glided the raven tress over his cheekbone.

"I had a vision about Atlanna. I think—I think she will soon die."

"Die? How?"

I swallowed. "I saw her prone, lifeless body on the ground, her blood seeping away from her." A tremor raked my spine. "My visions are never wrong."

His voice became as gentle as a summer rain. "Perhaps we will win this war, after all."

I should have felt tremendous joy at such a remark, but I didn't.

Sinking into him would have been so easy. Wrapping my arms around his neck and pulling him to me for a kiss would have been easier still. Yet I did neither of those things. I allowed him to offer the comfort.

His fingers cupped the back of my neck, and he did what I had not. He urged me back onto the mattress, allowing his lips to brush against mine. In the wake of such a sweet promise, I lost all sense of animosity and abandoned myself to his kiss. Gently, so gently, our tongues danced together. His tasted as pure and masculine as I remembered. His scent wrapped around me, evoking images of star-filled nights, expensive champagne, and chocolate truffles. On an achy moan, I slipped my hands under his shirt, willing to give him everything I had to give. His skin was soft velvet over hard steel.

His moan matched mine in intensity, but he tore his mouth away. His breathing labored, he said, "Lilla told me what happened. How you used your powers."

I drew in a shaky breath, and my arms dropped back to my sides. "A.I.R. thinks you killed those men. William Steele, Sullivan Bay, and even the woman, Rianne Harte. They're determined to hunt you down and execute you." My voice hardened with authority. "I want you to leave the city."

"How are they so sure I am guilty?"

"Your voice DNA is all over Bay's murder scene.

And the fact that you had contact with every victim doesn't help."

He cursed under his breath. "I did not have enough time to clean away the evidence of my presence the last time. I should never have gone, but I wanted you to see Atlanna's cruelty for yourself."

The doorbell sounded.

I jolted up. I knew instantly who stood outside, wanting entrance into Kyrin's home. A.I.R. Adrenaline pumped through my blood, giving me strength. "Get up. We have to go."

He remained casually lounged atop the mattress. "Worry not, little angel," he said as his lips curled. "I will send them on their way."

My hands anchored to my hips, and I leaned my face into his. Only a breath away. "I don't know how they found you, but they can enter your home with or without your permission. The fact that they're ringing your doorbell is only out of respect for me."

His shoulders lifted in a shrug. "I will simply make them choose not to enter."

Riding a wave of urgency, I latched on to his arm and jerked him to his feet. "Mind control isn't something you can do. Remember?"

"You are right." Still, he acted unconcerned.

"Kyrin! Work with me here."

He clasped my forearms and leveled me a glance. "Lilla is here, Mia. She can dissuade A.I.R. from entering."

"Oh." Just like that, amusement replaced my apprehension. A deep, true chuckle escaped. "I never thought I'd be glad for her ability."

"You are beautiful when you laugh. Like a goddess of love come to enchant all who gaze upon you."

"Enough," a female voice said from the doorway. "You are making me sick."

Both Kyrin and I reluctantly turned away from each other and toward Lilla, the sounds of revving engines in our ears.

"I will hear your thanks now," she said dryly. "I just saved both of you. I like roses."

"Go play," Kyrin said. He waved one hand through the air. "We are busy."

"No," I said. "Stay. We have work to do. We're going to visit Atlanna. Tonight."

Kyrin frowned. "You have not enough experience using your powers," he said. "We are not ready to face her."

"With enough pyre-guns, we'll be ready for three intergalactic wars." I shifted my gaze to Lilla, who still leaned casually against the doorframe. "Can we count on your help?"

"You set me free," she answered, her expression resigned. "I owe you. And an Arcadian always pays her debts."

I almost shook my head in surprise. These two aliens I had judged so harshly and fought so incessantly to destroy were becoming my strongest allies. That fact boggled my mind. I wanted to thank them, tell them I was sorry, and demand to know why all at once.

Kyrin sighed. "What should I do first?"

"Get a car ready," I said. "I know where we can get weapons." I grinned. "A.I.R. is about to make an anonymous contribution."

Sneaking through the back door, up an elevator shaft, and into A.I.R. storage took a little over an hour. I had to dodge cameras, guards, and ID scans. Not easy, and not fun. But I did it. I pocketed several pyre-guns and daggers from agents' lockers, and loaded myself down with top-of-the-line, state-of-the-art experimental gear from the lab. Exiting A.I.R. only required ten minutes. I just jacked the alarm in sector twelve and ran like hell.

As I turned toward the corner, five agents approached, guns drawn. I recognized three of them. They were hard, by-the-book A.I.R. If one of them tried to stop me . . . I knew I couldn't kill a fellow agent, so I increased my speed. Maybe they would be too busy to notice me, a suspended officer, striding as pretty as I pleased through this secured area. Right. I didn't know what would happen next, but I was prepared for anything. They passed by, heading toward the alarm without giving me more than a conspiratorial wave and a knowing grin.

God, I loved these people!

Once situated in Kyrin's SUV, where both Kyrin

and Lilla awaited me, I passed out weapons and said, "There's one more thing I need." I slipped my cell unit from my back pocket.

I rang Ghost, Kittie, and Jaxon on conference. I knew calling them was the right thing to do. They could get into places I couldn't, and having them at my back would give me a sense of peace.

"I need your help," I said after each man had answered.

They replied without hesitation, granting my request. Ghost even said, "I'll do whatever I can to help prove your innocence."

"Thank you," I said, and I meant it. I briefed them on the situation. I told them everything. About Atlanna. About Kyrin. About Lilla. "You still in?" I asked.

One by one, they all agreed.

These men might never know how much their support meant to me. "Meet me at the northeast corner of Michigan Avenue. One hour."

I slipped my phone into my back pocket and began strapping a recorder under my chest. This time, I was going to record Atlanna's voice. When I finished, I turned to Kyrin. Determination stiffened my spine. "Let's do this."

CHAPTER
23

Twenty-five minutes later, I found myself crawling over hills, around trees, and along icy embankments. Kyrin had explained the layout of the house, so we knew to enter through the basement.

Ghost and Lilla snagged the rear of our little train. Kittie and Jaxon had the middle, just behind me, and we all stealthily followed Kyrin. Some of us moved a little more stealthily than others. Apparently, Lilla did not know the meaning of the word silence. Her knees found and snapped every twig within a mile radius. And she'd slipped on the ice too many times to count. I couldn't believe this klutzy alien was the same one who'd once given me the slip.

When we topped the last hill, I gazed down at a beautifully landscaped garden that led to a circling wall and an equally beautiful home. Not a mansion like Kyrin's, but close. As white as Ecstasy, with a peaked roof that dipped and rose like the waves of an ocean.

"She keeps the men in the basement," Kyrin whispered to me.

"Excellent," I replied just as quietly. "Ghost and I will check for survivors. If we find any, we'll bring them here. Jaxon, you look for children, or any hint of children. All of you, grab any files—hell, any papers you see. Kyrin, stay here."

Kyrin's eyes narrowed. "You are not going inside that house without me."

"You're not trained for this type of mission, and I need someone out here, acting as guard. You can project your voice into my head and tell me if anyone else arrives."

"I go in."

"I'm not trained either. I do not mind waiting," Lilla offered.

I shot her a glance. "We may need your mind control."

She sighed. "This seemed fun in theory, but now that we are here . . ."

"Hey, babe, don't worry. I'll cover you," Ghost said, a lusty edge to his words.

She smiled over at him, even ran her nails over his

arm. "I like the thought of your body covering mine. You are so dark."

I leveled Ghost a warning glare. "Concentrate, people. Screw later."

Sheepish, he shrugged.

"I go in," Kyrin repeated.

"All right. Everyone goes," I said. "Just stay quiet." I directed the last to Lilla.

This time, Ghost and I led the way. Several armed men, all human, patrolled the outside wall. Lilla distracted their minds, and we were able to stride directly in front of them. They never saw us.

Remaining alert, we led our ragtag group inside the home's basement door, which Ghost expertly opened for us. Three female Arcadians were sauntering down a nearby hallway. Mind control wasn't what we needed here. I wanted these aliens incapacitated.

"Stun," I mouthed to my men. They might be pregnant, so I didn't want them killed. Each man nodded in turn. We set our pyre-guns to stun and fired on my count of three. The room lit for a split second, then one by one the women froze in place, their minds and bodies on hold.

Before any of us could blink, a fourth woman burst from the shadows, surprising us. Her expression wild, she stabbed Ghost in the thigh with a retractable knife. He groaned, the sound blending with the woman's screech as she raced away. I bolted after her and tackled her, knocking her to the plush carpet. The moment our bodies hit, she fought like a caged tigress. She scratched, bit, kicked, and clawed. I landed a solid punch to her chin, knocking her witless for a few seconds. Those seconds were all that I needed. I steadied my gun and fired. As the stunned woman lay motionless, I pushed to my feet.

Jaxon, Ghost, and Kittie all watched me expectantly. Lilla appeared distraught, as if I might attack her next, and Kyrin was shaking his head in exasperation.

"Can you not go one day without using your fists?" he asked.

I ignored him. "Playtime is over, kiddies. Follow me."

We worked our way through without further incident. Ghost dragged at the rear. There were several rooms, but only one was occupied. A lone man reclined upon a soft, decadent bed. Fat silk pillows of every color enveloped him. Wispy lace hung from the ceiling, cascading around X-rated portraits of couples having sex. The man was completely naked and reading a magazine. *Erotic Encounters*. His long, muscular legs consumed every inch of space, and his dark hair and dark eyes glowed with boredom. I didn't recognize him from the missing persons portfolio.

When he spotted me, he set his magazine aside with a sigh. "How do you want it?" he asked. Resignation dripped from his voice.

"Ssshhh," I hissed, scanning the room to make sure we were alone. Once I was satisfied that no other ears were listening, I crossed the room and positioned myself at the foot of the bed. "What's your name?"

"Terrence Ford."

"Are you here willingly?" Jaxon asked.

"No," Ford said. He kept his gaze directed at me. "Do you want to be on top?"

Behind me, Kittie chuckled. "Yeah, Mia. Do you want on top?"

"I'm here to save you," I told the victim. "Not screw you. Idiot," I muttered under my breath. "See this man here?" I motioned to Ghost. "He's going to take you to safety."

Ford stood so quickly, the sheet atop the bed whipped to the floor. His knees were wobbly, and he would have tumbled to the ground if Jaxon hadn't grabbed him by the forearm.

"Steady," Jaxon said.

I draped the comforter around the man's nakedness.

"Thank you," he gushed. "Thank you so much."

Ghost helped the poor, practically-screwed-to-death man from the chamber. I noticed Ghost was limping, and with every step the limp worsened. In fact, a trail of blood now followed him.

"Guard Ford, and wait in the car," I told him.

Ghost didn't argue. He nodded, for the first time looking like his name.

I turned to Kyrin. "All right. I'm ready to face Atlanna." Ready to face my mother.

CHAPTER
24

We entered several upstairs bedrooms. Like the rooms below, these were empty. We kept moving until we spotted a gathering of Arcadians huddled together in the middle of a hallway, laughing and talking. The carpeted flooring was congested with females, probably breeders, I realized.

Our guns were already set to stun, so we discharged a round of lasers. Blue lit the air like a midnight bonfire, and suddenly their bodies looked frozen by time, some standing, some sitting. Some were even poised with hands upraised, mouths open.

This almost seemed too easy.

Shaking my head, I studied the forked hallway ahead of me. Two choices. Left or right.

"Lilla," I said, "stay here. Detour anyone who comes this way."

She gulped and clasped a pyre-gun as if it were a precious diamond. "I will."

"Jaxon, Kittie. You take the right. Kyrin and I will take the left."

Everyone nodded, and we split.

Kyrin and I entered a large sitting room, making sure to stay in the shadows. A fireplace decorated the far wall, the only spot not covered by mirrors. A black velvet couch and two matching chairs flanked the center.

I sucked in a breath. There, in the second chair, lounged Atlanna. She wore a sheer lavender gown, mere wisps of fabric, and her snow-white hair hung down her body in erotic curls. A man was seated directly across from her, talking about their progress with the halflings.

I couldn't make out his features, but I knew from his short, inky hair that he was human. I inched a step toward them, my pyre-gun aimed at Atlanna's heart. Stun. I'd only stun her, I thought, squeezing the trigger. Blue lights erupted. Then fizzled. I watched, my heartbeat suspended. My mouth formed a small O. Shit, shit. Something was wrong. Atlanna remained completely unaffected. In fact, neither she nor the human had ceased their conversation.

Kyrin fired off a round of his own.

Nothing.

Atlanna shifted her body and faced me directly, as if she'd known I was there the entire time. "I'm so glad you decided to join me, Mia. Sorry I had to destroy your weapon." She waved her fingers in the man's direction. "Leave us," she said.

He instantly obeyed and disappeared behind a mirrored door. Before I could receive a clear look at his features, a sharp pain lanced through my hand. With a gasp, I dropped my gun, and the metal fell limply from my fingers and thudded on the carpet. Kyrin's features were contorted with pain, I noticed, and he too dropped his gun.

"Much better," Atlanna said, and the pain stopped.

"Our battle will end here and now, Atlanna," I told her, straightening to my full height.

"You disappoint me," she said. "I thought you'd kill Kyrin and help *me*. Instead, you do the opposite. Foolish girl."

A swarm of Arcadians burst into the room from the mirrored door, surrounding us. The air circling Kyrin thickened, and I knew he was about to use his lightning-fast reflexes. I closed my eyes, willing myself to do the same, damn the consequences. Instantly, my powers sprang free. When my eyelids snapped open, I saw Kyrin fighting three Arcadians at once. They moved slowly, barely an inch per second, while he waltzed around them, punching and kicking.

I turned my attention to Atlanna. Her eyes were narrowed, and she was watching me. She strode a step in my direction, yet even *her* actions were slowed. It was as if she could see me, but couldn't force herself to move as quickly. Something deadly gleamed in her gaze.

Fighting my way toward her, I landed a quick kick to one man's neck and a hard jab to another's midsection. But my head began to ache, my muscles going lax, and I slowed the closer I came to her. I knew, *knew,* Atlanna was the source of my pain, just as before. The more the ache intensified, the more energy I lost, until finally I was jolted back into normal speed. Lethargy seeped into my every pore.

She grinned.

Before I could gather the strength to protest, four male aliens latched on to my arms and legs. They gripped me, and I used what little strength I had to try and jerk myself free. I failed. Where was Kyrin? Was he safe? I could no longer see him, but I knew he was there, knew he fought for my freedom. Two of my guards flew back against the wall, making me fly forward. Before the other two were felled, a mass of them converged around me and managed to apprehend Kyrin. Slowly, his image appeared.

My strength completely gone now, I sagged against my captors.

"My people have already gathered the rest of your team," Atlanna said. "How silly to think you could best me." She positioned herself directly in front of me.

"If you harm them, I will make your death as painful as possible."

Her hands came up, the nails long and clean, polished, and she caressed my jawbone. "I want a thousand more just like you. Think of the profit they would bring." Eager to brag, she said, "For years I thought the answer lay in science, but all along I was the answer. *Me*. My blood, like Kyrin's, has healing qualities that aid in the creation of halfling offspring. After I infused my women with my blood, they were able to produce healthy babies with Earth men."

"Where are they? Where are the children?"

"I'll never tell."

"You disgust me."

Fury flashed in her brilliant lavender eyes. "Whip him," she said, motioning to Kyrin. "And if you fight it," she told him, "I will punish Mia. I might anyway. She's proving to be quite a disappointment."

His expression dark and dangerous, he nodded. A guard stripped away his shirt and bared his back.

"I will be fine," he assured me with a strained smile.

That smile was almost my undoing. He thought to keep me calm, to assure me everything would be okay. We both knew it wouldn't be.

"He is able to heal quickly," Atlanna growled, "unless he is whipped until there is none of his precious blood left. Or . . . unless the whip is laced with poison. Which this one is. You see, the poison binds with the healing properties of his blood, and the more his body tries to recover, the more the poison destroys him."

A mixture of panic, dread, and helplessness

uncurled in my stomach, giving me a jolt of energy. I twisted and lunged; free for a moment, I raced toward him, but was quickly grabbed again and subdued. "Leave him the hell alone," I screamed.

"Continue," Atlanna said to the whip wielder.

The first blow landed on his back, and Kyrin flinched. Then the next and the next were delivered in rapid succession. Sweat dripped from his temples, and blood flowed like a crimson river down his back. Again, the long, thick length of the whip cracked through the air. He moaned.

"Let him go," I shouted, kicking and jerking. I just didn't have the physical strength to fight my way free. "I'll kill you. Do you hear me? I'll kill you."

Atlanna's eyes narrowed menacingly. "No, you will not. You will help me breed more."

I stilled. "I'm your daughter, and you would do that to me?"

"Absolutely. I hoped to gain your willingness, but if you will not give it, I will take it by force. Lock her up," she snarled to the guards who held me. "Perhaps some time alone will help her adjust to her new fate."

I fought for my life, Lilla's, my agents', and most importantly Kyrin's, as six Arcadian warriors dragged me into a cold, dank cell. A cot lined the far wall, the only piece of furniture. No blankets, no toilet. This prison was nothing like Terrence Ford's. His had been meant for seduction. Mine was meant for punishment. Perhaps death.

The door slammed closed. A lock clicked in place, and red lasers formed bars, illuminating the small area with an eerie cerise glow. Alone now, I felt terror slice through my mind. Escape. I had to escape. The walls were closing in, faster, faster. Darkness all around. I heard a woman's screams, and realized moments later that they were mine. My throat was raw, my hands aching from clawing at the walls.

To my surprise, I felt a comforting presence enter my mind. I knew instantly that Kyrin was reaching out to me. He was alive.

"I'm here," he said inside my head.

Peace settled over me, as warm and welcoming as a winter coat. I am a fighter, I reminded myself. Atlanna would not defeat me. She would not break me. I patted down my body. The weapons I'd strapped to my thighs and waist were gone, taken during the trek here. I traced my palm over the edge of my boot, and a relieved sigh slipped from my lips. I still had one blade, small but just as deadly as any other.

With only one knife, how was I going to win this war?

The answer came to me like a gift from the God I'd thought I had forgotten. I straightened my shoulders, determination working through me. I knew what I had to do.

*   *   *

Hours passed, and still I remained calm. When I felt my energy had returned sufficiently, I stood directly in front of the door, the glow of the lasers nearly blinding me. They produced no heat, but I knew they'd burn the skin from my bones if I touched them.

I closed my eyes and allowed my powers to flood me. Stronger. Stronger still. I became saturated with it, and my lids flew open. I saw the blink of the lasers, realizing they vanished every other second. One, two, I counted, then shot out my hands and worked the blade into the lock. One, two. I jerked back, barely missing the flash of lights. One, two. I repeated the action many times before disabling the metal barrier.

I felt a flash of victory. Waiting until the lasers had disappeared again, I shoved past the thick doors and leaped into the waiting hallway. Just as I steadied myself, the lasers returned.

I zoomed through the house in search of Atlanna. I found her moments later. Too self-assured to require a guard, she stretched atop the black velvet couch in the same mirrored room she'd occupied before, her eyes closed. For one prolonged moment, I remained at the threshold. My God. She needed time to recuperate. After using her powers, she became weakened, just as I did.

My movements still quickened, I quietly shut and bolted the main door, as well as the mirrored door, then rushed at her. I struck her with my fists, toppling her to the floor before she had even opened her eyes. Then I sprang on top of her and hit her again and again. She kicked, hit, bit, and scratched, unable to concentrate long enough to gather her powers.

I drew back to punch her, and by luck or precision, she landed a kick to my stomach. Air burst from my lungs in a mighty heave as I was propelled backward. My arm hit a marble vanity table, and I would have cried out if I'd had the breath. A vase crashed onto the floor, shattering into a thousand tiny pieces.

"Where is Kyrin? Where are the others?" I gasped, laboring for every molecule of oxygen.

"Dead," she shouted, jumping up. "Dead."

From a mirror panel, a man rushed into the chamber.

The moment I saw his features, I forgot about everything else in the room. My mouth floundered open and closed, and I was unable to stop the motions. Dare. My beloved brother was alive. Not Kane, as I'd assumed, but Dare. It was like looking into the past. He was tall and strong and possessed the same dark curly locks and wide-spaced blue eyes as he had at eighteen. The same high cheekbones and straight nose. The same innocence.

My momentum slowed, as did my speed. I shook my head, certain if I cleared my vision, I'd realize this couldn't possibly be my brother. After all, I'd seen his dead body all those years ago. That was perhaps my first mistake. I shouldn't have allowed my speed to slow, for already I was growing tired again. I fought against it.

"Dare?" I said. My first instinct was to rush to him and wrap my arms around him as I'd done as a child. Atlanna's words stopped me. My second mistake.

"That's right," she said. "My blood saved him, and in return I have his devotion."

Devotion? My eyes narrowed. No, she controlled him with her mind. His features were blank. Unemotional. The same look Isabel had worn when she'd shot Dallas. Atlanna had controlled her as well, I realized. The woman's sins increased with every minute that passed.

Dare didn't spare me a glance, but watched Atlanna. "Are you hurt?" he asked her.

Even his voice was the same. Familiar, only slightly different from the loving laughter I remembered from fourteen years ago.

"Never." Atlanna wiped a small trickle of blood from her lip. Already the wound was closing.

Dare finally glanced in my direction. Not a single spark of happiness touched his eyes. I stood frozen, wondering what to do, what to say.

"Shall I whip her?" he asked Atlanna.

I spied the three-pronged, bloodied whip draped across the edge of the couch and, without thinking, dove for it. I knew what I had to do.

"No," Dare shouted, realizing my intent.

Before he could react, I was on my feet and advancing. I knocked him aside, kicked out my foot, connecting with Atlanna's ankles. All in one motion. Atlanna tripped and launched to the floor, her back to me. As she screamed and tried to crawl away from me, I gathered every force within me and whipped her until the fabric of her gown was torn, until her blood flowed around her. Until Dare grabbed my arm and forced the whip from my grip.

Panting, I blinked down at the floor. Her body was slumped in unconsciousness. Disgust—for myself, for Atlanna—filled me. I'd only just found my mother, only just found my brother, and I'd lost them both. I swallowed back a lump in my throat. My hands shook, and I pressed my lips together.

Dropping the whip, Dare sank to his knees in front of her. "What have you done?" he said, brokenly. "The whip was laced with Erolan. Even Atlanna cannot withstand such a poison."

I didn't answer him. The war was over. Except for the missing children, the case was closed. I'd done my duty, just as I always had. Why didn't I feel victorious?

Dare jumped to his feet. He glared down at me, but he didn't say another word. He simply scooped Atlanna up in his arms and quietly strode from the chamber. I let him go. She was dead, no longer a threat, and I couldn't bring myself to do more. Hopefully, in the coming days, Dare's mind would clear from her monstrous influence, and he would come back to me.

Right now, I had to find my friends. My strength slowly draining, I moved from the room. Only two guards were stupid enough to try and stop me. Because of my loss of energy, one managed to knife a wound from my sternum to my navel. When they were unconscious from my chokehold, I battled past the pain and stanched the flow of blood with a scrap from one of the women's gowns. I stumbled through the rest of the house, finding Jaxon and Kittie inside a cell. I disabled the lasers, and Jaxon was able to pick the lock.

They rushed through the doorway, then ground to a halt when they saw my blood-soaked shirt.

"Are you okay?" Jaxon asked.

"I'm fine," I managed. "Someone else's blood," I lied. "Help me find Lilla and Kyrin."

Ten minutes later, Kittie called, "In here. They're in here."

My footsteps were slow, but I made my way inside a bedroom. Lilla stood over a large, bare bed, staring down at an unmoving body. She slowly turned and faced me. Tears ran down her cheeks.

"He is dying," she whispered brokenly. "Kyrin is dying."

CHAPTER
25

J axon and Kittie dragged Kyrin outside to the vehicle where Ghost and Terrence Ford awaited us. Ghost had his thigh wrapped with cloth, and I knew he was going to be okay. But Kyrin . . . I was fighting to stay calm. I desired this man, this alien, maybe even loved him. Yet he'd been wounded so badly, he might not survive.

"I called for backup and medical," Ghost admitted weakly. "Be here any time now. Told Jack the whole story." His gaze zeroed in on my stomach. "Mia? You okay?"

"I'm fine," I said. Trees and sky swam before my eyes. Concerned faces faded in and out, and their voices seemed so far away. For one brief moment, flashing lights and sirens penetrated my senses.

I collapsed.

I don't remember the drive to the hospital. I just know that when I opened my eyes, I'd lost my clothes, and several doctors were standing over me, examining my abdomen.

"You're going to be okay," one of them said.

"I hurt like hell," I said, my voice raspy.

He grinned, causing his mustache to twitch at the corners. "Understandable. But you're healing faster than anything I've ever seen."

Within the hour, they had me stitched up. I refused pain medication. I needed my head clear. "Take me to see Kyrin," I said. I had to see him, had to know how he was.

The doctors and nurses ignored me.

I refused to be ignored. I screamed profanities at the top of my lungs until one of the nurses ran to get me a relaxant. Before she returned, Jaxon rushed into the room. Dallas followed, his progress slowed by a cane. His light blue eyes still gave me pause. If anyone else had noticed, they hadn't said anything to me.

"Is everything okay?" Jaxon demanded, weapon drawn.

"Hell, no," I said. "Where's Kyrin?"

"Is that what all the commotion is about? He's here," he answered, putting his gun away.

"Is he alive?" I probed, my hands clenching, my stomach twisting.

"Yes," he evaded.

Everything inside me relaxed, rejoiced. I couldn't help but smile. "Take me to him," I said. "Please."

He gulped, looked away. "Maybe—"

"Please, Jaxon, Dallas. I'm begging you here."

Jaxon glanced at Dallas. Dallas glanced at me, those lines of tension still firmly etched around his mouth. "You'll be happy to know Ghost is healing nicely," Dallas said.

Fine. They didn't want to take me, I'd take myself. With my wound shrieking in protest, I ripped the IV off my arm, shoved myself from the bed, and plopped into a nearby wheelchair.

"Stubborn as always," Dallas said. "Help her out, Jaxon, before she kills herself."

With a sigh, Jaxon grabbed the handles of the wheelchair and ushered me to Kyrin's room. Dallas hobbled beside us.

Jaxon said, "Damn, I'm glad this is over."

"Me too," I whispered. "Me too."

As dread and hope mingled inside me, we entered Kyrin's room. I glanced around, noticing that Kyrin was the only patient. He lay stomach down on the bed, his chin tilted toward the door, toward me, his eyes closed. Lilla stood vigil beside him, just as she'd done at Atlanna's.

A tear—my own freaking tear—slipped down my

cheek. I hadn't cried in so long, the single drop stung my tear duct. God, it felt so good to see him alive. I'd thought all my tears dry, but now, seeing him, I was unable to stop the torrent of emotion that flooded me. Relief. So much relief. Happiness. So much happiness.

"There's something you should know, Mia," Jaxon said.

"Don't," Dallas said, cutting him off. "Not yet."

Lilla said softly, "She has a right to know. He's dying, Mia. Kyrin is dying."

My joy instantly shriveled, but I gave no outward reaction to her words. I didn't believe her. I wouldn't believe her. This man, my man, was not going to die. I wouldn't let him. Slowly I rose from the wheelchair and hobbled to the bed.

"Leave us," I said to the men, not even glancing behind me.

Dallas patted my shoulder, then limped from the room with Jaxon at his side. They shut the door behind them. My tears trickled free at last.

"What are we going to do?" Lilla asked. "I cannot live in this world without him."

"He's not going to die," I said through clenched teeth, gazing down at him. His skin was pallid. His cheeks were hollow, and there were blue shadows under his eyes.

"Look at him, Mia. How can he survive?" Lilla caressed his brow with loving fingers. "When we were children, it was he who cared for me. He who taught me how to use my powers. His love has always given me strength."

"I once had the same type of relationship with my brother," I said. "His name is Dare, and he loved me when no one else would. He played hide-and-seek, rescued me when my dad became abusive. When Dare died, I wanted to die with him. And now I discover he's alive, but it's as if I'm dead to him."

My tears splashed onto Kyrin's chin, then trickled onto his neck. I buried my face in my hands and wept for all I had lost. And all I might lose.

"Please don't die, Kyrin. Don't die."

Two days dragged by, feeling more like two years. Every moment I grew stronger, Kyrin grew weaker. I'd been back to Atlanna's house, looking for any lead as to where the halfling children were, but the home had been ransacked, everything taken. Whether it had been done by Atlanna's underlings, by A.I.R., or by some other government agents, I didn't yet know. But I planned to find out as soon as the chaos in my life settled.

Lilla and I continued to talk to each other. Ironically, I found comfort in sharing my feelings with her, feelings that I was only now beginning to understand. She shared her own feelings with me. We'd formed a tentative sort of friendship.

I couldn't come to terms with Kyrin's approaching death. I needed to fight for him, but I didn't know how. Helplessness consumed me as I stared down at his thinning body and pallid skin.

"I love him," I said to Lilla. Each of us occupied a seat beside his hospital bed. "He has brightened my life. I'm different when he's around. With him I'm a . . . woman. Not a huntress."

She sighed. "I wish there were something we could do. But the poison is slowly destroying him."

I asked her the same question I'd asked her a thousand times before. "Is there no antidote?"

"No," she answered raggedly, the same answer she'd given each time.

The next day, I hadn't slept properly, and my brain felt like it had gone on sabbatical. I plopped myself next to Kyrin's bed, meaning to steal a quick nap. If only he had normal human blood, I thought wearily. Then I straightened. Shit. Shit! Hope sparked inside me and erupted like wildfire. That was it. That was the answer.

As Atlanna had said, the poison was binding and destroying the healing properties of his blood. What if his blood was replaced with average human blood?

Risky, I thought. Extremely dangerous—but he would die if we didn't try something.

I pitched my idea to the specialist in charge of Kyrin's care, and at first he refused. With a little persuasion—in the form of bodily threats—he decided to test my theory. He used a blood sample from Kyrin and a human, and studied both under a microscope.

"My God," he said incredulously, "this just might work."

That was all the encouragement I needed. I couldn't ask Dallas; he now had the same type of blood as Kyrin. So I called Jaxon from my cell phone, because he was the first that leaped into my head, and explained what I needed.

"Darling," Jaxon said, "for you, I'll do anything."

"Thank you," I said. "Thank you."

"I'll be there in fifteen minutes."

Since Jaxon and Kyrin were of different species, blood compatibility tests were unnecessary. We knew they wouldn't match. The doctors drained all of Kyrin's blood that they dared, then hooked him and Jaxon to a connecting tube. I watched the crimson blood flow from Jaxon to Kyrin. Would it work? My eyes widened as Kyrin's color slowly returned. Then . . . his heart monitor stopped.

A voice I didn't recognize sounded, "Code blue. Room four-one-nine."

"He's rejecting the blood," someone said. More doctors and nurses rushed inside. One man pounded on Kyrin's chest, while another wrapped his legs in a thermal blanket. *No,* I screamed silently. *No!*

"I'm sorry, but I need to ask you to leave," a nurse said to me, trying to usher me to the waiting area.

"You can ask," I growled. "But I'm staying."

She left me alone after that, and I remained exactly where I was, watching Kyrin through horror-filled eyes.

This was his last chance. His only chance. If he didn't make it—

The monitor beeped. Then beeped again. And again. And again. Finally steadying out.

Someone laughed. "He's going to be okay."

I collapsed to my knees in a relieved heap. I covered my mouth with shaky hands, halting my cry of happiness. He was going to be okay. I knew it. Felt it. He was going to live.

When he regained consciousness the next day, relief and happiness consumed me.

Kyrin's eyes were feverish, but he managed to clasp my hand. "You did well," he said, as if we were still at Atlanna's and not a single day had passed since. "You defeated her. Something no one else has ever done. I know she is your mother, but—"

My fingers pressed against his lips, stopping his words. "My only concern is for you."

I lifted my hand, and he offered me a soft smile. "I will live, Mia. I will live and spend the rest of my life loving you."

"You'd better," I said, wiping away my tears. "Or I'll kill you."

He chuckled. Our palms met, and we held each other, knowing we might never let go.

The day Kyrin was released from the hospital, healthy and whole, was the same day he and Lilla were exonerated of all charges. Smiling—I just couldn't seem to stop doing that lately—I drove him to his house. I thought to give him a little time alone, to heal, but he took my hand and led me inside.

"There's something I want to show you," he said.

"Please don't tell me it's a feather boa and a cowboy hat."

He chuckled. "Nothing like that, I promise you." He ushered me into his office and placed a *kalandra* in my hand. His *kalandra*. "Look," he said.

Brow furrowed, I glanced down. I gasped. Inside the locket was a lifelike picture of me, and I was embracing Kyrin. I blinked up at him. "I don't understand."

"I told you each necklace holds a legacy for the owner. You have always been my destiny, Mia. Always." With that, he enfolded me in his embrace. "I knew it the moment I saw you. You are a dominating, powerful halfling with attitude, and our time together will certainly be interesting."

I pushed him onto the couch. "You better believe it will." I had a feeling our adventure had only begun.

UP CLOSE AND PERSONAL
WITH THE AUTHOR

WHAT INSPIRED YOU TO WRITE THIS BOOK?

I'm fascinated by the possibilities of "what if." That question alone—what if—opens a vast world of exciting/dangerous/erotic situations. What if otherworlders walked among us? What if we discovered aliens in our own bloodline? What if we fell in love with a darkly seductive alien? The list of questions could go on forever. Writing books allows me to explore and play with those questions, giving them a life of their own.

WHAT'S YOUR PROCESS FOR WRITING A BOOK?

I plant my butt in a chair and write. Just write. I don't plot out my stories beforehand, but let the characters lead me where they want to go. Sometimes they take me to very strange places—but I'm never bored.

DO YOU BELIEVE ALIENS ARE REALLY OUT THERE?

I believe in the possibility. The universe is a vast place, more so than we might ever realize. I don't think there's sufficient proof to say with one hundred percent surety that yes we are alone, or even no we are not alone. How's that for a non-answer?

YOUR CHARACTER MIA SNOW IS A STRONG, TOUGH WOMAN WHO ISN'T AFRAID TO BATTLE A MAN. ARE YOU TOUGH LIKE HER?

If by tough you mean do I curl in a fetal ball, suck my thumb and cry for my mommy at the first sign of trouble, then yes. Yes, I am as tough as Mia. I have a quiz on my website titled "Do You Have What It Takes To Be An Alien Huntress?" and I have to admit I scored pretty low.

SPEAKING OF MIA'S TOUGHNESS, DO YOU REALLY THINK A WOMAN COULD KICK A MAN'S ASS?

Depends on the woman. Depends on the man. For the purpose of the book, however, I like to think of it this way: This is a fantasy of female power just like male-led action-adventure stories are male fantasies of power.

DO YOU HAVE PLANS TO WRITE ANOTHER BOOK ABOUT MIA?

Right now I'm working on a darkly erotic book about Alien Assassin Eden Black and her battle with human and alien slavers. However, I do plan to continue Mia's story. After all, there are halflings out there she's determined to find.

YOU REALLY TORTURE SOME OF YOUR CHARACTERS. ARE ANY OF THEM BASED ON REAL PEOPLE?

Absolutely. As much as I hate to admit this, I'm an emotional person. When I wrote this book, I was at a very dark place in my life and used my writing as a vent. Sort of like cheap therapy. Every time I got mad at someone, I wrote a new fight scene. The real question is, what the hell am I going to do now that I'm happily content?

Naughty Girls

Proudly Presents

Enslave Me Sweetly

Gena Showalter

Coming soon from Downtown Press
Published by Pocket Books

Turn the page for a preview of *Enslave Me Sweetly*. . . .

I spent the next two hours stretching on the mat and centering my energy, forcing my body past the barriers my injuries had set. At times, I found myself unsteady and shaky. A good shaky, though. The kind that let me know I was alive. I'm sure Lucius would have preferred I make use of the weights, maybe the virtual boxing ring.

Usually, I did train in the ring. I didn't want to go that route today. Instead, I sashayed off the mat and to the bar warm-up anchored across the far wall. I stretched one leg up, glancing over at Lucius. I nearly gasped when I realized he was watching me, his eyes heated and intense.

My gaze slitted on him. "Enjoying yourself?"

"Let's practice," he barked. "If you think you can handle me."

"I've been handling men like you for years, sparkie."

A muscle ticked in his temple. "Let's get a few things straight, *cookie*. You don't like me and I don't like you. You don't want a partner and I sure as hell don't need one—especially an arrogant female other-worlder with no talent that I can see."

"Then why did you agree to work with me?" I ground out.

"A paycheck is a paycheck, baby, and your daddy is paying out the ass to have me here."

"We're paid by the government, *baby*. Get your facts straight."

His lips pursed, and he cut off his next words.

"At least you got the better end of the deal," I muttered.

"How's that?" He arched a brow. "You failed your last mission, and I've succeeded every damn time."

I worked my jaw in irritation. Like I really needed a reminder of my failure. Like it wasn't front and center in my mind twenty-four hours a day. "In six years, that's my only failure. One I plan to rectify."

"You've succeeded at easy cases, sugar. That's nothing to be proud of."

My teeth ground together. "Have you even made a single kill?"

"If you have to ask, you're not a good judge of character."

Cold, hard death gleamed in his eyes, speaking of innumerable kills. My hands clenched at my sides. "I've made kills, too. Many, in fact."

"I'm curious," he said. "How did you eliminate those targets of yours? Annoy them to death?"

Scowling, I closed the distance between us until we were nose to nose. Our breath mingled, and I could feel the vibration of his strength. I could not seem to hold my usual cool facade with this man. I responded to him whether I wanted to or not. "Why annoy them when I can use my knife—when I can take a human like you, cut you up, and sauté you for breakfast?"

He studied me for a long, silent moment, his eyes raking over my curves with heated intent. "That's one glorious ego you've got there."

"I've earned it. You, however, have probably never—"

"That's enough, children," Michael said, suddenly filling the doorway.

We both spun around and faced him. With a feigned nonchalance, he leaned against the thick wooden frame. He held a cup of steaming coffee in one hand and an unlit cigar with the other. "I leave you two alone for a few hours and you turn on each other. Work together on this or find yourselves new jobs." He shook his head and gave me his complete attention. "I meant to give you more time but something's come up." Now he turned to Lucius. "Finish your training, then explain to Eden what I want done today."

With that, he left us alone.

"Explain now," I said, glaring at Lucius. I would have run after Michael, but that would amuse my *partner*, I'm sure.

"Anyone ever tell you if you're nice to a man, he's more likely to be nice to you?"

"Please explain what Michael wants me to do," I said, the words ripped from my throat.

"Not until after we train," he said, drawing out each syllable with relish. He eyed my injured side. "You, cookie, are in desperate need of it."

I had to swallow back a rush of curses. How did he keep getting the upper hand? "I'm ready when you are," I said through gritted teeth. As a Raka, I didn't have special, instinctive fighting skills. As a trained assassin, I *did*. I would not be the easy mark he obviously considered me. Injured or not.

He claimed his place on the large blue mat in the center of the gym.

Gathering my energy, centering at last, I placed myself just inches away from him. My strength was not at the level I wanted it, but for now it would have to do. I reminded myself of my battle strategy. Focus. Keep my thoughts clear. Never allow an emotional reaction.

"I won't go easy on you," he said. "I don't care that you're a woman, and I don't care that you're injured."

I'd trained with holograms more fierce and lethal

than this man, so his warning didn't frighten me in the least. "You plan to take me down all by your little self?" I laughed. "Good luck, sparkie."

Uttering a low growl, he sprung at me.

In one fluid motion, I leaned to the side, effectively avoiding impact. He whizzed past me and tripped on his own feet. "Tsk, tsk, tsk. You let your emotions get the better of you."

Pivoting, he advanced on me. I kicked him in the stomach, but that didn't slow him. He reached me all too soon and grabbed me by the shoulders. This time I couldn't evade him; he moved too quickly. He tossed me down, and I hit the mat with a smack. I winced at the sharp ache in my side but quickly leaped to my feet. And just like that, before I could drag in a breath, he was on me again, shoving me down, his hands wrapping around my throat to choke me.

"You're too slow," he said.

I knew that. The slower I moved, the more time my opponent had to consider his next action. I broke Lucius' hold with a quick thrust to his elbow. Not enough strength to break his arm into two pieces, but enough to hurt. Then I kicked him in the chest to send him stumbling backward. When he regained his momentum, he launched at me. Twisting, I sprang up and sidestepped. Gave another fluid twist. Kick.

Contact.

My shoe slammed into his stomach, knocking the air from his lungs. As he doubled over, trying to suck in air, I lunged, elbow raised. With one downward slice, I connected with his cheekbone.

He howled.

I grinned. "Still too slow?"

"Not a bad move," he said, rubbing his cheek. After a moment of staggering, he stood to his full height. "Let's see what else you've got." He went low, spinning on his heels, at the same time performing a booted strike. Anticipating such a move, I jumped.

Not far enough away, however.

The heel of his boot ground into my calf. My knees knocked together, buckled, and I was propelled onto my face. Cool foam met hot skin.

He jumped on me, his chest pinning my face to the floor. His warm breath fanned my ear, my cheek. Everywhere his skin touched mine acted as a live wire, singeing me, making me ache—not in pain, but in lust. I had trouble drawing in a breath, but when I did I inhaled the savageness of his scent. The wildness.

"What should you do in this position?" he said calmly.

I should place one palm against my cheek, then extend my other arm and roll myself over. But his long, thick fingers were surprisingly gentle as they slid down my arms, and I remained in place, doing nothing. His touch wasn't like that of an enemy, but like that of a lover.

An unwanted wave of need and desire crested inside me, growing hotter, hotter still. It didn't help that he had an erection. Thick. Hard. Hot.

He didn't want *me*, I knew. Not really. Men were simply turned on by physical contact. And we'd definitely gotten physical.

Knowing he would have desired any woman under him failed to diminish my own lust as it should have. Dark, dangerous fantasies sprang to life. Naked bodies, moans of surrender . . . Without thought, I arched my butt toward him, seeking more of his heat, craving deeper contact.

And that's when a fragrant cloud of cinnamon and honey surrounded us. The moment I smelled it, my cheeks burned a bright red and I fought frantically for release. If Lucius knew anything about Rakas, he'd know we only emitted that scent when desperately aroused.

"Let me go," I suddenly shouted. I couldn't have erected a calm, cool mask if my life depended on it. "Let me go right now." I extended my arm as I should have done earlier and tried to roll over.

He pressed me down with more of his weight, keeping me immobile.

"What's wrong with you?" he barked. "Be still, woman. And when the hell did you put on that perfume?"

He didn't know.

I immediately relaxed. It was one thing to desire him, but quite another for him to know about it. He seemed like the type of man who would use that against me, to mock me.

"Get off me," I said more calmly. "Or I'll kill you."

"What are you going to do if I don't?" he asked. "I've got you pinned, and you know what? There's not a damn thing you can do about it. So it looks like you've got yourself a bit of a problem."

"You think so?" I replied, nearly breathless.

"I do," he said confidently. There was a pause, then, "Was I too rough?" he asked gruffly.

I forced myself not to struggle. "I happen to like it rough."

"Liar." His voice was now low and husky. Full of sexual energy. "I think you like it slow and tender."

My God, if he kept talking to me like that, I was going to rip off his shorts and demand he take me right here. "Damn you. Don't you want to teach me a lesson?"

"Maybe next time." He paused. "When a man has you pinned like this, the best thing you can do is bite his arm and use the distraction to twist yourself around." Before I could take his advice, he jumped off me and stood to his feet.

I wrenched to my back and kicked, swiping his feet out from under him. Down, down he tumbled. I laughed when he hit. "To do something like that?" I asked him.

His laughter mingled with mine, the sound of it raw and genuine. He didn't move to rise, but remained in place. "Good move."

"Thank you."

When our amusement died, he linked one of his arms behind his neck and frowned. "I want that bastard EenLi killed. Not because it's our assignment, but because he deserves to die."

I glanced over at his profile; it was as harsh and savage a view as full frontal. "You make it sound personal."

"Every mission is personal, but I'm sure Michael told you EenLi used to work here."

"He did."

"When he left, he killed several agents. Agents who were my friends." Lucius turned to face me, the glint in his eyes feral, hard. "If, at any time, I think you're holding me back, I swear to God I'll kill you myself, cookie."

My eyes narrowed. "I'm only going to say this once." I held up one finger, just in case he needed a visual. "I'll speak slowly so you understand. If *you* hold me back, I'll send you crying back to your mommy—cut up like a little girl."

Another flash of amusement played at the corners of his lips. "Good with knives, are you?"

"Very," I said with utter confidence.

"Fair enough. Warning received." Quick as a snap, he rolled on top of me and pinned my shoulders to the mat with his knees.

I quickly brought my legs up behind him and wrapped my ankles around his neck. My thigh muscles ached when I jerked him backward. Down he went, up

I went. The moment his back hit, I used the momentum to pull myself the rest of the way up and planted my elbow in his stomach.

His breath whooshed out. "That's the second time you've elbowed me," he panted.

"Has EenLi showed up anymore?" I asked, quickly pushing to my feet. Just for fun, I dropped and thrust my elbow into his lungs again.

"Damn it!" When he caught his breath, Lucius said, "A few more times in New Dallas. We think he murdered a human female."

"That's not his usual MO. EenLi abducts, rapes, and tortures. He rarely kills. There's no profit in a dead body."

"I know. I think he's desperate and made a mistake." Lucius spun and lashed out, his foot suddenly slamming into my forearm. Into my wound.

I winced, but maintained my balance. My God, that hurt. He wanted me to cry "unfair," but I didn't give him the satisfaction. I leaped, whirling in the air, one fist cocked and ready. Contact. I nailed him in the temple.

His chin whipped to the side.

"It usually takes him months to round up the right slave candidates since he only wants those that meet his buyers' specifications," I said. "Why act hastily now?"

"From what you told Michael," he said, dancing to the side when I came at him again, causing me to miss him, "some of his last shipment died from some sort of sickness. His buyers wouldn't have liked that. They asked for a certain number, I'm sure, so he has to supply that exact number. And don't forget, you killed his top man, so he's doing some of the dirty work himself now."

"Makes sense." Since the move worked for me before, I went low, kicked out. My leg connected with his ankles. When he went down, I jumped and pinned his shoulders with my knees, my crotch near his face.

He met my eyes before his gaze slid downward. "Nice view."

I shivered and tried to halt the new flicker of awareness sparking within me. Short, inky locks of hair spiked over his forehead, giving him a just roused from bed appearance. "Look, I'm not like other women you know. I'm tougher than you think. I've done things and been places most people only fear."

"You're still a woman," he said, as if that explained every secret of the universe. "And you're a Raka, the most peaceful race ever to slink their way onto this planet."

Slink? I ground my teeth together. "I'm a Rakan woman who kills people for a living. I'm not afraid of you, and I'm not afraid of EenLi. I *will* kill him."

Good girls go to heaven...

Naughty Girls go Downtown.

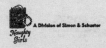